The
Animal Ark
Treasury

Ben M. Baglio

Illustrated by Ann Baum

Scholastic Inc.

New York   Toronto   London   Auckland   Sydney
Mexico City   New Delhi   Hong Kong   Buenos Aires

Special thanks to Jennie Walters, Linda Chapman, and Susan Bentley. Thanks also to C.J. Hall, B. Vet. Med., M.R.C.V.S., for reviewing the veterinary information contained in this book.

ISBN 0-439-31720-7

12 11 10 9 8 7 6 5 4 3 2 1   1 2 3 4 5 6/0

Printed in the U.S.A.   40
First Scholastic printing, November 2001

This book is dedicated to the Royal Society for the Prevention of Cruelty to Animals in recognition of the wonderful work it does, helping animals everywhere have better lives.

Contents

 # RABBIT AT RISK?

"I wonder if Robbie will be there?" Mandy said to her best friend, James Hunter, as they rode their bikes along Walton Road. They were going to visit Robbie Grimshaw, who lived on a small farm outside the town, up near Lamb's Wood. Robbie was a retired poacher who had once helped Mandy and James relocate a whole colony of wild rabbits.

"We haven't seen him for ages," James said.

"I hope we can hold his ferrets again," Mandy said. Robbie kept three beautiful ferrets — Kirsty, Marlon, and Sable. "They're so sweet."

James stood up on his pedals. "Come on. I'll race you to Woodbridge Farm Park!"

Small stones flew off the wheels of their bikes as they charged along the road. They reached Woodbridge Farm Park in a dead heat and then, laughing and panting for breath, turned up a narrow, bumpy road. A tunnel of overhanging trees shut out the blue April sky.

"I always think this place feels a bit creepy," James said as they jolted along the road.

"Just the right place for a poacher to live," Mandy agreed. "All cut off and alone." She imagined Robbie in his younger days, stealing off down the path in the dead of night. What she didn't like to imagine was him returning home, a couple of rabbits in his sack. She shivered. *I'm very glad that he's an ex-poacher now,* she thought.

They reached Robbie's gate and got off their bikes. Beyond the gate was a range of rickety sheds and a small cottage, the white paint peeling off its wooden sides. A clutch of hens pecked at the mud by an old wagon and Robbie's sow grunted in her tumbledown sty.

Mandy and James left their bikes leaning against a tree and went through the gate.

"Hello!" Mandy called, expecting to see Biddy, Robbie's black-and-white collie, come racing out at the sound of her voice. But nothing happened.

She walked farther into the muddy yard. "Robbie!"

There was still no reply.

"It doesn't look like he's here," James said, frowning.

"He might be around the back," Mandy suggested. "Or in one of the sheds. Let's have a look."

While James went to check the barn, Mandy looked into the ferret shed. The three ferrets — Kirsty, Marlon, and Sable — scurried over to the doors of their wire cages, their small, bright eyes shining as they stood up against the wire. Mandy stopped to say hello and then went outside. "He's not in here," she called to James.

"Or here," James shouted back from behind the barn. There was a pause, and then Mandy heard her friend's voice suddenly change. "Mandy! Come and look at this."

Wondering what it was, Mandy hurried around the barn.

She found James crouching by a makeshift wooden hutch. He looked over his shoulder, a slight frown between his eyes. "It's a rabbit," he said. "Look."

Mandy crouched down beside him and looked through the chicken-wire fence. A small brownish-gray rabbit was huddled in the back of the hutch. It stared at them with big, scared eyes, its nose twitching frantically.

"It's a wild rabbit, isn't it?" she asked.

Their eyes met. "What's Robbie doing with a rabbit?" James said slowly.

A horrible thought sprang into Mandy's mind. "You don't think . . ." Her voice trailed off. No, surely Robbie hadn't gone back to his poaching ways. "It could be a pet," she said quickly.

"It can't be a pet," James said. "Look at it. It's obviously scared stiff of people, and anyway, if it was a pet Robbie wouldn't keep it all the way back here."

Mandy knew he was right.

"Maybe Robbie's started poaching again, Mandy," James said, looking worried.

"But it's alive," Mandy said, seizing a ray of hope. "He hasn't killed it."

"Yet," James said, his brown hair flopping on his forehead as he looked at the frightened animal. "Maybe he's just fattening it up for the pot."

"He can't be!" Mandy said, her stomach flipping as she looked at the little rabbit's brown eyes and imagined anyone doing such a thing. "Robbie wouldn't do that."

But even as she spoke she knew that her words didn't ring true. Robbie had spent over half his life hunting rabbits and putting them into his pot.

"But what if he is?" James said. "What are we going to do?"

Mandy looked at the frightened rabbit. There was only one answer. "Set it free."

Just then they heard the sound of a dog barking. They both jumped guiltily.

"It's Robbie!" Mandy said. "He's back!"

"We can't do anything now," James said, looking alarmed. "Come on! Quick!"

They ran back around the barn. They had just reached the ferret shed when Robbie came stomping up the yard with Biddy trotting at his heels. He stopped when he saw them. He was a small man, with a weather-beaten and wrinkled face, wearing a battered cap and pants held up with rope. "Morning," he said gruffly. "I saw your bikes outside."

"Hi, Robbie," Mandy stammered. Her heart was racing.

"Been looking at my lovelies, have you?" Robbie asked, looking at the ferret shed, a rare smile suddenly flickering across his wrinkled face.

"Yes," Mandy said quickly. After all, it wasn't a lie. She *had* been to see the ferrets. She wondered what to say and do next.

"Do you want to come and take them out then?" Robbie said, walking toward the shed.

"Um . . . we've actually got to go," James said. From the faint pink flush on his cheeks, Mandy could tell that he was finding the meeting as awkward as she was. He looked at her. "Don't we, Mandy?"

Mandy nodded. She was desperate to ask Robbie about the rabbit but she didn't dare. What if somehow they had it wrong? He might be terribly offended. Worse still, what if they were right and Robbie really did intend to eat the rabbit? What would they do then?

Robbie looked slightly surprised at their sudden departure. "Okay then," he said as they hurried to the gate. "Bye."

"Yes . . . bye!" Mandy said.

Getting on her bike, she began to pedal as fast as she could down the bumpy lane, her thoughts racing. James quickly caught up with her but they didn't speak until they reached the main road and were safely out of earshot.

"What are we going to do?" James said, stopping his bike and looking at her.

"Perhaps we're wrong," Mandy said desperately. "Maybe he isn't going to eat it after all." But she could see from James's face that he didn't believe her. "I know what you're thinking — we'll have to set it free."

"But what if he's gone back to his poaching ways? He'll just catch another rabbit and the whole thing will happen all over again," James said.

Mandy was silent. She knew that he was right. "There must be something we can do!"

"But what?" James replied.

Mandy didn't know.

Their faces serious, they biked down the hill.

When they got back to town, Mandy left James at the corner of Fox and Goose streets and went back to Animal Ark. It was time for her to start helping at the afternoon clinic. As she worked, all she could think about was the rabbit's big, frightened eyes.

After she had gotten flea spray instead of worming tablets and eardrops instead of fungicide cream, Dr. Emily took her to one side.

"Are you okay, honey?" she asked, her green eyes concerned.

Mandy nodded. "I'm fine, Mom."

"Sure?" Dr. Emily asked.

Mandy nodded again. "Positive." She was sure that if she told her mom about the rabbit her mom would just tell her not to interfere. After all, technically Robbie hadn't done anything illegal or cruel. He was just keeping a rabbit in a cage. But it was what he was intending to do with the rabbit that was worrying her.

Just then, Jean Knox, the Animal Ark receptionist, called from the waiting room and her mom had to go.

Mandy fetched a broom to sweep the floor in the residential unit. Had Robbie gone back to poaching again? She hoped with all her heart that he hadn't.

* * *

Mandy didn't sleep well that night, thinking about Robbie, and she woke up early. Lying in bed, she watched it slowly become light outside. Suddenly, she made up her mind. Swinging her legs out of bed, she jumped up and pulled on a sweatshirt and jeans. There was only one thing to do. Difficult as it would be, she and James had to go and talk to Robbie.

She ran downstairs and checked and fed the patients in the residential unit, a job she did every morning. There were just three animals who had stayed overnight — Thomas, a rat with a ripped tail, Hercules, a Dalmation who had just had to have one of his toes amputated to stop a nail infection from spreading, and Tina, a pretty gray cat recovering from a car accident. Mandy fetched their food and then, after leaving a note for her mom and dad to say where she was going, set off to James's house on her bike.

The curtains at James's house were still drawn when she got there. Mandy wondered what to do. She didn't want to wake up Mr. and Mrs. Hunter, but she was desperate to speak to James and tell him what she had decided.

She looked around. Mrs. Hunter had recently replanted a flower bed in the front yard and around the plants was a thick layer of gravel. Mandy picked up a few pieces and went to stand under James's window. She threw the gravel up. It made a rattling sound against the glass and then fell to the ground. Mandy held her breath and waited. *Come on, James,* she thought.

Picking up a few more pieces, she tried again.

Suddenly, James's face appeared at the window. He was wearing his pajamas, his hair was rumpled, and his glasses were crooked. Seeing Mandy, his eyes widened in surprise. "Mandy!" he said, opening the window. "What are you doing here?"

"Can you come down?" Mandy said, keeping her voice as low as possible. "I don't want to wake up your mom and dad."

A few minutes later, James appeared at the kitchen door and let her in. He had put on some clothes, but his hair was still standing up in tufts. "It's seven-thirty in the morning!" he said, leading the way into the kitchen.

"I know, but I want to go and see Robbie Grimshaw," Mandy said. "I think we should talk to him — I can't stop thinking about that rabbit."

To her relief, James nodded. "Me, neither. I couldn't get to sleep for a long time last night."

"Well, let's go then," Mandy said. She turned and headed for the door. "Come on! What are you waiting for?"

*   *   *

They biked quickly out of Welford. As they turned onto the narrow road that led to Robbie's house, James began to look anxious. "What are we going to say to him?"

"We'll just have to ask him bluntly," Mandy said, feeling determined. "Ask him if he's started poaching again."

"But what if he gets angry?" James said.

"I don't care," Mandy replied. "We can't let him eat that rabbit, James — we just can't."

They reached the gate. Biddy came bounding down the yard, barking loudly.

"It's okay, girl, it's only us," Mandy said.

As she opened the gate, Robbie came out of his weather-beaten cottage looking surprised. "This is an early visit." Mandy saw his face suddenly crease in concern. "Nothing's the matter, is it?" he asked suddenly. "You're not in any trouble?"

"No," Mandy said quickly. "We're fine." She paused, wondering what to say next. Glancing at James, she saw that he didn't know how to start the conversation, either.

There was an awkward pause. "So what's the reason for this visit then?" Robbie said, looking from one to the other. "Not that I'm not pleased to see you," he added quickly, "but looking at your faces, I'd say something particular has brought you here. Come on," he said. "Out with it."

Mandy swallowed. "Um . . . it's . . . well, it's . . ." she stammered, feeling herself begin to blush.

"Come on, spit it out," Robbie said.

"Well, it's . . ." Mandy took a deep breath and suddenly the words rushed out of her. "It's about the rabbit!"

"The rabbit?" Robbie echoed.

"The rabbit behind your barn," James said quickly.

Robbie's cheeks flushed red. "Oh. That one," he replied, suddenly looking embarrassed.

"We saw it yesterday," Mandy said. "We were looking to see if you were around and that's when we found it." Seeing the guilty look on Robbie's face, she felt her stomach plummet. It looked as if they *had* been right — he *had* been keeping it for the pot! She couldn't bear the thought. "Oh, Robbie!" she cried, the words bursting out of her. "Please don't eat it!"

"Eat it?" Robbie exclaimed. He looked from Mandy to James in astonishment. "You think I'm going to eat that rabbit?" he said. "The one in the hutch?"

Mandy nodded. Seeing the surprise in Robbie's eyes, she felt hope suddenly surge through her. Could she and James have been wrong? "You're not going to?" she asked.

The suspicion of a smile twitched at the corner of Robbie's lips. "No, dear, I'm not."

"What are you keeping it for, then?" James burst out. "And why is it hidden away behind the barn?"

"Follow me," Robbie said and, turning, he began to walk through the yard.

Mandy and James glanced at each other, then followed him.

Robbie led them up to the rabbit's hutch. The rabbit was crouching in the corner, looking just as scared as the day before.

Robbie undid the flap at the top of the hutch and lifted out the rabbit. It struggled wildly for a moment but Robbie controlled it expertly, holding it gently but firmly against his chest. "Now, now, my beauty," he said, "stop that." He glanced up at Mandy and James. "So you think I'm going to eat him, do you?" he said, grinning. "Well, look at this." He pointed to the rabbit's right hind leg with his gnarled fingers.

"It's injured!" Mandy said, seeing a nasty welt.

"Yes. Libby Masters from Blackheath Farm found it when she was out playing on the moors behind her farmhouse one day," Robbie told her. "She'd heard I knew about rabbits and brought it to me to see if I could help." He grinned. "Of course, what Libby *hadn't* heard was *how* I came to know so much about rabbits!"

"So you said you'd look after it for her," Mandy gasped, looking at the little rabbit in his arms.

"Yes, I said I'd look after him until he was well enough for Libby to set him free again. That's why I've been keeping him around here. I didn't want him to get too used to humans, not if he's going to go back into the wild. I've been dressing his leg every day, though." Robbie shook his head. "I guess I must be getting soft in my old age," he muttered gruffly.

So Robbie hadn't started poaching again. Delight overwhelmed Mandy and she rushed over and kissed him on the cheek. "Oh, Robbie! I'm so glad!"

Looking rather awkward, Robbie took a hasty step backward. "Now, now," he said.

Mandy grinned, knowing that secretly he was rather pleased. "I'm so glad you're not going to eat him," she said. She looked at the little rabbit's leg. "The wound seems to be healing well."

"I've been using comfrey ointment, an old country remedy that my father showed me how to make. It works wonderfully on wounds." Robbie bent and carefully put the rabbit back into his hutch. "There you go, Bugs. You go back in there for a while."

"Bugs?" James echoed.

Robbie straightened up. "That's what Libby calls him. She visits when her dad can bring her. She likes to check that he's all right."

Just then, there was the sound of a car horn honking. "That's her right now, I believe," Robbie said.

Mandy and James followed him through the yard. A girl with dark curly hair, several years younger than Mandy and James, was letting herself in through the gate.

"Hi, Libby!" Mandy said.

"Hi, Mandy," Libby replied, looking surprised. "What are you doing here?"

"Stopping me from putting Bugs in the pot," Robbie said, shooting a sly grin at Mandy and James.

Libby looked shocked. "But you wouldn't do something like that, Mr. Grimshaw, would you? You *like* rabbits!"

Mandy saw Robbie's cheeks go pink as Libby skipped up to him and took his hand. "Come on! Let's go and see Bugs!" she said happily.

Mandy and James watched as Robbie allowed Libby to drag him to the barn.

James turned to Mandy. "Looks like Robbie *is* getting soft in his old age, after all," he said with a grin.

Mandy grinned back. "I think he was always that way."

Three weeks later, Mandy and James stood on the moors behind Blackheath Farm with Libby and Robbie. Libby was holding a cardboard box. "Should I do it, Mr. Grimshaw?" she said, looking at Robbie.

He nodded. "Yes, dear. If this is where you found him, then this is his home."

Libby put the box carefully down on the ground and lifted the top flap up just enough to look inside.

Mandy and James peered over her shoulder. Bugs was crouching in the box, his dark eyes blinking. His leg was now completely healed.

"Bye, Bugs," Libby said. "It's time to set you free."

Mandy saw Libby's eyelashes shine with tears. She gave the younger girl's shoulder a comforting squeeze. Libby looked up at her. "He'll be happier being set free, won't he, Mandy?" she whispered.

"Much happier," Mandy said softly. "Bugs is a wild animal, Libby. This is where he belongs."

Libby took a deep breath, then carefully tipped the box over on its side and opened the lid. There was a pause, and then a sudden rush of movement as Bugs shot out. His hind legs kicked as he raced away in a zigzag pattern across the ground.

"There he goes!" James cried.

Bugs reached the entrance to a burrow and stopped. Sitting up on his hind legs he paused, his ears twitching. For a moment the little rabbit seemed to look at them and then, with a delighted flick of his white tail, he disappeared happily into the ground. Robbie was right — he was home at last!

Claire McKay Tells You All About Guy and Other Hedgehogs

Did you know that . . .

- hedgehogs have been around for over 15 million years!

- hedgehog spines are grown, shed, and replaced continuously, like hair.

- the spines not only protect the hedgehog against predators but also cushion them against falls and blows.

- hedgehogs are often badly flea-infested. The average animal has about 100 fleas at any one time — though the record is over 1,000 on a single animal!

- hibernation isn't vital for hedgehogs. In warmer countries they sometimes don't hibernate at all. During hibernation, the hedgehog's body temperature can sink to 33.8° F (one degree Celsius) and several minutes may go by between breaths, though they usually wake up every seven to 11 days.

- a hedgehog can move at speeds of almost two miles per hour. For us, that may only be normal walking pace, but for such a tiny creature it's pretty fast!

- hedgehogs eat earthworms, beetles, and other invertebrates and can smell their food buried beneath more than an inch of soil!

- hedgehogs have almost no natural predators, thanks to their prickly protection. Only badgers are known to be able to penetrate their spiky defenses.

 DOLPHIN DRAMA!

Mandy crouched on the beach. Grains of sand stuck to her warm face as she peered into the rock pool. Slipping her fingers into the cool water, she gently eased up the largest stone. A crab scuttled sideways. Mandy dried her hands on her shorts and quickly made a note on her clipboard.

James would love it here, she thought. James Hunter was her best friend and Mandy was sure that he would have enjoyed scouring the rock pools with her. But James was a year behind her at school and the two-day biology field trip to the Cumbrian coast was only for Mandy's class.

She stood up and looked to where the headland jutted out, shielding the next bay from sight. "I'm going to go over there," she called to her friends Tania Benster and Susan Collins.

"We'll come, too," Tania said, picking up her bag. "Come on, Susan."

She and Susan joined Mandy, and together they started making their way across the rocks.

"Girls!" They stopped and looked around. Ms. Temple, their biology teacher, had seen them. "Don't go too far," she called.

"We won't," Mandy promised.

Just then, Katherine, one of the other girls in their class, came hurrying up to Ms. Temple. "Ms. Temple! Angela's sick!"

Mandy saw Ms. Temple's face crease in concern.

"Oh, dear," the teacher said. "Where is she, Katherine?"

"Over there. By the steps."

Forgetting about Mandy, Tania, and Susan, Ms. Temple hurried off.

Mandy and her friends continued walking across the rocks. "Should we go around to the next bay?" Susan suggested. "There might be some good rock pools there."

"Okay," Mandy said.

Tania nodded, too, and they started walking around the headland.

"Hey, there!" a man's voice shouted. Mandy looked around. At the foot of the headland, three men were sorting through piles of heavy-looking nets by the side of an upside-down dinghy. One of them was looking over at them. "Watch where you go!" he called. "The tide's high and it comes in quick. Don't go too far out."

"We won't," Mandy shouted back with a smile. "Thanks!"

They left the men and rounded the headland. The little beach in front of them was empty except for two girls sunbathing on the sand, their sneakers kicked off and their shorts rolled up. "It's Becky and Vicky," Susan said, recognizing their classmates.

The two girls jumped up guiltily at the sound of her voice, but when they saw it wasn't Ms. Temple, they visibly relaxed.

"Oh, it's you," said Vicky, who was the taller of the two girls and had a broad, freckled face and bobbed brown hair.

"What are you doing here?" Becky asked them in an unfriendly tone.

"We're doing our project," Mandy replied. She glanced at their clipboards lying on the sand. "Like you should be — or have you forgotten?"

"Thanks for reminding us, Mandy," Vicky said mockingly. "You wouldn't possibly think about sunbathing instead of doing your project, would you? Everyone knows you're Ms. Temple's little pet."

"Just because your parents are vets," Becky said.

Mandy shook her head in exasperation, but turned away. She knew better than to let Vicky and Becky get to her. "Come on," she said to Susan and Tania, pointing to a group of rock pools farther down the beach. "Let's go over there."

As she started off across the sand her eyes suddenly caught a glimpse of rough sea in the distance — just one patch in an otherwise calm-looking ocean. She stopped and looked harder. White spray plumed up into the air. Suddenly she remembered something she had read in the information pack that Ms. Temple had given them. Her heart sped up. It couldn't be, could it?

"What is it?" Tania asked, looking around to see why she wasn't coming.

Mandy caught sight of a gray shape leaping out of the water. *It was!* "Dolphins!" she gasped. "There's a school of dolphins out there!"

"Dolphins!" Susan echoed, looking at her as if she had gone crazy.

"Yes!" Mandy exclaimed. "In the shallows where the sea meets the beach. Look at that patch of rough water. Can you see them?"

Susan and Tania both peered at the sea. "I guess it could be," Tania said doubtfully.

"It is," Mandy insisted. "I'm sure."

Becky and Vicky must have noticed them acting

strangely because they came over. "What's the matter?" Vicky demanded.

"Mandy thinks there are dolphins out there," Susan told her.

Vicky laughed scornfully. "Yeah. As if!"

"There are!" Mandy said. "Where those white-crested waves are."

"But you don't get dolphins in England!" Becky said.

"Yes, you do," Mandy replied. "In that pack Ms. Temple gave us it says that bottle-nosed dolphins have been spotted off the coast here before. Look! If you watch carefully you can see them jumping."

There was silence as everyone stared at the patch of sea. Suddenly they all gasped. A dark gray shape could be seen leaping up above the water.

"It *is* a dolphin!" Vicky cried in amazement.

"Not one dolphin," Mandy said in excitement as her eyes caught a second dolphin leaping. "A whole *school* of them!"

"Come on!" Tania cried. "Let's go and see them!"

Mandy didn't need any encouragement. Stuffing her clipboard into her bag she raced after Tania, the surface water splashing against her slim, bare legs as she charged through the saltwater puddles.

"I've never seen dolphins in the wild before," Susan gasped, catching up with her.

"Me, neither!" said Vicky, running along behind them.

They reached the water's edge and came to a panting stop. A group of six dolphins were milling around in the water near the beach, their triangular dorsal fins cutting through the waves, their gray tail flukes stirring up white plumes.

"Aren't they wonderful?" Mandy breathed. She glanced quickly out at the sea. "Look, there's more of them out there," she said. "That must be the rest of the school." She had once spent a summer in Florida and had helped out at a dolphinarium. She tried to remember what she had learned about dolphin habits. "This group here is probably a group of young males," she said, looking at the way the six dolphins were slipping through the water — so close that their fins were almost touching. "Females would be in a larger group with their calves."

Suddenly, one of the dolphins in the group picked up speed. In one easy movement he leaped out of the sea, arched up and over, and then returned headfirst into the water. He surfaced and, swimming closer to the shore, looked directly at Mandy and the others.

"He's seen us!" Susan exclaimed.

Mandy couldn't resist. She began pulling off her sneakers.

"What are you doing?" Tania asked.

"I'm going in the water!" Mandy replied.

The others stared. "You can't," Vicky said.

"Why not?" Mandy said, her bare toes sinking lightly into the damp sand.

"What if it attacks you?" Becky said.

Mandy laughed. "Dolphins don't attack people. They're friendly. I swam with them often when I was in America." She hurried down to the water. It was cold, and her shorts were going to get wet, but she didn't care. The dolphin seemed to be waiting for her. She waded through the water until she was up to her knees.

"Hi there, boy" she said in a soft voice. She hoped the dolphin wouldn't swim away. She knew that he wouldn't attack her, but she also knew that not all dolphins were confident with humans.

The water reached her hips. Mandy was bracing herself to start swimming, when suddenly the dolphin dived under the water and started coming toward her!

Mandy gasped in delight as the dolphin poked his head up beside her.

She heard the gabble of her friends' excited voices but she didn't look around. Her eyes were riveted on the beautiful creature. Very slowly, she reached out and touched his wet body. The dolphin pushed at her hand with his beak. Mandy tickled his head. The dolphin opened his mouth wide, as if he was smiling at her.

Mandy glanced over her shoulders. "Come into the water!" she called to the others. "He's really friendly."

Susan was the first to throw her bag down and kick off her sneakers. She waded through the sea and joined Mandy. "He's beautiful!" she said, sounding thrilled, as the dolphin swam around her legs. "I can't believe he's letting us get so close!" She turned to the others who were still hesitating. "Come on!"

Leaving their bags on the sand, Tania, Becky, and Vicky joined them in the sea.

Mandy bobbed down in the water and stroked the dolphin's side. He gave a neat flip and rolled over, exposing his pale silver belly.

"What's he doing?" Becky asked.

"He wants his tummy tickled," Mandy said, grinning.

The girls crowded around and stroked and tickled the dolphin's belly. His powerful muscles could be felt under his smooth skin.

"Doesn't he feel soft!" Becky exclaimed.

"Really smooth," Vicky agreed. "Not at all slimy." Her face had lost its normally sulky look and her eyes were shining as she gently scratched the dolphin's belly.

The dolphin flipped over in one fluid movement and surged away from them through the water. A few seconds later he bobbed up again, his mouth opening.

"Wwwwwuuuuuu," he whistled and then, with a flick of his tail, he turned and swam out to the other dolphins.

"He's gone," Tania said in disappointment.

"No, look. I think he's coming back," Mandy said.

She was right. Suddenly all six of the dolphins started surging through the water.

"They're all coming!" Becky said in delight.

Mandy gasped as the dolphins surrounded them. They swam around in circles, brushing against their legs, curious and inquisitive.

"How come they're so friendly?" Tania said, turning to Mandy.

"Most dolphins are," Mandy explained. "They just don't seem to be scared of humans; in fact, they really seem to like us."

"So how come you know so much about them?" Becky asked.

Mandy explained about her time in Florida. "My friend Joel and I helped set a dolphin free," she said.

As she spoke, one of the dolphins dived between her legs and knocked her over backward. She rose spluttering from the water, her T-shirt soaked, her blond hair plastered to her head. The dolphin surfaced and opened his mouth as if he was grinning.

The others burst out laughing. "Look at you!" Tania giggled. "You're soaked."

Mandy didn't care. She grinned and dived into the water, swimming after the dolphin. He swam easily out of her reach, surging underneath her legs and surfacing near the other girls. They crowded around, petting him. Mandy was sure it was the same dolphin who had first approached her. He seemed to have a particularly mischievous glint in his eyes.

"Ms. Temple's going to be mad when she sees you!" Becky said as Mandy swam back.

Susan's eyes widened. "Ms. Temple!" she gasped. "She told us not to go too far away. I bet she's looking for us."

They all turned and looked back at the beach, half expecting to see an angry Ms. Temple striding toward them. To their relief, there was no sign of their teacher.

"I guess we should go back," Tania said reluctantly.

They all looked at each other. Mandy could tell from the others' eyes that they wanted to stay with the dolphins as much as she did. They were such magical creatures. In Florida, she had heard all sorts of stories about dolphins helping people and had actually seen one of her own friends being rescued from drowning by a school of dolphins.

"Where are our bags?" Vicky asked suddenly.

Mandy looked at where the beach started a little way away from them. There was nothing except sand. Their bags — and their sneakers — had vanished! "They're gone!" she exclaimed.

"They can't be," Susan said.

Looking at each other they started wading out of the water. Suddenly Becky tripped and fell forward heavily. She landed in the knee-deep water with a cry.

Mandy reached her first. "Becky! Are you okay?"

Becky shook her head. "My ankle!" Tears welled in her eyes as she crouched in the water. "I've hurt my ankle."

"Here," Susan said, reaching for her arm. "Let's get you onto the beach." As she stepped forward, she stumbled, too. She looked down. "Our bags!" she exclaimed, her concern momentarily replaced by astonishment. She pulled a dripping duffel bag out of the water.

"But how did they get here?" Vicky began.

Mandy suddenly realized. She looked around at the beach. While they had been playing with the dolphins, long fingers of sea had been creeping across the sand on either side of them. "The tide's been coming in," she said.

"Our books will be ruined!" Tania cried.

Becky tried to stand but gasped in pain and almost fell again. Mandy grabbed her just in time. "Susan! Give me a hand."

Together they got Becky out of the water and onto the sand. They helped her sit down. Mandy bent over her ankle and examined it gently. "Can you move your toes?"

Becky gritted her teeth in pain but managed to move her toes slightly. "It's probably not broken then," Mandy said, feeling relieved.

"Well, I can't walk on it," Becky said. She bent over her ankle, her face pale.

Tania and Vicky came wading out of the sea with the five dripping schoolbags. "What are we going to do?" Tania asked, dropping them on the sand.

"Some of us should go and get help," Susan replied.

"But the tide's coming in," Mandy pointed out. "Becky can't stay here." She looked down the beach. She didn't like what she saw. On either side of them the sea was moving toward the headland. They were no longer standing on a wide sandy beach but on a strip of sand — surrounded on three sides by sea. It wasn't very deep at the moment, but Mandy remembered the fisherman's warning. *It comes in quick,* he had said. She glanced around behind her and saw the ocean swelling. A shiver of fear ran down her spine. It was a long way back to the safety of the headland.

Vicky also seemed to have noticed the problem. "We're going to be cut off if we're not careful!" she said. "Come on, Becky! You've got to try and walk." She put her hands under her friend's arm and helped her up.

"It hurts!" Becky cried as she put her foot on the ground.

Susan took her other arm. "We'll just go slowly."

Mandy felt water lapping at her feet. Already the

sea had crept up behind them. Picking up the bags, she handed two of them to Tania. "Come on!"

Susan and Vicky started to help Becky across the sand. The progress was painfully slow. Every few steps, Becky had to stop.

"Mandy, look!" Tania said in a low voice. The two long fingers of water on either side were almost meeting in front of them now.

Mandy nodded. Her stomach was churning. The water was getting deeper and deeper. What if they had to swim? There was no way Becky would be able to get back.

"That's it, and another few steps," she heard Susan encouraging Becky.

Mandy looked around desperately. The waves were flowing in faster now on either side of them. The piece of sand they were on was rapidly shrinking in size. What were they going to do? She scanned the cliffs. If they spotted someone they could wave for help. But there was no one there.

"I can't go any farther!" Becky said suddenly. She stopped and looked up. Mandy saw her eyes widen with horrified realization. "The beach!" Becky exclaimed. "It's gone!"

They all looked at each other in fear. There was no escaping from the truth. They were completely encircled by sea.

"What are we going to do?" Vicky cried. Her voice high.

Mandy dropped the bags. There was only one thing to do. "I'm going to try to get back around the headland and get help," she said.

The others stared at her, aghast.

"You can't!" Tania said. "You'll have to swim. What about all the rocks? You might get injured."

Mandy felt her throat tighten in fear as she thought about the rocks they had climbed across earlier. But she knew she had no choice. "We need help. I'm a strong swimmer. I'll try and reach one of the fishermen we saw." She didn't want to, but someone had to get help. Ignoring their protests she ran into the water. It covered her ankles and then her knees.

"Wwwwwuuuuuu!"

Out of the sea bobbed a broad gray head and a rounded beak. It was the dolphin! Seeing him there gave Mandy the courage she needed. "I'll be back soon!" she called to her friends, and plunged farther into the cold water.

"Mandy!" she heard Tania and Susan cry.

But Mandy kept going, her eyes fixed on the headland. The water suddenly deepened. There was nothing to do but swim. Her heart pounding, Mandy took a breath and dived into the waves. If she could just reach the fishermen, then they could come get them in their boat.

The waves lapped against her, splashing her face, dragging her in toward the rocks. Mandy kicked with her feet, fighting against the water. *Come on! Come on!* she willed herself.

Suddenly a muscular gray body surged up in the water beside her. It was the dolphin. "I can't play right now, boy," Mandy gasped, trying to push him out of the way. "I've got to get around the headland and find help."

The dolphin dived underneath her and came up on the other side of her, pushing her away from the swell of the rocks. As he swam beside her, her fingers brushed against his dorsal fin. He pushed against her again. Suddenly Mandy realized what he was doing. In some mysterious, instinctive way the dolphin had realized that she was in trouble and was trying to help!

Once more he dived under her, this time coming up directly underneath her. Feeling his fin graze against her stomach as he came up to the surface, Mandy grabbed it with both hands. The dolphin kicked the water with his muscular tail and they surged forward with a burst of power.

The waves parted as the dolphin glided through

the water. The white spray flew up in the air beside them, half blinding Mandy as she clung on desperately. She couldn't see where she was going. All she could do was hang on and place her trust in the amazing animal who was pulling her. The waves battered her face but she didn't care. Exhilaration charged through her veins as the dolphin sped through the water faster and faster. He was in his element — his territory — and he was helping her.

All at once the moment ended, and the dolphin seemed to slip swiftly beneath her. Losing her grip on his fin, Mandy found herself floundering in the water, her arms splashing desperately, her eyes burning from the stinging salt.

"Hey! You!" Mandy vaguely heard men's voices. She forced her eyes open and saw that she had reached the headland. Three fishermen were wading through the water toward her. Putting her feet down she realized that she could stand.

"The dolphin!" she cried, swinging around. A gray head bobbed up out of the water from far away.

"We saw!" one of the men said, reaching her. It was the same man who had shouted out to her and Tania to be careful of the tide. "What's going on?"

Suddenly Mandy remembered that there wasn't a second to lose. "My friends!" she gasped. "You've got to help! *Please!*"

*   *   *

Ten minutes later, she was watching her friends being ferried around the headland in the fishermen's dinghy. "Here they come," Jim, the fisherman, said to Mandy as his friends Gary and Tony expertly brought the yellow dinghy to a stop and started to help everyone out. They were wet, but safe. Gary lifted up Becky and carried her through the water.

Mandy hurried forward. "Are you okay?"

"Are *you*?" Tania said. "Wasn't the dolphin amazing?"

Mandy nodded. "He was wonderful!"

"I've seen some things on this beach," Jim said, scratching his gray head, "but that beats everything."

"You girls were very lucky," Gary said, his face grave as he put Becky down. "You know, if it hadn't been for that dolphin . . ." His voice trailed off.

Mandy shivered. She didn't like to think what might have happened.

"Girls!" Ms. Temple's voice rang out, high-pitched and anxious. "Where have you been?" Their biology teacher came hurrying toward them. Her face was pale. "We've been looking for you everywhere." She saw their wet clothes. "What *have* you been doing?"

It took some explaining. However, Ms. Temple was so relieved that they were all safe that she didn't get angry with them. "Oh, goodness!" she said, hugging them all. "Thank goodness you're okay."

"Our schoolbooks aren't," Susan said ruefully.

"That's the least of our worries," Ms. Temple said briskly. "Now, let's get you back to the hotel and into some clean, dry clothes and then we better get you to the hospital, Becky, and get that ankle checked out." She turned to the fishermen. "Thank you so much for rescuing them."

"Yes, thank you very much," the girls said gratefully.

"I think it's the dolphin who deserves the real thanks," Jim said.

Mandy looked out to sea to where the group of six dolphins were playing in the waves, their gray bodies surging effortlessly through the water.

Suddenly there was a plume of white spray. One of the dolphins leaped into the air, his wet skin gleaming in the sunlight as he arched in a flowing teardrop shape over the sea. He came up again headfirst and looked directly at the shore.

"*Thank you,*" Mandy whispered.

The dolphin's mouth opened in a wide dolphin grin and Mandy was sure that she saw a glint in his eyes.

Lydia Fawcett Tells You All About Houdini and Other Goats

Did you know that . . .

- goats are the most common farm animals
  in the world and have been used by man
  for their meat, milk, and wool for over
  5,000 years.

- goats were first domesticated about 9,000 years ago!

- goat milk is the most consumed milk worldwide. A dairy goat produces six to eight pints of milk per day.

- goat milk is good for the treatment of ulcers, asthma, and eczema.

- goats are often used as pack animals to carry baggage.

- a female goat is called a doe, a male a buck, and the young, kids.

- goats have no top teeth at the front of their mouths, so they cannot bite.

 DOGGY DILEMMA

"Okay, Ernie, you can bring Twinkie in now," Dr. Adam Hope said to the man who was sitting in the waiting room. It was the end of Saturday morning office hours at Animal Ark and the only animal left to see was Twinkie, Ernie Bell's young black-and-white cat.

Ernie picked up the wicker traveling basket. "Come on then, my dear."

Mandy, who had been tidying up behind the desk, came around to look at the little cat. "You'll be okay, Twinkie," she said. "Dad will make your ear feel much better."

As she moved aside to let Ernie and his cat pass, the clinic door suddenly flew open as if it had been hit by a hurricane.

Mrs. Ponsonby staggered into the waiting room.

She was wearing a purple-and-yellow dress and a large hat. In her arms she carried a brown mongrel. "Dr. Adam!" she cried, tottering slightly on her high heels. "I need to see you urgently!" The fake cherries on her hat quivered as she stared dramatically at Dr. Adam.

Mandy saw her dad quickly swallow his surprise. "Well . . . er . . . good morning, Mrs. Ponsonby," he began. "If you'd just like to take a seat and . . ."

"This *cannot* wait!" Mrs. Ponsonby exclaimed. "It's about Toby."

"Well, Mr. Bell *was* here first . . ." Dr. Adam began.

"Eee, Doctor, forget about us," Ernie Bell said good-naturedly, starting to move back to his seat. "I'm sure Twinkie won't mind waiting a little bit longer."

"That's very kind of you, Ernie," Dr. Adam said quickly. "But we do have a strict policy here to deal with clients in the order they come in, unless, of course, it's an emergency. So, if you'd like to bring . . ."

"Dr. Adam! This is an emergency!" Mrs. Ponsonby interrupted him. Her hat was quivering so much that Mandy thought the fake fruit was about to fall off. "Thank you, Mr. Bell," Mrs. Ponsonby declared, and with that she swept into the consulting room, her dress billowing out imperiously behind her.

"Thanks, Ernie," Dr. Adam said in a low voice.

Ernie grinned at him. He knew Mrs. Ponsonby well. Everyone in Welford did.

"Here we go," Dr. Adam said to Mandy.

Mandy grinned. "It's not going to be *that* bad, Dad."

Her dad didn't look convinced. At least once a month, Mrs. Ponsonby turned up at the clinic convinced that something was fatally wrong with Toby, or with Pandora — her spoiled Pekingese. So far, every time had been a false alarm.

Mandy followed her dad into the consulting room. Mrs. Ponsonby had put Toby down on the examination table and was fussing around him. The mongrel wagged his tail happily when he saw Mandy.

"So, Mrs. Ponsonby, would you like to tell me what the trouble is?" Dr. Adam asked.

Mrs. Ponsonby glanced over her shoulder as if to check that there was no one listening. "Toby has . . ." She glanced around again. "A *problem*, Dr. Adam." She almost hissed the word.

"Okay," Dr. Adam said. He waited a second, but Mrs. Ponsonby didn't say anything else. "Exactly what *sort* of problem, Mrs. Ponsonby?"

"It's . . . he's . . ." Mandy saw Mrs. Ponsonby's cheeks flush. She looked agitated.

"Yes?" Dr. Adam asked encouragingly.

The words came out of Mrs. Ponsonby in a rush. "He's started doing wee-wee on the floor, Dr. Adam!"

Mandy had to bite the inside of her cheek to stop herself from laughing at the horror in Mrs. Ponsonby's voice.

Her dad cleared his throat. "Okay," he said, in his professional voice. "So we appear to have a urination problem. Mandy, would you hold Toby for me while I examine him, please?"

Mandy held Toby carefully while her dad examined the dog's gums, checked the glands in his neck and underneath his back legs, and then took his temperature.

"Good boy," Mandy whispered, scratching the mongrel's chest as her dad worked. Toby was one of her favorite dogs. She loved him almost as much as Blackie, her best friend James's dog. He was always so happy and inquisitive.

"How often does this happen, Mrs. Ponsonby? Every day or just occasionally?" Dr. Adam asked.

"Just occasionally — maybe once every few days," Mrs. Ponsonby said. She leaned closer to Dr. Adam. "And it's always in the same place in the kitchen! Oh, Dr. Adam. Can you tell me what's wrong? Is it serious?"

Dr. Adam put the thermometer down. "Well, Toby

seems to be in great shape, Mrs. Ponsonby. A clean bill of health."

"So why's he . . . he . . ." Mrs. Ponsonby's cheeks went bright red as she struggled with the words.

Dr. Adam helped out. "Urinating in the house?"

Mrs. Ponsonby nodded gratefully.

Dr. Adam stroked Toby. "I think it's probably a behavioral problem. If there was a physical cause, it would happen every day and in all different places, not just in one specific place. Adult dogs can act like this if they are troubled in some way. Can you think of anything that might be making Toby stressed or unhappy, Mrs. Ponsonby?"

Mrs. Ponsonby thought hard, her double chins wobbling slightly.

"Any reason for him to be feeling particularly bored or in need of attention?"

"That's it!" Mrs. Ponsonby exclaimed, her eyes lighting up. "I know what it is. He must be jealous of Pandora." She went over to Toby and kissed him on the top of his head. "Oh, Toby, has Mommy been paying too much attention to your older sister?" She turned. "Pandora's being entered into a photographic competition for Yorkshire's prettiest pet," she explained. "I've got a professional photographer coming tomorrow to take her picture and I've been busy getting her ready — brushing and combing her and" — she smiled coyly at Dr. Adam — "practicing her camera poses, of course." She turned to the brown mongrel. "So my poor little Toby-woby's been feeling jealous, has he?" she gurgled.

Pandora the Pekingese was going to be in a prettiest pet competition! As much as Mandy loved the snub-nosed, snuffling little dog she couldn't imagine her winning the title of Yorkshire's prettiest pet. She glanced at her dad. His beard was shaking and he looked like he was trying not to laugh.

"Well, it looks like the solution is obvious," Dr. Adam said, quickly swallowing his laughter. "Toby simply needs more attention."

Mrs. Ponsonby looked at the mongrel doubtfully. "Do you think *he* wants to be entered in the prettiest pet competition?"

"No!" Dr. Adam said in alarm. "I was thinking more of playing games with him, taking him for some long walks . . ."

"Oh, Dr. Adam. All walks are off at the moment," Mrs. Ponsonby interrupted, shocked. "I can't have my little Pandora getting muddy or risk her catching a chill. Toby has a big yard to play in."

It was true. Mrs. Ponsonby lived in a large old house just outside Welford. Mandy had been there quite a few times. The yard was massive.

"Even so," Dr. Adam said firmly, "I think you should take him out. Dogs need the mental stimulation of getting out and seeing new things — particularly young dogs like Toby."

"But I don't have time this week," Mrs. Ponsonby said. "I have to get Pandora ready for the competition and I'm in charge of organizing the Women's Club rummage sale. Oh, Toby, what are we going to do?"

"Maybe you could get someone to help you for the week," Dr. Adam suggested. "You know, take Toby out for a few walks."

Mandy had an idea. "I could do it," she offered. "James would help, too. We're on vacation now."

"Oh, Amanda!" Mrs. Ponsonby exclaimed in delight. "That would be *so* kind of you!" She took a step toward her, looking so pleased that for one horrible moment Mandy thought she was about to be hugged.

She took a hasty step backward. "I'd enjoy it."

"Sounds like the ideal solution," her dad said, beginning to wash his hands. "And I'm sure it's just what Toby needs. Although if this doesn't clear up his little" — he cleared his throat — "problem," he said delicately, "then you should bring him back in for further tests, Mrs. Ponsonby."

"Certainly, certainly," Mrs. Ponsonby said, nodding hard. "Thank you, Dr. Adam. Thank you. I'll see you later, Amanda." And with that, she picked up Toby and sailed out the door.

"We're doing *what*?" James exclaimed when Mandy told him later.

"We're going to Mrs. Ponsonby's house to keep Toby happy over vacation," Mandy repeated. They were sitting at the Animal Ark kitchen table.

James stared at her. "But that means seeing Mrs. Ponsonby every day!"

Mandy nodded. It was undoubtedly the drawback of the whole plan. "Well, maybe she won't be there much," she said, trying to look on the bright side. "She said that she's going to be busy with Pandora and we can take Toby out for lots of walks. We don't have to see her *that* much."

"I guess you're right," James sighed. He ran a hand through his brown hair. "I *hope* you're right." His face brightened slightly. "Can Blackie come?"

Mandy nodded. "He can play with Toby and keep him company."

James looked happier. "So when do we start?"

"We could go over now," Mandy suggested.

James agreed.

After collecting Blackie from James's house they set off. Blackie galloped happily beside them as they biked along the winding lane that led up to Mrs. Ponsonby's house, Bleakfell Hall.

At last it came into sight. It was an enormous building, built out of gray stone with towers and turrets. As they biked down the driveway, the front door opened and Mrs. Ponsonby came out. Mandy recognized the hairy bundle in her arms as Pandora. Blackie trotted over to say hello.

"Hi, Mrs. Ponsonby," Mandy said, stopping her bike.

"Hello, Amanda, James. So kind of you to come."

Pandora struggled and squirmed under Mrs. Ponsonby's arm. It was obvious that she wanted to get down and play with Blackie. "Now, now, sweetums," Mrs. Ponsonby cooed, kissing Pandora's snub black nose. "We can't have you getting your beautiful coat all messy before you're photographed, can we?" She turned to Mandy and James. "The photographer's setting up in the garden. Pandora is getting very excited. She *loves* being photographed."

"Where's Toby?" Mandy asked.

"In the kitchen," Mrs. Ponsonby replied. "Let me show you the way."

"It's all right, I remember where it is . . ." Mandy began.

But Mrs. Ponsonby was already heading back into the house. "This way!" she called.

Mandy and James followed Mrs. Ponsonby along the dark, oak-paneled corridors. "The kitchen's over there," Mrs. Ponsonby said, pointing to a big wooden door at the end.

As they got nearer, they heard the sound of barking coming from the other side of the door. "Oh, no!" Mrs. Ponsonby gasped. She quickened her footsteps and flung open the door.

Toby was standing at one side of the large kitchen, barking. At his feet was a big puddle!

"Oh, Toby!" Mrs. Ponsonby exclaimed.

Mandy, James, and Blackie followed. Seeing Blackie, Toby gave a woof of excitement and bounded over.

"This is just what he does," Mrs. Ponsonby told Mandy and James. "I hear him barking and by the time I get here there's always a puddle on the floor, right there by the washing machine."

"Oh, Toby," Mandy said, stroking him. "You shouldn't make puddles on the floor. Would you like me to mop it up, Mrs. Ponsonby?" She was used to cleaning up puddles — it was all part of a day's work at a busy veterinary clinic like Animal Ark.

"Oh, thank you, Amanda," Mrs. Ponsonby said, looking relieved. "That would be most helpful. The mop and the disinfectant are in that cupboard over there." Mrs. Ponsonby turned to James. "James, would

you be kind enough to hold Pandora for me? I see
that the washing machine has finished its load."

James held Pandora as Mandy mopped and Mrs.
Ponsonby took the clean laundry out and put a new
load of laundry in. She had piles of it!

"I've got some friends coming to stay next week
and the house is such a mess. I thought I'd do a bit of
spring cleaning," she explained, seeing Mandy eyeing
the mound of curtains and bedspreads. She turned to

James and took Pandora back. "Now, sweetums, should you and Mommy go and see if that nice photographer is ready for us?" She patted the little dog and headed for the door. "Pandora and I will be outside if you need us," she called.

"Should we go into the yard?" James said after Mrs. Ponsonby had left. Mandy nodded and put the mop away.

As soon as they got outside, Blackie raced off to investigate and quickly found one of Toby's toys behind a tree. He shook it and then bounded up to Toby.

"He wants to play!" Mandy said.

Toby needed no encouragement. Soon the two dogs were racing around the yard. They played for a long time, at last flopping down together in a panting heap. "Doesn't Toby look happy?" Mandy said with a smile.

"Yeah, he looks like he's grinning," James said, looking at Toby's open mouth.

Suddenly Toby lifted his head. He pricked his ears. The next second he was running across the lawn toward the back door. "What's he doing?" James said in surprise, as Toby disappeared inside.

"Woof! Woof! Woof!" The sound of barking came from the kitchen.

Mandy and James looked at each other. "Surely he hasn't . . ." Mandy began.

They hurried to the back door. When they looked inside they saw Toby barking beside the washing machine, a large puddle at his feet.

"He has!" James said, speaking above the spinning of the washing machine.

"Oh, Toby!" Mandy exclaimed. The mongrel stopped barking and trotted over to her. "What did you do that for?" she said. "You weren't feeling bored, and you were being given lots of attention."

This time James got the mop and cleaned it up.

The washing machine was making a very loud noise. "Come on," Mandy said as he finished, "it's too noisy in here. Let's go back outside."

"Why do you think he did it?" James said as they went out. "I mean, if he'd wanted to go to the bathroom, he could have just gone outside. It doesn't make sense."

Mandy frowned. "I know. Maybe he's just gotten into the habit. We'll have to watch him carefully."

They walked through the yard. "I wonder what's down this path," said James, seeing a path that ran alongside a brick wall. They followed it.

As they reached the corner they heard a loud voice. "Now then, Pandora, be a good doggy and look at the nice man!"

Mandy and James exchanged looks.

They came to a gate. It led into a rose garden and

there, in one corner, was Pandora sitting on a pink cloth on a table with roses strewn artfully around her. Mrs. Ponsonby had even tucked a pink rosebud behind Pandora's left ear. She was fussing around, adjusting the cloth. "Are you ready, Mr. Hewson?" she called.

The photographer, a young man of about twenty-five, nodded in an exasperated way.

"Let's watch!" Mandy whispered to James.

The photographer took a picture.

"Now one from this angle," Mrs. Ponsonby said bossily, moving him slightly to the right. "And I'd like one from over there, and a close-up."

The poor photographer moved back and forth. Pandora looked very bored.

At last Mrs. Ponsonby was satisfied. "There!" she said. "Now, I'd like you to set up for the nautical photographs. Pandora has the sweetest little sailor hat — she *must* be photographed in that. We'll just go indoors and get it." Sweeping Pandora under her arm, she turned toward the gate and saw Mandy and James.

"Amanda and James," she said. "How's Toby?"

"Fine, Mrs. Ponsonby," said Mandy, deciding not to tell her about Toby's second puddle.

Mrs. Ponsonby opened the gate. Blackie and Toby bounded in. "I'm just going to get Pandora's sailor hat," she said to Mandy and James. "I'll be back in a minute." She hurried off.

The photographer bent down and patted Toby and Blackie, who had gone up to him to say hello. "Nice dogs," the photographer said, looking at Mandy and James. "Are they yours?"

"Blackie's mine," James said. "He's the Labrador."

"Toby belongs to Mrs. Ponsonby," Mandy explained. She smiled. "I'm Mandy and this is James."

"I'm Ted," the photographer said. "Pleased to meet you." He looked at Blackie and Toby. "I could take some pictures of them while we wait," he said.

"Won't it use up the film?" James asked.

Ted shook his head. "I'm using a digital camera," he said, holding the camera out for Mandy and James to see. "You take photographs and then look at them on this screen. Then you just choose to print the ones you want. The rest you delete." He put the camera to his eye and took a few quick photographs of Blackie and Toby sniffing in the bushes. "Look," he said, showing the screen to Mandy and James.

They saw a computer-generated picture on the screen. Ted pointed out the commands at the side. "I press this if I want to save the photo I'm looking at, and this if I want to delete it."

"It's really clever!" Mandy said, impressed.

Ted started taking some more photographs. "Here,

boys!" he called to the dogs, clicking away as the dogs pricked their ears and gamboled about.

"I like that one of Blackie by the bench," James said when Ted showed them the results one after the other on the screen.

"And this one of Toby's terrific!" Mandy said. Ted had captured the little mongrel coming out of a rosebush, his mouth open, his tongue hanging out happily, and a few rose petals caught in his wiry hair.

"It *is* good!" James said. "I bet Mrs. Ponsonby will like that one, too."

Ted took some more until Mrs. Ponsonby came back. Pandora was wearing a sailor hat perched jauntily over one ear. Saying a quick good-bye to Ted, Mandy and James made their escape.

As they walked back to the house, Toby suddenly raced past them and in through the back door.

Mandy and James looked at each other.

"Quick!" Mandy gasped.

They began to run.

"Woof! Woof! Woof!" Toby barked from inside.

Mandy and James charged in through the door.

"He's done it again!" James exclaimed, stopping dead in his tracks.

Mandy looked at the puddle around Toby's feet. "Toby! How could you?" she cried over the noise of Mrs. Ponsonby's old washing machine. "Bad dog!"

Toby looked at her in surprise. Mandy sighed. She knew that it was no use scolding him now. It was too late. He wouldn't understand. "We can't scold him unless we actually see him doing it," she said to James as she fetched the mop.

James nodded. "We should watch him until he makes another puddle, but I'm not staying in here with all this noise."

"I think it's almost finished," Mandy said, looking at the washing machine. She mopped up the puddle and then they went outside with Toby and Blackie until the washing machine stopped.

"So, what do we do?" James asked as they went back into the kitchen. "Just wait until Toby makes a puddle again?"

"I guess so," Mandy said, sitting down at the large pine table. "And then scold him so he realizes that it's wrong."

"But why's he doing it?" James puzzled. "He's not bored — we're here."

Mandy shook her head. It was a mystery. Why on earth *did* Toby keep running into the kitchen to go to the bathroom? It just didn't make sense.

*   *   *

They waited all afternoon, but Toby showed no sign of making another puddle. At four o'clock James looked at his watch. "I'd better go," he said. "I told Mom I'd be back by four-thirty."

Mandy sighed. "Maybe we'll have more luck tomorrow."

Just then the kitchen door opened. Mrs. Ponsonby came in with Pandora. "We're going now, Mrs. Ponsonby," Mandy said.

"Thank you so much for entertaining Toby today," Mrs. Ponsonby said, smiling. She put Pandora carefully down on the floor. The little Pekingese gave a relieved shake and immediately waddled up to Blackie and Toby to say hello. "It's been such a help knowing that he's had company."

"Well, actually, we haven't been that successful," Mandy admitted. She explained about the two puddles on the floor.

Mrs. Ponsonby looked worried. "But why would he do it when he had you two and Blackie to keep him company?"

"I don't know," Mandy said.

"I hope he's not ill," Mrs. Ponsonby said anxiously.

Mandy nodded. She was beginning to wonder if her dad had gotten his diagnosis right. "I'll tell Dad about it," she said.

"Thank you, Amanda. That would be very kind."

Mrs. Ponsonby looked at the washing machine. "Oh, dear, my machine doesn't seem to have drained properly. I'd better put it on again." She fiddled with the dial.

"Here, Blackie!" James said as the machine began to rattle into life. He clipped a leash onto the Labrador's collar. "Bye, Mrs. Ponsonby."

"See you tomorrow," Mandy said, following him quickly to the door in an effort to get out of the kitchen before the machine really got going. But she was too late. With a grinding, spluttering noise the machine started to fill with water.

"Woof! Woof! Woof!"

Mandy and James swung around. Toby had raced to the washing machine and was staring at the bottom of it, barking loudly.

"Toby!" Mrs. Ponsonby exclaimed. "What *are* you doing?" She put her hand on his collar and tried to pull him away.

"Woof! Woof! Woof!" Toby barked insistently.

"Mrs. Ponsonby! Look!" Mandy cried. Seeping out from underneath the washing machine was a creeping pool of water. It trickled down the uneven wooden floor and made a puddle. "It's the washing machine that's been making the puddles, not Toby!" Mandy exclaimed.

"Well!" Mrs. Ponsonby gasped.

"He must have been trying to tell you about the leak by barking," Mandy said.

"And that's why you always found him standing by the washing machine when you came into the kitchen," James said.

"Looking as if he'd made the puddle!" Mandy added.

"Woof! Woof! Woof!" Toby barked as if in agreement.

For once, Mrs. Ponsonby actually seemed lost for words. "Well, I never!" she gasped, shaking her head. "I . . . I can't believe it."

"So you *weren't* being a bad dog, after all," Mandy said, crouching down and hugging the mongrel. "Poor Toby! You just got all the blame."

Two weeks later, Mandy was tidying up the worming tablets in the waiting room when the door flew open and Mrs. Ponsonby swept in. "We've won!" she exclaimed, the red and yellow feathers on her brown hat bouncing up and down. Ignoring the clients who were waiting, she waved a photograph at Mandy. "Amanda, we've *won!*"

Mandy stared at Mrs. Ponsonby in astonishment. She could hardly believe it. Pandora had been chosen as Yorkshire's prettiest pet. It just didn't seem possible. "Gosh, Mrs. Ponsonby!" she managed. "Nice job!"

"I knew that he would win as soon as I saw the photograph," Mrs. Ponsonby said smugly.

"He?" Mandy echoed, wondering if she'd heard right. Mrs. Ponsonby thrust the photograph she was holding into Mandy's hands.

Mandy gasped. It was the one the photographer had taken of Toby coming out of the rosebush. The brown mongrel stared out of the photograph, his eyes bright, his mouth hanging open as if he was grinning. "It's Toby!" she exclaimed.

"Of course," Mrs. Ponsonby said, looking surprised. "I entered him in the happiest dog category as soon as I saw it on Pandora's entry form, and now his picture's going to be in all the doggy magazines. He won!"

"But what about Pandora?" Mandy said.

"Well, naturally my little darling is disappointed," Mrs. Ponsonby said. "Those judges simply had no taste. But my Toby," she smiled proudly at Mandy, "my Toby is Yorkshire's happiest dog!" Throwing her arms wide she hugged Mandy.

And for once, Mandy didn't mind. "Oh, Mrs. Ponsonby!" she gasped. "That's great!"

Ernie Bell Tells You All About Sammy and Other Squirrels

Did you know that . . .

- there are 365 species of squirrels or squirrel-like mammals in the world.

- the word "squirrel" originally comes from Greece, where *skiouros* means "he who sits in the shadow of his tail."

- the largest squirrel on earth, the Ratufa or Indian giant squirrel, can measure up to three feet in length, while the African Pygmy squirrel is only two inches long!

- the bushy tail of the squirrel is not only used as a balancing tool, a parachute, and a winter blanket but also to communicate with other squirrels. Squirrels should never be grabbed by their tails as they may come off, and once lost, the tails never regrow.

- squirrels always descend from trees headfirst.

- squirrels can hop or jump up to six feet in one bound on the ground, and even greater distances jumping from branch to branch.

- the sweat glands of a tree squirrel are located in its feet and it leaves wet tracks on dry ground when it is hot or excited.

- a squirrel's teeth grow about six inches every year. Luckily they are constantly being worn down, so they never get too long!

 GOLDFISH GALORE

"Game, set, and match!" James called to the boy on
the other side of the net.

David Teale was one of James's classmates. He lived
in a huge modern house in Walton and had invited
Mandy and James over for a game on the newly built
tennis court.

Mandy had been watching from behind the
baseline. She came over to congratulate the winner.
"Well done, James!"

"It was a close game," James said. "You're pretty
good, David."

"Thanks." His friend grinned, running a hand
through his short reddish hair. "But I think I need
more practice."

David's mom was placing a tray of drinks on the
patio, where pots of geraniums made a bright splash

of color. "I thought you might be feeling thirsty," she called across to them. "There's lemonade, Coke, fresh orange juice, iced tea . . ." She reeled off an endless list of choices.

"Wow. She could open a store with all that," James whispered to Mandy.

"I know." Mandy grinned. "She's really nice, isn't she?" James nodded.

"Have you invited Mandy and James to your party?" Mrs. Teale asked as they sipped their cold drinks.

David flashed Mandy and James a smile. "Not yet. I've been too busy trying to beat them at tennis! It's my birthday on Saturday and Mom and Dad are organizing a dance party for me," he explained. "Would you like to come? I'm going to ask nearly everyone from my class and a few other kids, too."

"We'd love to," Mandy and James both said at once.

"Oh, good!" said Mrs. Teale, gathering up the empty glasses. "It'll be wonderful for David to have so many friends here. We're having a DJ and a light show. And there'll be lots of food."

If today's choice of drinks is anything to go by, the food's going to be fantastic, Mandy thought.

David jumped up and twirled his racket. "Thanks for the drinks, Mom. Come on, you two. There's just enough time for a quick game before you have to go home."

*   *   *

Dusk was falling as Mandy and James bicycled back to Welford. It was a perfect summer evening, with a warm breeze playing through the trees.

"Phew! David's house is really fancy, isn't it?" James said, freewheeling down a gentle slope. "There must be acres of land."

"And did you notice the indoor swimming pool?" Mandy replied. "It's amazing that David isn't spoiled or stuck-up living in that place. I think his party is going to be great."

"Hmm," James said, sounding thoughtful.

Mandy frowned. "What's wrong? Have you changed your mind about going?"

James shook his head. "No way! I wouldn't miss it for anything!" He grinned. "But what do you buy the boy who has everything?"

"His own private plane?" Mandy joked, braking as she steered her bike around a curve. "Seriously, though, why don't we ask David's mom? She's bound to have some idea of what he wants."

"Good idea," James agreed. "I'll give Mrs. Teale a call when I get home."

"No luck with David's mom," James said to Mandy as they biked toward Walton Moor School the following day. "She says David can't think of anything he wants.

His parents are going to give him money so he can buy himself something later."

Mandy wrinkled her nose. "I don't want to give him money, do you?"

"No," James agreed. "It's a bit boring, isn't it?"

"Yes. We'll have to come up with something else," Mandy decided. "Let's see now. What's David interested in?"

James shrugged. "I don't really know him that well, but he seems to spend all his time outdoors or reading. I could try to get him talking about his hobbies between classes today."

"Good idea," Mandy said as they wheeled their bikes through the school gate. "I'll think about it, too. See you at lunch."

By lunchtime, Mandy and James still didn't have any ideas. They glumly went in for their afternoon classes.

"For homework, I'd like two pages about any member of the animal kingdom, please," Ms. Temple, James's biology teacher, said as the last class of the day drew to a close.

James sighed. Biology wasn't his best subject. Now computer studies, that was a different matter.

"Can it be a bird or a fish, Ms. Temple?" someone wanted to know.

The teacher gave the speaker a level look, but the corners of her mouth were twitching. "Wake up, Ben Lyman! Animal *kingdom*? You can pick dragonflies, bats, or dolphins if you like!"

A ripple of laughter ran through the biology lab.

James grinned at David. "What are you going to write about?"

"Piece of cake. Fish!" David said promptly.

"You're doing your homework on — fish cakes?" James joked.

David spluttered with laughter. "No, silly! Real swim-around-in-the-water kind of fish. I think fish are really neat the way they get oxygen from water through their gills. How about you?"

"Haven't decided yet," James replied with a secret smile.

He dashed out of class the minute the bell rang and cornered Mandy in the coatroom as she was putting on her sweater. "I've got it!" he announced, with a whoop.

Mandy grinned. "Is it catching?"

James raised his eyebrows. "No, listen. David's birthday present. I've got it. I found out in biology that he's crazy about fish. We'll get him some goldfish!"

"Goldfish?" Normally Mandy didn't agree with buying pets as presents but goldfish were easy to take care of. "The pet shop has loads of them. We could get him one each. You're brilliant, James Hunter."

James blushed and grinned. "Yeah, I know!"

Mandy got up especially early on Saturday morning so that she finished her chores in time to go and buy David's present before the party. She popped into the clinic to say good-bye to her mom.

"All set for the party?" Dr. Emily asked. She wore her white coat and was washing down the treatment table with disinfectant.

Mandy nodded. "I'm biking over now to meet James at the pet shop. We just have the goldfish to buy."

Her mom smiled. "David will be pleased. Mrs. Teale was in the post office yesterday. I heard her telling Mrs. McFarlane that David's fascinated with fish."

"So we're right on target? Great." Mandy kissed her mom's cheek. "See you later."

"Bye, dear. Have a good time," Dr. Emily called after her.

James was waiting outside the pet shop when Mandy arrived on her bike. They went inside and headed for the back of the shop where the fish were kept.

"Oh." Mandy looked down in surprise. There were only three fish left in the blue, plastic-lined pool.

"Wow!" James said. "What's happened? They had about fifty fish the other day!"

"Thank goodness we only want to buy two!" Mandy bit her lip. "Except . . . that means that the last fish will be left all alone, poor thing."

James began counting his money. "We don't have to buy wrapping paper and I could make David a computer card."

"Oh, yes!" Mandy had caught on fast. "With the money we save, we can afford all three fish!"

The shop assistant poured water into a large plastic bag, then gently tipped in the fish. "Here you are."

"Mission accomplished!" Mandy said triumphantly outside the shop. She checked the time on the church clock. "It's past one already. David's party starts at two. We have just enough time to go to your house and make that card."

Half an hour later, James sat back from his keyboard, pressed "Print," and watched David's card emerge. He held it up to show Mandy. On the front there was a bright yellow smiling fish. "Happy Birthday" was spelled out in a stream of bubbles.

"Impressive!" Mandy said.

"Glad you like it. Come on," James said, already heading for the door.

*　　*　　*

They were both out of breath by the time they had biked over to Walton. At David's house the long driveway was full of cars. They dismounted and crunched across the gravel to the front door.

David answered the door, a broad smile on his face. "Hi, you two. Come in."

"Sorry we're late," Mandy and James said politely.

"That's okay. I've only just finished opening my presents," David replied.

"Well, you haven't finished yet!" Mandy said, holding out the plastic bag.

"Happy birthday," James chipped in. "Here's your card."

"Gosh! Thanks . . . er . . . goldfish. Okay. Lovely," David stammered. He opened his birthday card and smiled broadly. "More fish!"

Mandy and James exchanged curious looks. David seemed rather embarrassed.

Just then Mrs. Teale appeared behind her son. "Why don't you show Mandy and James your other presents?" she suggested, her eyes twinkling.

"Okay." David turned and led the way.

Through some French windows, Mandy and James could see everyone else in the yard. They stepped into the modern kitchen. There, swimming in the sink, were about thirty other goldfish!

"Wow!" Mandy's eyes opened wide with surprise.

James looked puzzled. "But . . . how come?"

Mrs. Teale had followed them inside. She was smiling broadly. "This may have something to do with my telling a packed post office that David's crazy about fish!"

"I'm glad you did!" David said delightedly. "I love *all* my fish. My only problem is thinking up thirty-three names!"

Mandy and James laughed.

"At least you don't have to worry about where to keep the fish," Mandy said. "With all your birthday money you can buy a great aquarium!"

Mandy Tells You All About Moonbeam and Other Kangaroos

Did you know that . . .

- there are at least 69 species of kangaroo. A male kangaroo is called a boomer and a female is called a flyer.

- red kangaroo males can be as tall as six feet and as heavy as 200 pounds!

- when the first European explorers arrived in Australia, they asked the Aborigines what the strange hopping animal was called.

They replied "Kangaroo." But it was all a huge misunderstanding, because in Aborigine *kangaroo* means "I do not understand." Still, the name stuck!

- a baby kangaroo — or joey — is only about eight inches long and weighs less than an ounce when it's born. After birth, it crawls up its mother's body to enter her pouch, where it stays for several weeks before emerging. It doesn't leave the pouch completely until it is at least seven months old.

- the four teats in a kangaroo mother's pouch all contain a different type of milk — each suitable for a different stage of the joey's development.

- if a kangaroo mother gets pregnant while still carrying a joey in her pouch, the new joey doesn't grow. It waits inside the mother until the previous joey has left!

- if there is danger around, a kangaroo mother will accept any joey that jumps into her pouch!

- kangaroos can go for months without water. When they do need it, they dig their own "wells" — digging over a yard deep into the ground.

- kangaroos have been reported to jump heights of three yards and lengths of eight yards — as well as reaching speeds of up to 40 miles per hour!

- on land, kangaroos can only move their hind feet together, but when swimming they can kick each leg independently!

PANDA PANIC!

Animal Ark
Welford
Yorkshire
UK

Dear Mei Ling,

Hi! I hope you and your mom and all the pandas are well. How's Hua Hua? I guess he must be six months old by now. I just can't believe that it's three months since James and I stayed with you in China. Life here in Welford is great. I thought I'd write and send you some photographs. The first one is of Animal Ark, Mom and Dad's veterinary clinic. You'll recognize Mom and Dad (and me!). The woman with the glasses is Jean — she's our receptionist — and the other person is Simon, who's the veterinary nurse and is really nice. The black Labrador in the next photograph is Blackie, James's dog (James says hello, by the way), and then there's a photograph of my three rabbits — Flopsy, Mopsy, and Cottontail. I wish I could have more pets, but Mom always says we have enough sick animals to look after at the clinic without having any extra. If I had my way I'd have lots! You're so lucky having all those pandas around you.

How are the panda corridors, by the way? I hope the pandas move along them so that they start to mate with other pandas on the reserve. Is Rick still going to chase them "Quick, quick, quick"? Anyway, I'd better go now, because office hours are about to start. I help every evening after school and on the weekends. I'll finish this letter later.

Okay, I'm back! Office hours were really busy and then I had to help with the animals in the residential unit — that's where we keep the animals who are too sick to go home. There's a cat named Polly who was hit by a car. She has two broken legs and a broken jaw. Mom put her legs in plaster and wired up her jaw but we're not sure if she's going to get better or not. I'm really worried about her. And there's Harry, a West Highland terrier who has Perthe's disease — a disease that affects the blood supply at the top of the thigh. Mom operated on him this morning and he's got to stay until we see whether the operation worked.

Well, I'd better stop writing now and do my homework. Write soon and let me know how you and the pandas are.

Lots of love,
Mandy

P.S. James said that I can send you e-mails from his computer, so you can write to me at the e-mail address that I gave you.

◆   ◆   ◆

From: Mei Ling Yun
To: Mandy Hope
Subject: Pandas

Dear Mandy,

Hi! I'm supposed to be writing a history assignment but I decided that I'd rather e-mail you! Thank you for the photographs and for your letter. Animal Ark looks lovely — maybe one day I can come and visit *you*!

All the pandas are well although Hua Hua (you're right, he is six months old) is getting very mischievous. The other night, Rick and Mr. Chang camped out — they are trying to track a red panda. They set their tent up in Bai Lu and Hua Hua's territory, which is also where the red panda has been seen. They cooked themselves some soup and after they had eaten, they left the metal pot outside the tent. When they went to bed, they heard a clanking sound. Rick looked out and saw Hua Hua chewing the pot. He had soup all over his face and paws and had started gnawing at the metal. So much for pandas only liking bamboo! Mom told me that when people first wrote about pandas they used to think that pandas ate metal. Villagers would often find that pandas had been to their huts in the night and had chewed up the pots and pans, often crushing them to pieces. Of course it was only because they were trying to get to the food remains, but the people didn't know that then — they used to call pandas "metal-eaters"!

Anyway, I guess I'd better start my history assignment. Oh, yes, Tai An said to say hello. He's been working for Mom since you left, helping find deer traps, and he still wants to be a vet when he leaves school.

Write back soon!

Love, Mei Ling

P.S. How are the cat and the dog you told me about in your letter? Did they get better?

P.P.S. The panda corridors are just about finished. We're hoping that the pandas will start to move along them in about six more weeks. The bamboo at the sides of the corridors has grown well, so we're hoping the pandas will be tempted to walk along them and start mixing with the other panda groups in the reserve.

◆　◆　◆

From: Mandy Hope
To: Mei Ling Yun
Subject: Red pandas

Dear Mei Ling,

I just got your e-mail. What are red pandas? I've never heard of them. Are

they just like giant pandas but red?
Let me know!

Harry (the dog) and Polly (the cat)
are both getting better. Harry's gone
home now. Polly's still at Animal Ark.
She can't eat by herself yet and Mom's
worried about one of her legs. I'll let
you know what happens.

Lots of love, Mandy
P.S. I bet Hua Hua looked really sweet
with soup all over his face!
P.P.S. Do you like chinchillas? I know
a man who breeds them and one of his
chinchillas just had babies. They're
adorable!

♦ ♦ ♦

From: Mei Ling Yun
To: Mandy Hope
Subject: Red pandas

Dear Mandy,
Thanks for your e-mail. Red pandas
don't look anything like giant pandas.
They're much more like raccoons or

foxes. In fact, villagers here call
them "fire-foxes." They're about ten
inches high. They have thick red coats,
pointed ears, little dark eyes, white
eyebrows, and pointed muzzles — just
like a fox's muzzle, except white.
Their tails are thick and have darker
bands of color running all the way down
them like a raccoon's. They live on
bamboo like giant pandas. They're very
rare and hardly any research has been
done on them. But two weeks ago, one of
the workers at the research station saw
one!

Mom decided that we should keep track
of it, so we're trying to catch it and
attach a radio tag. That's why Rick and
Mr. Chang camped out the other night.
Red pandas usually come out at dawn and
dusk, and they thought that if they
camped out in the area where it had
already been seen they'd have more
chance of coming across it. So far it
hasn't worked.

Still, Mom's hoping that there might
be a few of them around. It would be
really good if she could tag a group of

them like she tagged the giant pandas. It would mean that she could learn more about their habits in the wild, which would help people to try and breed them in captivity. I'm going to help over the weekend. I hope we find one!

Lots of love, Mei Ling

P.S. I like chinchillas although I have never seen one in real life. I bet they're really cuddly to hold!

♦ ♦ ♦

From: Mandy Hope
To: Mei Ling Yun
Subject: Red panda hunt

Dear Mei Ling,

Good luck this weekend!

Lots of love, Mandy

♦ ♦ ♦

From: Mei Ling Yun
To: Mandy Hope
Subject: Zhen

Dear Mandy,

We found a red panda this morning! It was great. At dawn, Mom, me, Rick, Tai An, Mr. Chang, and lots of the other helpers all spread out in the area where the panda had been seen and started looking carefully around the undergrowth and trees. I was with Tai An. He thought we should go where the arrow bamboo grows.

We were creeping through the bamboo when suddenly there it was — a flash of red fur just ahead! The panda was eating the young leaves of a bamboo plant. It wasn't eating like a giant panda — sitting up and using its hands — it was standing up and snipping off each bamboo leaf carefully with its teeth! Tai An whispered that he'd go and fetch the others. I stayed and watched the panda. It was beautiful — its coat was a deep russet red and so fluffy. After a while, it stopped eating and went to sleep in a hollow tree trunk nearby! It just curled up like a dog with its muzzle resting on its tail.

Anyway, Tai An came back with Rick and Mom. They tranquilized it while it was asleep and then attached the radio tag and found out that it's a female. We're going to call her Zhen. We're going to go out looking tomorrow morning, too. Mom says it's their breeding season, so we're hoping that if we stay near Zhen we might see some others and be able to tag them, too. It would be great for Mom's research! No one's ever seen red pandas mating in the wild before!

Anyway, I'll write more soon.

Love, Mei Ling

◆　◆　◆

From: Mei Ling Yun
To: Mandy Hope
Subject: Good news and bad news

Dear Mandy,
   I just had to e-mail you again. So
much has been happening — good and bad.
Mom, Rick, and I went out at dawn again
this morning and waited near Zhen to see
if there were any other red pandas
around. We watched Zhen for ages and
then all of a sudden a male red panda
appeared! He was bigger than Zhen and
the fur around his neck was thicker. He
didn't go up to Zhen at first. He kept
his distance, following her, eating
when she ate, drinking when she drank,
and then finally he went closer. She
started to make a whistling, twittering
noise sort of like a bird and he did the
same.
   Rick got his camera out and started
taking some photographs and then they
mated. We should have red panda babies
in five months! After the mating, Mom
tranquilized the male and so now he has

a radio tag, too. That's all the good news. The bad news is horrible.

We were on our way back to the station, going through the bushes in case we found any signs of other red pandas nearby, when we found some blood on the ground. We followed it and in a little clearing saw a red panda lying on the ground, bleeding. I felt sick, Mandy — I thought he was dead! Mom went over to have a look. He wasn't dead but he was really badly injured with a huge gash on his neck. Mom tranquilized him and asked me to run ahead to radio the vet at the Wolong Panda Reserve for help while she and Rick stopped the bleeding and brought him back to the station. I got through to the vet and she said she'd come out right away. But it seemed like we waited for ages before she arrived.

Anyway, when the vet came she managed to clean the wound and stitch it up but she was worried about the amount of blood he'd lost and about infection setting in. Mom thinks that he must

have been injured by another male red
panda.

Red pandas don't normally fight over
females — each male has a territory with
several females — but the injured panda
is a young male and Mom thinks that he
must have tried to take over an older
male's territory and that's why he got
into a fight. We've put him in a large
compound while we wait to see if he

recovers. Oh, Mandy, he's so sweet. I hate seeing him looking so sick. I just hope he gets better.

Love, Mei Ling
P.S. We named him Wei Wei.

◆　◆　◆

From: Mei Ling Yun
To: Mandy Hope
Subject: Wei Wei

Dear Mandy,
   Bad news. Wei Wei's getting worse. He's very weak and the wound has become infected. We have to fetch bamboo leaves for him but even so he's hardly eating them. I just wish I could pet and cuddle him but I know I shouldn't in case it makes him too tame to go back in the wild when/if he ever recovers. Tai An said that he's going to ask his grandmother what herbs can be used to fight infection. She knows all about healing with plants. Mom says it won't work but it must be worth a try, right?

I'll write soon.
  Love, Mei Ling

◆   ◆   ◆

From: Mandy Hope
To: Mei Ling Yun
Subject: Wei Wei

Dear Mei Ling,
  Thanks for all your e-mails. I'm so
sorry not to have replied sooner, but
James went away with his parents for
the weekend and I only got to read them
this afternoon after school.
  It's so exciting about Zhen — I can't
believe you're going to get to see red
panda cubs, too! James and I were
really upset to hear about Wei Wei,
though. How is he today? Have you tried
the herbs yet? I think you should. It
must be awful seeing him so sick.
  Polly the cat's gone home now. I was
sad to see her go but I'm very glad
that she's finally getting better. James
is planning to enter Blackie, his

naughty Labrador, into the local dog show!

Write soon and tell me the news.

Lots of love, Mandy

◆   ◆   ◆

From: Mandy Hope
To: Mei Ling Yun
Subject: Wei Wei

Dear Mei Ling,

I guess you must be too busy to e-mail me. Is Wei Wei any better? Please let me know how he is. I can't stop thinking about him.

Lots of love, Mandy

◆   ◆   ◆

From: Mei Ling Yun
To: Mandy Hope
Subject: Wei Wei

Dear Mandy,

Good news! Wei Wei's getting better! Sorry I haven't written but I've just

been so busy getting him bamboo leaves
and watching over him that I haven't
had time to sit down at my computer.
Tai An's grandmother made a traditional
herbal ointment — she wouldn't tell us
what was in it — but it worked! Wei Wei
began to improve the day after we put
it on and now the infection is almost
completely gone. Mom doesn't think it
was the ointment but I know it was. Wei
Wei's still weak but eating well and
the vet thinks that soon he should be
ready to be released into the wild.
Isn't it great? I'm so happy. I don't
know what I would have done if he'd
died.

The other pandas are all fine, too. We
found two more red panda females, so it
looks like Mom will have plenty of data
for her research. I can't wait until
the cubs are born in June and July. I
bet they'll be really cute! I've been
taking loads of pictures of Wei Wei and
I'll send you one. I hope everything's
fine with you. I'm really glad that
Polly is better, too. Did James take
Blackie to the dog show?

Bye for now!
Love, Mei Ling

◆   ◆   ◆

From: Mandy Hope
To: Mei Ling Yun
Subject: Photographs

Dear Mei Ling,
  Thanks a billion for the photographs!
They arrived this morning. I love the
one of Wei Wei curled up on top of a
log, his eyes closed and his head on
his tail — and the one of him climbing a
tree and peeking out from behind the
branches is so sweet that I've put it
in a frame on my dresser. It's just
great that he's getting better. No
wonder you're happy! I couldn't stop
smiling when I got your e-mail. Thanks
also for the photo of Hua Hua. Is he
still up to mischief? Looking at his
sparkling eyes, I bet he is! You're
just so lucky to live with pandas, Mei
Ling — I must come and visit again SOON!

Anyway, I'd better go now — my homework's waiting. Blow Hua Hua a big kiss from me and write soon to tell me all your news.

Lots of love, Mandy

P.S. James entered Blackie in the show — not for obedience, but in the class for the best sausage catcher.

P.P.S. Guess what? Blackie won!

Jenny Tells You All About Nordica and Other Whales

Did you know that . . .

- whales are not fish but mammals that spend their entire lives in water. They have lungs, not gills, and have to come to the surface of the ocean to take a breath.

- whales have hair instead of scales!

- there are about 80 types of whales living in the oceans of the world.

- blue whales are the biggest animals that have ever lived on earth — bigger than any kind of dinosaur. They can be up to 30 yards long and weigh in at a whopping 220 tons or more!

- whales don't have eyelids. Their eyes are protected by thick, oily tears.

- whales use the magnetic field of the earth for navigation.

- whales don't go into a deep sleep like most mammals. They have to be partly conscious to breathe, so they let only one half of their brain sleep at a time.

- sperm whales have the largest brains in the world, nearly six times the size of an average human brain. Their brains can weigh up to 20 pounds, though this is only 0.02% of their total body weight.

- sperm whales are amazing divers and have been known to dive to a depth of almost two miles in search of food. The longest recorded dive was for one hour and 52 minutes in 1969.

* the fat — or blubber — of a whale living in very cold water can be up to 20 inches thick. The blubber acts both as insulation and as an emergency food store.

* whales are the loudest animals on earth. The sound of a human shouting is around 70 decibels, while the sound of a jet engine is around 140 decibels. But the sound of a whale call can reach up to 188 decibels — and can be heard thousands of miles away!

Beagle
— *in the* —
Basket

One

"Excuse me! This is the vets' office, isn't it?"

Mandy Hope looked up from the bicycle tire she had just finished pumping. A large man with a flushed, shiny face was calling to her from the open window of his sports car. "That's right — Animal Ark," she replied, pointing up at the carved wooden sign swinging gently in the breeze. "But we're not open yet — unless it's an emergency, of course."

"Well, the thing is, I can't hang around," the man said anxiously, mopping his forehead with a large polka-dot handkerchief. "I had a terrible time catching this little fellow, and I'm going to be late for my first appointment. Could you help me get him out of the car, please?"

With a great deal of effort, the man levered himself out of the driver's seat. Mandy couldn't help wondering how such a big person could possibly be comfortable in such a small car.

"Lovely set of wheels, don't you agree?" the man said proudly, following Mandy's gaze and patting the car's gleaming hood. "Drives like a rocket. I've had this car for fifteen years, you know — since I was a young boy. Can't bear to part with her."

That explains it, Mandy thought to herself, trying not to smile. *You're certainly not a young boy now.* "So what do you have?" she asked, leaning her bike against the wall and peering into the car. She was curious to see exactly what kind of creature he'd managed to catch.

"Well, I spotted the poor thing in a ditch by the side of the road," the man replied, not exactly answering her question. "His leg seems to be hurt pretty badly. I managed to scoop him up and put him in an old box in the car, but he found a way out of it. Now he's gone under the passenger seat and I can't reach him." He paused and looked at Mandy. "I'm Geoff Bates, by the way, sales rep for candy and chocolates. Must have driven past your sign a hundred times on my route. Never thought I'd stop by one day!"

He walked around to open the passenger door and raised his eyebrows. "I think you're just about the right size to reach the little fellow," he said. "Could you give it a try?"

"Well, I'll do my best," Mandy replied, going around to join the man at the other side of the car. There was no way she could hear about a sick or injured creature without wanting to lend a hand. Tucking her blond hair behind one ear, she crouched down to take a cautious look under the passenger seat. Wounded animals were often frightened and could lash out suddenly, so she was ready to retreat if necessary.

A pair of beady round eyes set in a glossy green head stared back at her. A male mallard was nestled in a shadowy cave under the leather passenger seat. The floor was littered with crumpled chocolate-bar wrappers, and he seemed to have made himself quite comfortable among them. He didn't look like he was going anywhere in a hurry.

"Can you see him?" Mr. Bates asked, from somewhere behind her. "What's he up to?"

"He's just sitting there. He looks happy, though," she reported, and she heard the man groan.

"I won't be in York until ten at this rate," he muttered.

Mandy sat back on her heels and wondered what to do. She could just about reach the duck, but if she

backed him into a corner he might become
aggressive. That strong beak of his could strike a nasty
blow, and she wasn't wearing gloves. Suddenly, she
had a brainstorm.

"Can you reach in from the other side and make a
noise behind the seats?" she asked, turning around to
look at Mr. Bates. "I think that way we might be able
to flush him out. I'll be ready to catch him here."

"Good idea!" he replied promptly, and he hurried
around to open the door on the driver's side. Mandy
took off her school sweater and held it high, ready to
throw it over the duck when he emerged.

"Out you come, little duckie," called Mr. Bates in a
high voice, making a scrabbling sound on the back of
the passenger seat with his fingers. His large bottom
was up in the air as he leaned headfirst into the car,
and his face was turning redder and redder with
effort. Mandy had a terrible feeling she was going to
burst out laughing, so she tried not to look at him.
Don't be mean, she told herself sternly. *At least he took
the trouble to stop and help — lots of people would have just
driven past.* She forced herself to concentrate on what
they were trying to do.

The duck gave a low, hoarse call and Mandy
prepared herself as she willed the bird to come out.
She watched intently as Mr. Bates called and thumped
more loudly on the back of the seat, beginning to lose

patience. And then, with a very indignant quack, the tip of a yellow beak emerged and the mallard struggled out into the open, dragging one webbed foot awkwardly behind him.

As carefully as she could, Mandy dropped her sweater onto his body and picked him up — holding him gently but firmly with his hurt leg facing away from her. "It's all right," she said comfortingly, feeling the frantic beating of his heart through her fingers. "No one's going to hurt you."

Carefully, she pulled her sweater free of the duck's head, so he could see where he was and she could take a closer look at him. The beautiful colors of his plumage shone in the sun. Below his gleaming green head, a sparkling collar of white feathers ringed his neck. His breast was a subtle purple, and soft gray feathers covered the underside of his body — contrasting with his dark tail. Mandy couldn't tell exactly what was wrong with the injured leg, but it looked swollen, and one broad, paddle-shaped foot hung uselessly. His eyes were dull, too. And then she spotted a telltale piece of nylon thread trailing from his leg.

"He's gotten caught up in some fishing line, poor thing," she told Geoff Bates, who'd straightened up in relief and was wiping his face again with the polka-dot handkerchief. "Can you help me take him inside?

We'll need to get it off as quickly as possible. I think the clinic door's locked, but we can get there through the house."

"Of course, of course," Mr. Bates replied, opening the gate for her and hurrying ahead down the path. "I'm so grateful to you for helping me. I'd never have gotten him out on my own." He lifted the latch and pushed open the front door, then stood back to let Mandy through.

*   *   *

The Hopes lived in an old stone cottage in the little Yorkshire town of Welford. The vets' clinic was in a modern extension at the back of the house, which Mandy thought was a perfect arrangement. It meant she could keep a close eye on any animals who had to stay in the residential unit for a few days, and she was often able to help out with surgery, too. Her parents, Emily and Adam Hope, were both vets, so animals had been an important part of her life for as long as she could remember.

The duck gave another harsh call of alarm and began to struggle in Mandy's hands as she carried him into the cottage. "It's all right," she said soothingly. "We're just going to fix that leg of yours." Her father had gone out to a nearby farm early that morning but she knew her mother was at home, ready to start morning office hours.

"What's all this?" asked Dr. Emily, coming out of the kitchen. Her eyes widened in surprise as she saw Mandy holding the duck, with the large figure of Mr. Bates hovering behind her.

"I found this duck by the side of the road," he told Mandy's mom, almost apologetically. "I couldn't think of what else to do with him so I brought him here."

"He's got some fishing line wound around his leg," Mandy said. "Can you see the end of it there?"

"Oh, yes. I see it," said her mother, holding back her long auburn hair as she bent forward cautiously to take a closer look at the mallard. He watched her warily from the safety of Mandy's arms. "Looks like he's rather dehydrated, too," Dr. Emily added, carefully prying open the duck's beak. "Yes, his mouth is very dry inside. Never mind, I'm sure we'll be able to fix him up."

"I can't pay a huge amount for his treatment," Mr. Bates said awkwardly, taking a small white card out of his pocket, "but perhaps you could let me know what it's likely to cost. Here's my address and phone number."

"Don't worry," Dr. Emily said reassuringly, taking the card from him. "I'm sure it won't come to very much." Mandy caught her mother's eye and smiled. Dr. Emily might be more businesslike than her husband, but she could still be a softie sometimes. Mandy felt sure that Mr. Bates wouldn't be charged anything at all for his kindness.

"Marvelous!" he said, with a look of great relief. "And now I really have to go, or I'll lose my job." He riffled through the other jacket pocket and came up with a couple of chocolate bars. Putting them on a side table, he winked at Mandy and said, "These are for later, since you've got your hands full now. Thanks for everything!"

As Mr. Bates left, the duck began to strain against Mandy's grip again. "Should I take him to the clinic for you, Mom?" she asked. "I think he's getting a bit agitated."

"No, thank you very much," Dr. Emily replied firmly, shutting the front door behind Mr. Bates and scooping the bird expertly out of Mandy's arms. "Unless you hurry, you're going to be late for school as it is. Simon's opening up the clinic now, and I'm sure we can manage one little duck between us." Simon was the practice nurse who helped the Hopes run Animal Ark, along with Jean Knox, their receptionist.

"But, Mom . . . !" Mandy protested. "Can't I stay and help you?"

"School! Now!" replied Dr. Emily over her shoulder, already on her way to the clinic extension. "Don't worry, I'm sure he'll still be here when you get back."

Mandy pedaled frantically along the road toward school. She usually biked with her best friend, James Hunter, who also lived in Welford, but there was no sign of James this morning. He must have thought she'd gone earlier and decided not to wait for her. Mandy took one hand off the handlebar to snatch a quick look at her watch. She'd already missed homeroom and she was going to be late for her first class. It was Friday, so that would be — oh, no, biology! She groaned, and urged her aching legs to pedal faster. Biology used to be her favorite subject, but it definitely wasn't at the moment. Their teacher, Ms. Temple, was recovering from an eye operation and wouldn't be back until after spring break. A substitute teacher named Mr. Marsh was teaching her classes while she was away.

It was a couple of weeks into the spring semester, and so far, Mr. Marsh and Mandy weren't getting along very well. The trouble was, she found it very difficult to concentrate during his lessons. Biology was full of interesting information about plants and animals, and her mind was always shooting off on tangents. Some fact Mr. Marsh was explaining might remind her of a patient back at Animal Ark, for example, or a conversation she'd had with her parents. But she soon discovered that their new teacher hated being interrupted — unlike Ms. Temple, who always enjoyed a lively discussion.

"Yes, that's all very interesting, Amanda," Mr. Marsh had said to her a couple of days before, when she couldn't resist telling him how dangerous chocolate was for small animals like hamsters. "However, I must remind you that we are talking about digestion in *humans.* And now can we please get back to the subject?"

As soon as she got to school, Mandy hastily flung her bike against the railing and dashed over to the biology lab. "Sorry I'm late, Mr. Marsh," she said breathlessly as she slipped into the classroom and took a seat by the front, trying not to make any noise.

"Just take your book out quickly," he replied in an irritated voice, "and write down this assignment. As I was telling the others, we'll be doing something different over the next couple of weeks. I want each of you to work on your own project. You can choose the subject, as long as it has something to do with the topics we've covered so far. And I want to see lots of research and scientific information, please — not rubbish. This task is to help you organize your work, which *some* of you . . ." — and here he glared at Mandy, who felt herself blush — ". . . need to do. You can work on your projects at home as well as in class, and I want you to start this weekend. Please choose a topic and write a short outline, ready to hand in on Monday. Now, any questions?"

As the class continued, Mandy tried to concentrate on the complicated diagrams Mr. Marsh was drawing on the board — but her mind was already racing. There were so many subjects she was interested in, she didn't know which one to choose. Perhaps she could write about how animals adapt to their surroundings. There was plenty she could say about that. Or maybe she could concentrate on animal travelers: birds who fly south in winter, or salmon who come back to the river in which they were born to lay their eggs. She was so busy thinking, she found it difficult to keep her mind on what Mr. Marsh was saying, and once or twice he caught her looking out the window. At the end of the class, he called her over.

"I think you and I need to have a chat, Amanda," he began, loosening his tie and rubbing his neck. He was quite young — about the same age as Ms. Temple, Mandy guessed — but he always wore a formal jacket and tie. Ms. Temple was much more casual, with her flowery cotton dresses and wavy brown hair that never managed to stay neatly tied in a ponytail. She loved her subject, though. Mandy sighed, wishing Ms. Temple was giving this assignment. They could have chosen a really interesting topic together.

She suddenly realized that Mr. Marsh had stopped talking and was fixing his hazel eyes on her. "You see?" he said in exasperation. "You haven't been listening to a word I've been saying, have you? *And* you missed the beginning of the class this morning. It's just not good enough!"

"I'm sorry, sir," Mandy replied, staring hard at her fingernails. She tried to explain. "You see, I was late because —"

Mr. Marsh held up one hand. "No, I don't want to hear any excuses!" he said, shaking his head. "Whatever happens at home, you must get to school on time. And when you *do* get here, you have to put everything else out of your mind and concentrate on what you are being taught. Is that clear, Amanda?"

"Yes, sir," Mandy said, her cheeks burning again. She felt angry and confused. It was so unfair! There were lots of others in the class who didn't work nearly as hard as she did. Why was Mr. Marsh picking on her?

Two

"Oh, come on, Mandy! Give it a rest," James said, buckling on his helmet. "It's the weekend now. No more Mr. Marsh for two days."

"I suppose you're right," Mandy admitted, adjusting her schoolbag before pushing off. Complaining to James had already made her feel better, and besides, there was always plenty going on at Animal Ark to take her mind off things. "Can you come home with me?" she called to him. "There's a new patient you have to meet!"

By the time they'd arrived back in Welford, her bad mood had disappeared completely. She and James dashed straight to the residential unit at the back of the clinic. Simon, the practice nurse, was just settling a sleepy-looking rabbit into one of the empty cages.

Mandy proudly showed James the duck. "Oh, he is

lovely," James said, admiring the bird as he looked out at them from the shelter of his cage. "Wouldn't that make a fantastic photo? Look at the color of his head!"

"He's looking a bit happier than he did this morning," Mandy said. "Did you manage to get all that fishing line untangled, Simon?"

"Eventually," he replied, running a hand through his spiky blond hair. "It was quite a job, though — the line had been there for such a long time it had actually cut into his leg." He shook his head. "It's horrible stuff, nylon fishing line. People ought to see the damage it causes."

The duck gave a hoarse, low call and shifted uneasily. "So what will happen to him now?" Mandy asked. "Could he fend for himself if we put him back on a river or pond somewhere?" She knew that wild creatures should be kept in captivity for as short a time as possible.

"Your mother has a plan," Simon said, walking back toward the clinic. "I haven't had a chance to ask her about it, but I know she's been talking to someone on the phone."

"Simon! You're needed," came a voice from down the corridor, and then Dr. Emily popped her head around the door. "Hi, dear," she said, smiling at Mandy. "And hello, James. What are you two up to?"

"Checking up on our duck," Mandy answered. "What's your plan for him, Mom?"

"Geraldine O'Meara," her mother answered briefly before she and Simon disappeared back to the clinic. "I'll tell you all about it later," she called over her shoulder as she went.

"So who's Geraldine O'Meara?" James asked, looking puzzled.

Mandy was smiling delightedly. "Oh, come on, James! You remember," she said. "She's that journalist who writes for all the country magazines. You know, the one with the beagle and the tabby cat. I must have told you about the two of them!"

"Oh, yes, that does ring a bell," James said, wandering off to inspect some of the other cages. "They get along really well together, don't they?"

"They're devoted to each other," Mandy said, taking one last look at the duck before following James. "Robbie was the runt of the litter, and his mother abandoned him. Martha — she's the cat — had just had kittens, so she suckled Robbie, too. He fed alongside the kittens, and Geraldine's convinced he still thinks Martha's his mother."

"But why does your mother think Geraldine can help with the duck?" James said, watching a big lop-eared rabbit nibble on a piece of carrot.

"Geraldine has a pond on her farm," Mandy

answered. "That must be what Mom has in mind — it would be the perfect spot for him." She grabbed James's arm. "Let's go to the house. You can call your mom and then, later on, we can persuade mine to take us with her when she goes to Geraldine's. You've got to come, James. Wood Vale is such an amazing place!"

"Now you're sure you can spare the time for this, Mandy?" Dr. Emily asked the next morning. She and Mandy were carefully loading the wire carrying-basket that held the duck into the back of the Land Rover. "What about that project of yours?"

"Oh, Mom, I spent time on it after breakfast," Mandy said, slightly uneasily. She had spent time *thinking* about the project, it was true, but her notebook was still only full of doodles. It was so difficult to choose the right topic — one that interested her but was scientific enough for Mr. Marsh. *I'll try it again tomorrow,* she thought, putting biology firmly at the back of her mind.

"Bye, Dad!" she called from the passenger seat as Dr. Adam's tall figure appeared in the cottage doorway to wave at them. "See you later!"

They pulled out of the driveway and onto the road. "This is such a good idea of yours, Mom," Mandy said, buckling up her seat belt. "What made you think of Geraldine?"

"Well, I saw her with Martha in the clinic a couple of weeks ago," Dr. Emily replied. "She mentioned something then about the pond at Wood Vale. Then yesterday, it suddenly hit me that it would be the perfect place for Mr. Duck. Luckily, when I phoned Geraldine she agreed at once. She's more than happy to keep an eye on him over the next few weeks."

"Is Martha okay?" Mandy asked anxiously. "Was it anything serious?"

"Just a case of conjunctivitis," her mother said. "Her eyes did look quite sore, but antibiotic drops should have cleared up the infection by now. She's getting older," she added in a gentler voice. "Do you remember the very first time you saw her?"

"Just barely," Mandy replied, rolling down the car window and taking in a deep breath of fresh air. It was a fine day in spring, and all the town gardens were bright with sweet-smelling blossoms. She closed her eyes and tried to focus in on the memory. "I think I remember Martha lying in her basket, with lots of furry little bodies next to her. It's all a bit hazy, though."

"Well, you were only three," said her mother, smoothing back a strand of curly auburn hair that the breeze had blown into her eyes. "Just think — we've been looking after Geraldine's pets for over nine years now! I really don't know where the time goes."

"Have you ever seen that happen before, Mom?" Mandy asked. "A mother cat bringing up another baby animal, I mean."

"Oh, yes, it's quite common," Dr. Emily replied, braking as she steered around a sharp corner. "Cats are such motherly creatures, they'll happily feed all sorts of orphans. I've even seen a newborn squirrel tucked in among a litter of kittens. But it *is* unusual that Robbie and Martha should still be so close now."

Mandy smiled affectionately, thinking of all the times she'd seen the tabby patiently putting up with Robbie as he bounded around her. Once she'd caught Martha tapping him smartly on the nose when she was tired of the rough-and-tumble, but her claws were safely sheathed.

"Beagles are pack animals by nature," her mother went on. "But Robbie's quite different. Geraldine's often told me that he doesn't want to mix with other dogs — he'd much rather be with Martha." She grinned. "They're like an old married couple."

"Like you and Dad, you mean?" Mandy teased. "I bet they don't argue all the time about who's going to do the dishes!"

"All right, it's your turn next, then," said her mother promptly.

Mandy was about to protest when they turned into

the Hunters' driveway, and James came out to meet
them. His pet Labrador, Blackie, was rushing around
his heels and Mr. and Mrs. Hunter had to stop him
from jumping up into the Land Rover, too.

The mallard gave a couple of quacks, as if asking
whether they'd arrived. "Not long now, Mr. Duck,"
Mandy said, turning around to check that his cage
was still wedged securely. "Wait until you see your new
home. You're going to love it!"

Twenty minutes later, they were driving along a
winding lane that led steeply downhill. "There it is!"
Mandy cried, pointing back to a wooden sign nailed
onto a huge yew tree at the side of the road. "You've
just gone past the gate, Mom."

"Thanks, love," her mother replied, reversing the
Land Rover a few yards. "Why do I always manage
to miss that turn? You'd think I'd know the way by
now."

Mandy jumped down to open the gate and her
mother drove through. As the Land Rover crunched
over the gravel driveway, there was a volley of excited
barking and a tan-and-white dog dashed out of the
house to greet them. Mandy shut the gate behind her
and hurried over to say hello, crouching down on her
knees to give the beagle a big hug.

"This is Robbie," she said as James climbed out of
the car to join them. "He's gorgeous, isn't he?"

"Lovely," James agreed, bending down and patting Robbie, too. "I think he can smell Blackie on me," he added as the beagle began sniffing his hand with great concentration and then licking it.

"You're always pleased to see visitors, aren't you, Robbie?" Mandy said, taking the dog's tawny head between her hands and gazing into his shining eyes while he wagged his tail furiously. He had a white muzzle, tapering up to a stripe between his eyes, and soft, toffee-colored ears. His chest and legs were white, as was the tip of his jaunty tail, while the rest of his body was the same shade of caramel, splotched with darker patches of brown. Mandy particularly loved the way a furrow between Robbie's eyes sometimes made it look as though he was frowning, intent and busy, as he followed some enticing scent.

"I'd say you were the favorite, Mandy," said a cheerful voice with a soft Irish lilt to it, and she looked up to see Geraldine O'Meara smiling down at her. "But it must have been a while since you were last here," she added as Mandy jumped up to introduce James. "I believe you're taller than I am now!"

Geraldine might have been on the small side, but she was a bundle of energy. She reminded Mandy of a firework, fizzing with enthusiasm and never still for a minute. Her clear blue eyes always seemed to be sparkling with life. "You only have to look at

Geraldine to tell she's Irish," Mandy's mom had said many times. "Dark hair and pale skin, with those amazing blue eyes." As usual, she was wearing a faded pair of jeans and a T-shirt. Today she'd topped them off with a pair of thigh-high waders, which were draped in pondweed.

"I hope we haven't caught you at a bad time," Dr. Emily called as she came over.

"Not at all," Geraldine replied warmly, taking her hand and giving it a squeeze. "It's always wonderful to see you! I was only checking over the pond to make sure it's shipshape for our new guest. Let me just put Robbie inside while we take the mallard down there."

"We'll see you in a minute, I promise!" Mandy said, giving Robbie one last pat before he was taken away. Then she and James carefully slid the traveling cage out of the back of the Land Rover.

"Well, he doesn't look too bad, considering his journey," Dr. Emily said as the duck watched her steadily with his beady black eyes.

Geraldine closed the front door of the cottage safely behind her and came over to join them. She'd taken off her waders and replaced them with an old pair of sneakers. "Oh, that's a fine fellow," she said, looking at the mallard. "I think he'll do very well with us."

"How many other ducks do you have at the

moment?" Mandy asked, holding the cage securely, as she followed Geraldine through a side gate and into the backyard.

"There are five mallards, and their families," Geraldine began, counting on her fingers as she led the way down a cobbled path between the trees. "Two males and three females with six ducklings. Plus a couple of tufted ducks I got in the spring."

"What a fantastic place!" James exclaimed behind them. "It looks like something out of a nature film."

"See? I told you," Mandy said, steadying the cage against her knee and turning back to grin at James's wondering face as he gazed around.

The yard at Wood Vale looked like a clearing in some enchanted forest. Half of it was taken up by a large pond, fringed with reeds and bushes. A neatly fenced vegetable garden lay opposite, and beyond that was a lawn the size of a small meadow, dotted with wild flowers among the grass. Some chickens wandered here and there, scratching at the ground, while others pecked busily in two large, wire-covered runs. The orchard stood on the other side of a bushy lavender hedge that ran along the far side of the garden.

"I'm glad you like it," Geraldine said warmly. She stopped by a wooden bench close to a willow tree that looked out over the pond and added quietly, "Most people thought I wouldn't be able to manage the place after my father died. I knew I could never sell it, though."

Mandy settled the duck in his cage at her feet and followed Geraldine's gaze. A group of tall yellow irises was blooming among the rushes on the far side of the pond, and a rippling carpet of lilies opened their creamy white flowers on the quiet water. She could understand just how Geraldine felt. If Wood Vale belonged to her family, she wouldn't want to leave, either.

Noticing James's puzzled expression, Geraldine explained, "I grew up at Wood Vale, but my mother died when I was young. Ten years ago my father became ill, so I moved back home to look after him. And I'm still here!"

"Keeping it up beautifully, too," Dr. Emily added, sitting down on the bench. "Oh, look, Mandy! James! Over there!" She pointed to a couple of mallards who had just emerged from a clump of rushes, followed by a bobbing line of fluffy ducklings.

"Come on, everyone!" Mandy said, suddenly reminded of why they were there. "Let's set this duck free. I bet he can't wait to get his feet wet again."

"Of course! What am I thinking, rambling on like this!" Geraldine exclaimed, tearing her eyes away from the pond and looking down at the duck. "And why did I take my waders off? I'll just run back to the house and get them. Then I can take his cage down to the water and let him come out in his own time."

"Don't worry!" Mandy said, kicking off her canvas shoes. "I'll do it." She rolled up the legs of her jeans and scrambled down to the edge of the pond with the cage in her arms. Soft, silky mud oozed between her toes. "Here you are, Mr. Duck," she said, setting the cage down and opening the front flap. "Welcome to paradise!"

The mallard gave another of his low, husky calls. For a while he stayed still, staring out as though he couldn't believe his eyes. After a moment, he moved forward slowly, one step at a time, his bad leg dragging behind. Mandy held her breath. The duck paused for a second at the mouth of the cage. Then, with a stream of hoarse quacks, he sailed out onto the water, looking all around with what she thought was a very satisfied expression.

"Success!" she called to the others, swinging the empty cage and making her way back up the bank to join them. She wiped her feet on the springy grass and jammed her shoes back on. They all watched as their duck stretched his wings with a whir and a flap, then started busily searching for food.

"He can swim just fine," James observed. "His leg doesn't seem to bother him at all in the water."

"Will the other ducks accept him?" Mandy asked Geraldine.

"I think they should," she replied. "Now if it was swans we were dealing with, that would be a very different matter. They're much more territorial — won't accept a stranger on their patch."

A few minutes later, their mallard had joined the other ducks on the pond, and Mandy had to look carefully to tell him apart.

"Of course, he'll lose that glossy green head very soon," Geraldine said, shading her eyes with one hand as she stared into the sun.

"What do you mean?" Mandy asked in alarm. "Will the others pick on him? I thought you said they'd be okay."

"It's nothing like that, to be sure," Geraldine said, laughing as she put her arm around Mandy's waist. "No, he's going to be losing his feathers — molting! He'll look much more like the females in a month or so, and he won't be able to fly. The experts call it 'being in eclipse.'"

"I'm sure he'll have settled in by then," Mandy said, watching as the ducks set off in stately procession toward a clump of bright green weeds. "He won't want to go anywhere else."

"Well now, everything looks fine on the duck front," Geraldine said briskly, turning away from the water. "So you can all come along to the orchard with me." She stretched out a hand to pull Dr. Emily up from the bench and declared, "There's something I want to show you — and I promise it's worth seeing!"

Mandy took one last look at the pond and then followed the others over the long grass with a spring in her step. The duck seemed happily settled, and she couldn't wait to discover what Geraldine had in store. She usually had some new scheme on the go, which she would write about for the country magazines she worked on. Added to that, Robbie and Martha were waiting for them up at the house. In fact, the day seemed pretty much perfect, so far!

Three

"Here we are!" Geraldine said, throwing out one arm with a flourish. "My newest exciting enterprise!"

Mandy and James looked toward the patch of rough ground at the edge of the orchard, and then back at each other. "What exactly are those?" Mandy said uncertainly. She didn't want to disappoint Geraldine, but she didn't have a clue what the two small wooden houses were for.

And then James let out a cry. "Beehives!" he said. "That's what they are, aren't they? Look, you can see a couple of bees flying around the roof."

"They are indeed," Geraldine said proudly. "By next year, Wood Vale Organic Honey should be up and running. Isn't that wonderful?"

"Fantastic," Mandy agreed politely, but without much enthusiasm. She was rather wary of bees, and she'd been expecting something different — a couple of goats in the orchard perhaps, or even a pony, or a nice fat pig who could root about under the trees. You couldn't exactly bond with a bee, could you?

"Oh, c'mon!" Geraldine said, taking Mandy's arm and gently pushing her forward. "You can do better than that, Mandy Hope! Come and have a look. When I've told you what amazing creatures bees are, you'll understand why I'm so excited. Don't worry — we won't get too close."

"Okay," Mandy said, prepared to give Geraldine the benefit of the doubt. "And you come, too, Mom," she added, pulling Dr. Emily along with them. It wasn't that she was frightened exactly, but she did feel nervous.

James was already standing at a safe distance opposite one of the hives. "So what's going on in there?" he asked Geraldine. "I can see the bees going in by that little entrance," and he pointed to a tiny hole above a wooden shelf at the base of the hive, "but I don't know what they're up to inside."

"Those are some worker bees," Geraldine told them. "They've been off looking for flower nectar to bring back to the hive. Now, inside, there are other worker bees making honeycomb out of wax. The queen bee will lay an egg in each of the cells of the honeycomb. And can you guess how many eggs she can lay in a day? Go on, try to guess."

"Twenty?" Mandy tried, interested almost in spite of herself. Geraldine shook her head. "All right then, fifty," Mandy guessed again. "No, make that a hundred."

"*Two thousand!*" Geraldine told them, her eyes shining. "Isn't that amazing?"

"Wow!" James breathed, pushing his glasses back up his nose as he peered forward. "She must be worn out."

"She has attendants to look after her," Geraldine said, putting her hands in her pockets and leaning back as she watched the bees coming and going. "They feed her and groom her, while other bees look after the grubs as they hatch. Oh, I can't tell you how fascinating it is, once you start learning how the hive works."

"So what about the honey?" Mandy asked, coming nearer to the hives and standing next to James. "How's that made? And where is it, exactly?"

"Well, the worker bees come back to the hive with pollen, nectar, and water, too," Geraldine said. "It all gets mixed up in their honey stomachs, and then they seal it in other cells in the honeycomb and leave it to ripen."

"Do you talk to your bees, Geraldine?" asked Dr. Emily with a smile. "Don't the country folk say you should talk to them and tell them all your news?"

"Would you believe, I do talk to them," she confessed, looking slightly embarrassed. "I know it's crazy, though. Bees can't hear," she explained to Mandy and James. "They communicate through smell and vibration."

"How, exactly?" James asked. He was always eager to find out the precise facts behind any statement.

"Just listen to this," Geraldine began, her face alight with interest. "When a worker bee finds a new source of nectar — say my lavender bushes have started to bloom — she comes back to the hive and does a special dance on the side of the honeycomb. It tells the others precisely where the nectar is — how far away *and* in what direction. And of course they can smell the pollen on her, too, so that helps them find it."

"That's incredible!" Mandy said. "Hey!" She took a couple of quick steps backward as a bee buzzed a little too close to her face for comfort.

"Maybe it's time for a snack," Geraldine said, laughing and putting an arm around her shoulder. "I could talk about bees for hours, but I'm sure Robbie's wondering what we're up to. Still, I hope I've whetted your appetite."

James nodded enthusiastically, and Mandy had to agree. There *was* something fascinating about bees, even if they weren't particularly cuddly.

"And how's Martha doing?" Mandy asked Geraldine as they walked up the path toward the house. "Has her conjunctivitis cleared up?"

Geraldine frowned slightly and jammed her hands in the pockets of her jeans. "It's better than it was," she said. "She's not herself, though — she doesn't seem to want to do anything. Still, I suppose that's normal for an old cat like her." She looked at Mandy and summoned up a smile. "Why don't you look her over and tell me what you think."

"Of course I will," Mandy replied, worried by the sad look in Geraldine's eyes. "And even better, so will Mom. Her bag's in the Land Rover."

Geraldine was about to say something else when a volley of loud barks sounded from inside the house. "Would you listen to that!" she said. "Somebody's feeling left out."

She opened the back door and immediately Robbie bounded toward them, only pausing for a second to pick up a rubber ball that was lying in the flower bed. He dropped it at Mandy's feet, looking up at her appealingly and wagging his tail.

"All right," Mandy said, smiling. "Just one quick throw, okay?" She had such a soft spot for Robbie, and it was impossible to resist his dark, shining eyes. He was a beautiful-looking dog, but on top of that, there was a sweetness in his nature that made him extra special. Although she'd often seen him teasing Martha, frisking around her and nuzzling her with his nose, he was always careful not to hurt her. And he was so affectionate! Mandy knew that as soon as she sat down, Robbie would be next to her, trying to snuggle up as close as possible and laying his head on her lap.

"You'll be here all day now." Geraldine laughed from the doorstep as Mandy threw the ball in a wide arc over the vegetable garden and onto the grass beyond. Robbie tore off down the path in hot pursuit.

"Can you take over now, James?" Mandy asked. She was anxious to have a look at Martha as soon as possible.

"Sure," he replied, before whistling Robbie back so that Mandy could follow her mother and Geraldine through the back door.

It was easy to tell from the state of the kitchen that Geraldine was more interested in the outside of Wood Vale than she was in the house. Mandy liked the shabby, comfortable feel of the room, though. Everything looked old and well used. Pots and pans were hooked to a circular rack that hung down from the ceiling, and a huge wooden dresser held Geraldine's collection of china, in every color of the rainbow. The walls were covered in framed black-and-white photographs of the O'Meara family, while more recent color shots took up every inch of space between.

Mandy usually enjoyed looking at the photos, but today she went right over to a large wicker basket in one corner of the kitchen. "Hello there, Martha," she said softly, crouching down to stroke the gray tabby cat who was lying there asleep. Immediately, she could tell that Martha had lost weight. The cat's ribs and knobbly spine stuck out prominently.

Martha opened her eyes, and Mandy could see that her eyelids were red and inflamed. "You don't look very happy, poor old girl," she murmured to Martha, scratching her behind the ears. The tabby pushed her head against Mandy's fingers, and then closed her eyes again.

Mandy looked over to where her mother was standing, leaning against the dresser and watching her, while Geraldine filled the kettle and put it on her old stove. Something in Mandy's expression must have showed her alarm, because Dr. Emily came over to the basket right away. She took one look at Martha and then lifted her out gently. "Do you mind if I give Martha a quick examination, Geraldine?" she asked, setting the cat down on a newspaper that was lying on the kitchen table. "Perhaps you could hold her for a minute while I wash my hands?"

"Of course," Geraldine replied, going over to the

table. "Soap's in the dish and there's a towel hanging up by the door." When she saw Martha, she added worriedly, "Oh, dear, oh, dear. She looks much worse all of a sudden. Why didn't I check up on her more often? I just got so carried away with the pond, and then the bees and everything . . ."

"I'll get your bag from the Land Rover, Mom," Mandy offered. She felt a cold hand clutch at her stomach as she hurried through the house and out of the front door to the car. They'd been so carefree before — now all she could think about was what might be wrong with Martha. By the time she returned to the kitchen, James was standing by the table, too, with Robbie next to him. He shot her an anxious look, while the beagle sniffed at Martha's feet and whined quietly.

"Here you are, Mom," Mandy said, putting the bag down on the table and then going to wash her hands in the sink, too, in case she was needed to help.

"Thanks, dear," Dr. Emily murmured, probing Martha's stomach gently with her fingers. "She's certainly very thin," she went on, turning to Geraldine. "How's her appetite?"

Geraldine shook her head. "She hasn't been eating much for the last couple of days," she said, running one hand through her mop of dark curls and frowning again.

Martha stood on the kitchen table with her legs bent and her tail lowered. Dr. Emily carefully opened the cat's mouth, looked at her teeth and gums, and took her temperature. Robbie barked a couple of times and looked inquiringly up at Mandy, as though asking what was going on.

"Don't worry," she told him. "We're just trying to find out what's the matter with Martha, that's all."

"We won't hurt her," James added, patting Robbie reassuringly.

"Could you pass me a syringe, please, Mandy?" her mother said while she waited for Martha's temperature to register. "I'd like to take a blood sample," she explained to Geraldine. "That'll be the most accurate way of finding out exactly what's the matter with Martha. I'd rather not make a diagnosis until I'm absolutely sure, and it won't take long. I can run the test myself back at Animal Ark and have the results the next day."

"Of course," Geraldine replied distractedly. "Whatever needs to be done. I'm so sorry — I should have brought her in to see you before now, obviously. I just thought she might have had a touch of cat flu. She does get it now and then, but she usually manages to shake it off after a day or so."

Mandy located a syringe in the bag and removed the sterile cover before passing it to her mother. Dr. Emily was looking at Martha's temperature on the thermometer, but her face gave nothing away. "Don't be too hard on yourself," she said to Geraldine while she took the blood sample. "Martha could have taken a turn for the worse with very little warning."

"I'm sure Mom will be able to sort everything out," Mandy added sympathetically. She knew how much Geraldine loved Martha, and she could imagine just how awful she was feeling.

"Okay! All done," said Dr. Emily, after she'd finished by giving Martha an antibiotic injection. "I'll leave you some antibiotics and eyedrops, and here's a sample pack of some liquid food that she might like to try. Perhaps you could pop her back in the basket now, Mandy?"

"Sure," Mandy said, picking Martha up as carefully as she could. Immediately Robbie whirled around and dashed over to the basket, settling himself in it and looking up at her. "Hey, Robbie!" Mandy exclaimed. "Don't you think you should let Martha have the best place?"

"That's exactly what he's doing," Geraldine said. She came over to stand beside them, and Mandy saw that there was a tear on her cheek. "Martha likes to sleep next to him," she explained, dashing one hand quickly over her eyes and then giving a dim smile. "Robbie takes his duties very seriously, you know. He's just getting into the right position."

"Well . . ." Mandy began doubtfully. Surely if Martha were ill, it would be better for her not to be with Robbie in the basket? She looked over to the sink, where her mother was washing her hands. But Dr. Emily quickly nodded her head.

"Okay, you're the boss," Mandy said. She lowered Martha's thin little body carefully into the basket. Immediately, the cat curled herself into a neat ball against Robbie's clean white stomach and closed her eyes. Gently, he licked her ear a couple of times and then laid his own head next to hers, forming a protective curve around her body.

Geraldine looked tenderly at them both and then tucked a faded soft toy between Robbie's paws. "Mouse has to go in the basket, too," she confessed, with an embarrassed smile.

"Just like an old married couple," Dr. Emily repeated, walking over and putting a comforting arm around Mandy's shoulder.

Mandy tried to reply, but the lump in her throat made it difficult to speak. *Oh, please, let Martha get better!* she said silently to herself.

Four

"Do you have any idea what *might* be the matter with Martha?" Mandy asked her mother worriedly after they'd waved good-bye to Geraldine and pulled out of the driveway at Wood Vale.

"Well, I didn't want to say anything to Geraldine until we knew for sure," Dr. Emily said slowly, "but I've got a strong suspicion that Martha might have FIV — Feline Immunodeficiency Virus, to give the condition its full name. Quite a mouthful, isn't it?"

"What's that, exactly?" Mandy asked. "Is it serious?" The nagging sense of worry in the pit of her stomach was growing stronger by the second.

"Yes, it is, I'm afraid," Dr. Emily admitted as she drove the Land Rover slowly up the steep hill. "FIV affects the immune system, you see. It makes cats more prone to other infections that they don't have the strength to shake off — like Martha's conjunctivitis."

"Poor Martha," James said, sitting back. "But how would she catch FIV in the first place?"

"Well, it's spread through body fluids — so probably from saliva," Dr. Emily explained. "Martha might have been bitten by an infected cat at some time or other. The virus could have been in her system for a while before she developed any symptoms. Unfortunately, there's no vaccination against it."

"So what happens now?" Mandy asked her mother. "How do we treat her?"

By now, they had reached the top of the street and were waiting to join the main road. Dr. Emily Hope put on the parking brake for a moment and laid a hand over Mandy's. "There isn't a cure for FIV," she said gently, a sympathetic look in her green eyes. "We can treat the secondary infections Martha's developed with antibiotics, but there's no getting rid of the virus itself. If she *does* have FIV, that is. We can't be certain until her blood's been tested."

"But you're pretty sure she has it," Mandy said miserably. "You wouldn't have mentioned it to us otherwise." She felt tears beginning to sting the backs of her eyes. She'd known Martha for most of her life.

It was awful to think of the motherly tabby cat being so ill — and beyond their help, too. "Surely there must be something we can do for her?" she added fiercely, quickly brushing her eyes with the back of her hand.

"We can make sure she doesn't suffer too much pain," her mother said, looking to her left and right before edging the Land Rover out into the road. "Martha's had a long and happy life, after all. Between us, we'll be able to give her a peaceful and dignified end."

Mandy stared out of the window without taking in what she was seeing. It was almost unbearable to imagine Robbie lying all alone in the basket, with no Martha to cuddle up against him.

Nobody said very much for the rest of the journey back to Welford.

"Come on now, dear," Dr. Emily said, breaking the silence as they approached the town. "Try not to get too sad and mopey. That won't do any good, will it?" And she patted Mandy's knee.

"I suppose not," Mandy said, giving herself a little shake and doing her best to cheer up. She tried to think of something that might stop her brooding. "Could James stay for dinner tonight?" she asked her mother. "Maybe we could go out for pizza or something."

"Good idea!" Dr. Emily replied. "What do you say, James?"

"That would be great," James said enthusiastically. "I don't think I can stay very late, though. We're visiting my grandmother tomorrow, and we have to get up early."

"I'll give your parents a call as soon as we get in and tell them we'll be sure to bring you home early," Mandy's mother promised as they walked up the path to the house. Then she stopped and sniffed the air. "Hang on, we may have to hold that pizza," she added. "I think Dad's started cooking already." A savory smell had come wafting out to greet them.

"Just as long as it's not cabbage soup," Mandy groaned. Her father was always trying to lose weight and keep fit. He'd made so much cabbage soup for his latest diet that Mandy and her mom had eventually protested. "If I eat another bowl of cabbage soup, I'm going to start turning green!" Dr. Emily had said.

"You haven't gone back on your word, have you, Dad?" Mandy asked once they were all in the cozy, oak-beamed kitchen. "You're not by any chance making something that begins with C and S?" She looked at him sternly and folded her arms.

"Now what could that possibly be?" Dr. Adam replied, his eyes twinkling as he scratched his dark beard and tried not to smile. He was wearing an apron and his face was flushed with heat from the stove. "Cheese soufflé, perhaps? Or chop suey? Chicken stew, maybe? No, it's none of those." Then he stopped frowning and put on a pained expression. "Surely you don't mean my tasty cabbage soup? But I bet James would just love to try some!"

"Dad!" Mandy warned, poking him with a wooden spoon. "You promised . . ."

"Don't worry! I've decided cabbage soup's too good for you." Her father grinned, turning back to the stove and stirring a bubbling saucepan. "You'll have to make do with vegetable lasagna instead. I'll just have to go for a jog tomorrow and work it all off."

"Sounds perfect!" Dr. Emily said, giving her husband a quick hug. "I'll go and call the Hunters quickly to see if James can stay. Mandy, you need to clear all those books off the kitchen table, please, so we can start setting it."

"You know, I have an idea," James confided, as he helped Mandy put the books back into her schoolbag. "I was thinking about Geraldine in the Land Rover just now, and I wondered whether you might want to write about bees for your project. I thought they were fascinating, didn't you?"

Mandy stood still for a moment with a file clutched against her chest as she considered his suggestion. "You're brilliant!" she exclaimed after a few seconds' thought, her eyes shining with enthusiasm. "Geraldine can tell me all about them, and I can make it really scientific. We've studied pollination in class already. Thanks, James! You're super!"

"That's all right," James said, blushing to the roots of his hair as he stuffed a couple of textbooks into the bag. "I'm glad you think it could work."

"Mom's visiting Geraldine tomorrow to see how Martha is," Mandy went on. "I wanted to go with her anyway. Perhaps I could talk to Geraldine about it then. I bet she has some books I could borrow."

But Dr. Emily looked doubtful when Mandy explained the plan to her over dinner. "I don't know, dear," she said. "We should have the results of Martha's blood test by tomorrow. If it's bad news, I'll need to break it to Geraldine and discuss Martha's treatment with her. I think she might have other things on her mind apart from bees, don't you?"

"Maybe," Mandy admitted, chasing a slice of carrot around her plate. Perhaps it would be insensitive to expect Geraldine to help with her project at such a difficult time. It was a pity, though. James had suggested the ideal subject and she couldn't wait to get started. Mr. Marsh would be furious if she hadn't done any research, and although she and James had searched through all the books in the study, they'd only found one short paragraph about bees.

She tried to think back to what Geraldine had told them that afternoon, but it wasn't enough to build up a whole picture. And then she remembered Geraldine's look of pride and enthusiasm as she'd shown them the hives. What had she said? "I could talk about bees for hours." That was it. And she'd seemed so forlorn as they left, turning to go back into the house.

"I don't know," she began slowly. "I got the feeling this afternoon that Geraldine was rather lonely. She was so pleased to see us, and do you remember how eager she was that we stay for a snack? She might be glad to have some company tomorrow — especially if there *is* bad news about Martha."

"You may have a point there," Dr. Adam said, waving his fork at her and sending a piece of lettuce flying across the table. "I've often thought how isolated Wood Vale must be for someone as lively as Geraldine. I know she's got lots of friends, but there's no one close by for her to visit."

"Besides," James added, "she knows so much about bees. Helping Mandy with her project might be just what she needs to take her mind off things."

"Well, you could be right," Dr. Emily said, putting her knife and fork together and sitting back.

"Geraldine's certainly the kind of person who likes to be busy doing something, rather than sitting around brooding. Why don't you come along with me tomorrow then, Mandy, and we'll see what she says about it."

Mandy began to clear the empty plates, thinking about what the next day might hold. Tomorrow they would find out for certain whether her mother's diagnosis was right. If it was, they would have sad news to bring to Wood Vale.

It took Mandy a long time to get to sleep that night, and she didn't wake up until much later than usual on Sunday morning. By the time she'd gotten dressed and gone downstairs for breakfast, her mother was already coming out of the clinic. Mandy took one look at her face and realized the news wasn't good.

"It's just as I thought, I'm afraid," her mother said sadly, shaking her head. "Martha's blood shows she does have FIV, and she's extremely anemic, too. No wonder she's very thin and weak."

Mandy put down the cereal box, her appetite suddenly gone. She felt so sorry for Martha — and for Geraldine and Robbie, too. "We'd better go over there right away," she said to her mother, getting up from the table.

"When you've had something to eat," Dr. Emily

replied firmly, putting a hand on Mandy's shoulder and pushing her gently back down in the chair. "You can't do anything useful on an empty stomach. Besides," she added, looking at her watch, "Geraldine's not expecting us for another hour or so."

When they arrived at Wood Vale a little while later, it took Geraldine a few minutes to answer their knock at the door. She was looking pale and anxious, much different from her usual cheerful self. Robbie was overjoyed to see them, though. He bounded around their heels, barking excitedly and wagging his tail.

"How's our patient?" Dr. Emily asked as Geraldine took them to the kitchen.

"Not good," she replied. "I've given her some of that liquid food you left yesterday, and the antibiotics, of course, but she doesn't want to get up. I took her basket down to the pond this morning so she could lie in the sun for a while, and she seemed to like that." She smiled, looking down at Martha, who was still curled up in the basket, and added, "It's her favorite spot, you know, sitting with Robbie at the foot of the willow tree and looking out over the water."

"Well, at least her eyes are looking better," Dr. Emily said. She rose to her feet and put an arm around Geraldine's shoulder. "Come and sit down," she went on. "I've got the results of Martha's blood test. We need to talk about her illness, and how to treat it."

Mandy stayed where she was, crouching down by the basket and scratching Martha comfortingly behind the ears. She knew what her mother was going to say, and she didn't feel like hearing it all over again. Robbie sat next to her, resting his head against her side.

From time to time, phrases floated over from the kitchen table. She heard her mother say ". . . no resistance to infection . . . can only treat the symptoms . . . make her as comfortable as possible . . ." and Geraldine's soft Irish voice murmuring something she couldn't quite catch. Eventually she couldn't bear only hearing snippets of the conversation and got up to join them. Robbie followed close behind.

Geraldine's eyes were red and she was blowing her nose with a tissue. "Would you look at me being so foolish!" she told Mandy with a watery smile. "Anyone would think I'd expected Martha to live forever. It's just that we'll miss her so much. Won't we, Robbie?" And she buried her face in the beagle's silky coat.

"Of course you will!" Mandy exclaimed, biting her lip as she tried hard not to cry, too. If *she* was feeling miserable, it must be a hundred times worse for Geraldine — and for poor Robbie, who had no idea what was happening to Martha. "I just wish there was something we could do," she added unhappily.

"Oh, but you've done so much already," Geraldine replied, straightening up and blowing her nose again. Then she looked almost fearfully at Mandy's mother. "Unless you think the time's come . . . ?"

"No, I don't think Martha's in so much pain we should put her to sleep," Dr. Emily replied. "We'll continue with the antibiotics for the time being and see how things go. I'll come and see her as often as you want me to." She gave Mandy a quick glance and added, "And now perhaps we should leave you in peace, Geraldine."

"Oh, no, don't go yet!" Geraldine said at once, jumping to her feet. "You must stay for a cup of tea, at least! Or why don't we all have an early lunch? Please, I'd like that. And besides, I haven't even taken you down to the pond to show you how that fine duck's doing."

She genuinely seemed to want them to stay, and Mandy was certain her gut feeling had been right. Geraldine would rather have their company than be left on her own.

Her mother seemed to be thinking the same thing. "The trouble is, I've got a pile of paperwork at home I need to catch up on," she said. "But I know Mandy's been wondering if she could talk to you about something."

"Of course," Geraldine said, tucking the tissue away in her sleeve. "Fire away, Mandy. Ask me anything you like."

"Well, we have to do a project at school, for biology," Mandy began, not quite sure if Geraldine was really ready for such a quick change of subject. She was looking at Mandy expectantly, though, so she decided to press on. "We thought it was so interesting yesterday — everything you were telling us about your bees, that is. James suggested I should write about them, and I wondered if you —"

"Oh, Mandy, I'd love to help!" Geraldine beamed. "There's so much I can tell you — all about how the hive is organized, the different jobs the bees have, and how they make honey. And I've got a couple of excellent books you can borrow. We could get started right away!"

"It's settled, then." Dr. Emily smiled as she kneeled by the basket to say good-bye to Martha. "If you're sure it's okay with you, Geraldine, I could leave Mandy here and pick her up in a couple of hours."

After Dr. Emily had gone and Geraldine had given Martha a quick cuddle, she took Mandy to her study. "Okay," she said briskly. "Before you start writing

anything down, why don't I explain how the hive
works and show you those books I mentioned? If
there's anything you don't understand, just ask me."

Mandy was delighted. It was nice to sit in the quiet,
sunny room, with Robbie asleep at her feet, and listen
to Geraldine talk.
She had the knack
of explaining
things so clearly
that Mandy hardly
ever had to
interrupt.
Geraldine had
given her a pad of
paper to take notes
if she wanted, but
Mandy was so
absorbed in what
she was saying that
she forgot to write
anything down.

After what
seemed like hardly
any time at all,
Geraldine looked
at her watch and
exclaimed, "Oh,

you poor thing! I've been talking to you for nearly an hour. Why don't we have a break now?" She reached up and took a couple of books down from the shelf. "Here," she added, handing them to Mandy, "have a look at these while I go and make us a sandwich. You must be starving." And she hurried off to the kitchen, Robbie trotting hopefully along with her.

Mandy was browsing through the books when, a few minutes later, Geraldine came bursting back into the study. Her face was chalky white. "Oh, Mandy, I think we'd better call your mother right away," she gasped in a panicky voice. "Martha's in bad shape. Please, come and see!"

Five

Mandy looked anxiously into the basket. Martha was still lying curled on her side, but her breathing had become very uneven. She seemed to be taking much longer inward breaths than normal and struggling to breathe out again. She looked very ill.

"You're right, I think we should phone Mom immediately," Mandy said to Geraldine, who was kneeling beside her.

"I'll go and call right now," Geraldine said, jumping to her feet. "Can you stay with Martha? I don't want her to be by herself."

"Of course," Mandy replied. She tried to think what she could do to help in the meantime. Perhaps she should check Martha's heart rate — that might be useful for her mother to know. She'd done this before. It was just a question of finding the right spot to feel the heartbeat. At last she located a rapid, faint

fluttering on the left-hand side of Martha's chest,
behind her elbow. She looked at her watch and tried
to count the beats for fifteen seconds. The pulse rate
was dangerously fast.

"Your mom's on her way," Geraldine said, coming
back into the kitchen and crouching down again by
the basket. She stroked Martha gently and
murmured, "Hold on, little girl."

Robbie had pushed his way in between Mandy and
Geraldine. He nudged the basket with his nose and
whined, as though wondering what was the matter
with Martha.

"You must be very gentle now," Mandy told him.
"Martha's not feeling so good."

Robbie gazed up at her with his deep brown eyes.
He gave a short bark and then turned around,
padding purposefully across the kitchen. Pausing by
the back door, he gave another urgent bark and
looked at Mandy again. "Do you want to go out?" she
asked him, tearing her eyes away from Martha. "Okay,
I'm coming." Geraldine was there to keep the tabby
company, so she might as well make herself useful.

She opened the door for Robbie and he bounded
off down the path, heading straight for the pond.
Mandy watched curiously as he sniffed around the
willow tree. It looked as though he were searching
for something. Then suddenly his body stiffened and

his tail wagged excitedly. He barked again and pushed his muzzle into the long grass, then turned around with something in his mouth and trotted back up the path.

"What do you have there?" Mandy said curiously as she let him into the kitchen again. She couldn't see what he was holding so carefully. "Hey, come back!" she called anxiously as he pushed past her.

"It's all right," Geraldine said as Robbie dropped his offering into the basket. "Look! He's found Mouse." And she held up the shabby soft toy Martha loved.

"Mouse must have fallen out of the basket this morning," Geraldine said, a catch in her voice, "I hadn't even realized she was missing. But you knew, didn't you, Robbie?" She stroked the beagle's ear.

"There's a clever boy," Mandy exclaimed, hurrying over and crouching down to give Robbie a hug. The beagle looked at her with such a hopeful expression, she could hardly bear it. *I've done what I can*, he seemed to be saying. *Now it's up to you two to make Martha better.*

Geraldine put the faded stuffed mouse between Martha's paws. The old cat opened her eyes for a second and focused on the worn gray material before closing them wearily again. And then Robbie put his head into the basket they shared and gently began to lick her thin body.

Mandy looked at Geraldine, uncertain whether they should allow him to continue. Geraldine shrugged and raised her eyebrows. "He seems to be helping her relax," she murmured.

It was true. Mandy was taking in air much more naturally now and she wasn't fighting to breathe out again, either. Then gradually, Mandy became aware of a faint rumbling sound coming from Martha's chest as Robbie carefully massaged it with his clean pink tongue.

"Geraldine!" she said softly, nudging her side. "Martha can't be purring, can she?"

"She is!" Geraldine whispered, her blue eyes brighter than ever with tears. "Who'd have believed it?"

A weak, rusty purr hung in the air for a few seconds longer. Then the sound slowly faded away until Mandy could no longer hear a trace of it, no matter how hard she strained to listen. Robbie stopped licking and sank down beside the basket, his head between his paws.

"She's gone, isn't she?" Geraldine whispered, the tears spilling down onto her cheeks.

Mandy nodded wordlessly. She felt for Martha's heartbeat again, just in case there was a chance she

was still alive. In her heart, though, she knew it was hopeless.

"I'll go and wait for Mom outside," she said, getting heavily to her feet. Geraldine and Robbie would want to say a last good-bye to their old friend.

Mandy slept badly again that night. She'd started to write an outline for her project when they came back from Geraldine's, even though it really wasn't what she felt like doing, and her mind wouldn't stop racing when it was time for bed. Besides the bees, she couldn't help thinking about everything that had happened that day and worrying about Geraldine and Robbie. She'd called James that evening and broken the sad news about Martha. His class — which was the year behind Mandy's — was going on a geography trip on Monday, and she wanted to tell him what had happened as soon as she could.

Luckily, Dr. Adam was going through Walton the next morning. After taking one look at the dark shadows under Mandy's eyes, he offered to give her a lift to school. Mandy yawned as she unpacked her schoolbag in the classroom. They had double English first — that wasn't so bad — and biology after recess. Then her hand flew up to her face and she groaned. The outline for her biology project was still lying on the kitchen table at home. Mr. Marsh would be so angry at her!

When she made her confession to him at the start of class, Mr. Marsh stared at her. "I can't believe you haven't brought in your outline!" he exploded. "Have you forgotten everything we talked about last week already? You probably haven't even begun your project."

"Oh, but I have!" Mandy exclaimed, feeling outraged. After all the work she'd done yesterday! "I decided to write about bees," she went on, feeling the color rise in her cheeks, "and I've drawn up a really detailed plan of the whole thing. Honestly!"

She had to stop talking at that point, because she

could feel a big lump forming in her throat. There was no way she was going to cry in front of Mr. Marsh!

He looked at her for a few seconds without speaking. Then he said, a little more calmly, "That's not a bad choice. Well, I'll look forward to seeing your outline tomorrow. I'll check it over as soon as I can and you'll just have to work on your project in the meantime. But I'm going to have to give you a detention for Friday, Amanda. You've left me with no alternative!"

"Yes, Mr. Marsh. Sorry, sir," Mandy muttered, too tired to argue. As she turned to go back to her desk, she felt as though things couldn't get any worse.

The day seemed to drag on forever, and even when her dad appeared at the end of it to give Mandy a ride home, it didn't lift her spirits. They drove along in silence for a while, until Dr. Adam suddenly smiled.

"I know what might cheer you up," he said. "We've got a new arrival in the residential unit. Or should I say, arrivals?"

"Oh? Who?" Mandy asked, making an effort to shake herself out of this dark mood.

"Wait and see," her father replied. "It'll be worth it!" He wouldn't say any more, no matter how much Mandy nagged. As soon as the Land Rover arrived at Animal Ark, she hurried through the clinic to the residential unit.

"Oh, isn't that wonderful?" she breathed, looking into one of the cages.

A beautiful chocolate-brown Burmese cat was lying in a blanket-lined box, fast asleep. Four tiny kittens lay sprawled against her stomach in a tangled heap. Their eyes were shut tight, and they looked only a few hours old.

Mandy gazed at the little family in delight. She always found newborn animals particularly special. "They're absolutely gorgeous," she said, taking in every detail of the kittens' damp, tousled bodies. Their thin, fragile legs were like twigs, and the fur was still sparse over their pink skin. As she watched, one of the kittens gave a reedy meow and began to struggle blindly toward its mother's teat. She opened one golden eye and helped nudge it into place with her nose.

"I thought you'd like to see them," said Dr. Adam. He put an arm around Mandy's shoulder and added quietly, "The miracle of new life. It helps make up for the sad times, doesn't it?"

"Yes, it does," said Mandy, resting her hand on his. This time the tears in her eyes were happy ones. "Is anything wrong with them, Dad?" she added, turning to her father with a suddenly anxious look. "Why are they here?"

"Don't worry, they're fine," he replied. "We had to perform a Caesarean on their mother this morning, that's all. She's not a big cat, and we thought she wouldn't be able to deliver the kittens alone. Those three males might look small, but they're actually quite hefty for newborns."

"Will they turn darker brown, like their mother?" Mandy asked. Two of the kittens were a soft fawn color, one was a darker gray, and the smallest of the litter had a pale, creamy coat.

"Well, their father was a blue Burmese," Dr. Adam said. "I think those two males will be chocolate and that one blue, like his dad. The little female looks as though she'll be lilac, though. That's a sort of silvery, pinky gray — quite beautiful." He watched the litter for a moment and then added, "We're going to have to keep an eye on her, I think."

"Oh, why?" Mandy asked, looking at the tiny kitten at the end of the row.

"Her brothers seem intent on pushing her out," Dr. Adam replied. "I think they've decided she's the runt of the litter, and they're taking all the milk."

As they watched, the female kitten began to struggle toward her mother's teat to feed. She kept slipping, her thin legs too weak to push herself forward over her brothers' sleeping bodies. Mandy would have loved to reach in and help, but she knew this would probably upset the mother cat. It was her job to nudge the babies into place. She didn't seem too interested in her daughter at the moment, though.

Come on, you can do it! Mandy urged silently, willing the tiny creature on with all her heart. She knew how important these first few hours were if the little kitten was going to survive.

The next morning, Mandy raced to the residential unit as soon as she was dressed. She found her father sitting on a chair in his pajamas, with a dropper in one hand and a scrap of pale fur in the other. There was no need to ask which kitten he was trying to feed.

"So she's been rejected," Mandy sighed. "You thought that might happen, didn't you, Dad?"

Dr. Adam nodded. "I think the mother cat feels those three big males are enough for her to cope with," he replied. "This is her first litter, so she's inexperienced. This one was pushed out of the nest by her brothers last night and Mom's lost interest in her."

"Poor thing," Mandy said, sitting on the arm of the chair and watching as Dr. Adam patiently coaxed the kitten to eat. She was meowing with a thin, reedy cry, but she hardly seemed strong enough to swallow the drops of milk. "Do you think she's going to pull through?" Mandy asked doubtfully.

"I'm not sure," her father answered. "Sometimes

when a mother rejects one kitten, it's because she knows there's something wrong with it. We've given her a thorough check over, though, and there aren't any obvious problems — no cleft palate to interfere with her feeding or anything like that. We'll just have to wait and see how she does."

"How are the others?" Mandy asked, going over to the cage and looking at the mother cat. She was awake and purring loudly, while the three male kittens were firmly latched onto her teats.

"They're fine," Dr. Adam said, glancing over. "It's a case of survival of the biggest in that family, I'm afraid."

"It seems awful they've just pushed her out," Mandy said, looking back at the tiny female. "She's got as much right to live as they do."

"Well, Mother Nature can seem cruel sometimes," said her father, yawning. "That's where us vets come in handy." He held the kitten at arm's length and they both laughed as it sneezed a drop of milk from the end of its bright pink nose.

"Why don't you let me take over, Dad?" Mandy asked, quickly washing her hands. "Looks like you're the tired one this morning."

"Thanks, dear," he replied, carefully handing her the kitten. "I don't think she's going to take any more

milk, but can you try and get her to relieve herself
before she goes back in the incubator? There's some
cotton here."

Mandy held the little creature in the palm of one
hand. The kitten's ear canals were still closed, as well
as her eyes, so she couldn't hear anything. Mandy
tried to keep her movements as calm and smooth as
possible. She stroked the kitten gently under her tail
with the ball of damp cotton. Normally, the mother
cat would lick her babies and encourage them to
urinate and open their bowels, but this also did the
trick.

"The trouble is, I don't think the owners will be
prepared to bother with all this business," Dr. Adam
went on. "When they came to look at the kittens
yesterday afternoon, I could tell they weren't really
interested in this one."

Mandy was horrified. "They can't abandon her,
too!" she said. The kitten had managed to produce a
small puddle by now, so she laid her back in the warm
incubator and covered her up with a blanket. "What
do they think will happen?" she asked, turning back
to her father.

"I get the impression they're hoping she'll just
fade away," Dr. Adam replied, stretching as he got up.
"They're planning on selling the kittens, and they

probably think the runt of the litter won't go for very much, even if she does pull through. I doubt they'll want to hand raise her."

"How can people possibly be like that?" Mandy asked, outraged. She couldn't believe anyone could be so callous. After watching Martha's life coming to its end, this new beginning seemed even more precious to her than ever. She knew that the odds were stacked against this little kitten — hand-raised animals often didn't survive — but she was determined to do everything she could to help her. In a strange kind of way, she felt as though she owed it to Martha.

Six

"How's the kitten?" Mandy asked her mother anxiously as soon as she and James arrived back at Animal Ark that afternoon. "James has come to have a look at her, too. We stopped by his house on the way, so his mom knows all about it."

"Good." Her mother smiled, sipping a mug of tea. "And as for our little reject — Simon's been feeding her every hour or so and she seems to have taken to the bottle quite well."

"That's great!" Mandy beamed, putting down her schoolbag. "I've been worrying about her all day."

"Just remember, though, it's still early," her mother warned. "You know how quickly things can go wrong with newborns. And we don't have any idea what's going to happen to her over the next week or so. There don't seem to be any nursing cats nearby who might be able to foster her, I'm afraid."

"Is it worth talking to the owners again?" James asked. "Won't they change their minds about hand raising the kitten if she seems to be doing better?"

Dr. Emily shook her head. "They've definitely decided against it," she said. "You should have seen their faces when I said she'd need feeding at least every two hours during the night! I told them how rewarding it could be, but they were horrified at the very thought."

"They don't know what they're missing!" Mandy said. "How can they turn down the chance to save her life? It's the most fantastic thing they could ever do." She turned to James. "Do you remember when we looked after Delilah's kittens? It was great, wasn't it?"

Delilah was a Persian cat who'd been injured on the road when her kittens were only a few weeks old, so James and Mandy had helped raise them during their summer vacation. It had been hard work, but wonderful to see the tiny animals growing stronger every day.

"It was a struggle to get them to take the bottle at first," James reminded her. "They were much happier when Blossom took them in, weren't they?" Blossom was a stray tabby who'd just had kittens of her own and managed to feed Delilah's, too.

"Yes, and they'd already had Delilah's milk for a few weeks, which gave them a good start," Dr. Emily said. "Their chances were a lot better than our little reject's." Noticing Mandy's worried expression, she added more cheerfully, "Still, at least she's feeding well now, and she seems comfortable in the incubator."

"And we'll give her all the love and care she needs, since the Brewers can't be bothered!" Mandy declared. "James and I could look after her at night, if Simon can feed her during the day. We'll take turns —"

"Now, Mandy, that's just impossible and you know it," Dr. Emily broke in firmly. "You two couldn't be up all night during school! You've been looking tired enough recently as it is. No, if anyone's going to feed her at night, it'll be your father or me. For the time being, anyway."

Mandy opened her mouth to argue, but one look from her mom made her close it again. "Well, at least we can do something now," she said, turning to leave. "Come on, James — let's go to the residential unit."

"Fine," Dr. Emily replied, rinsing her mug in the sink. "The Brewers are coming to take the mother and her male kittens home tomorrow, so you might as well enjoy them now. Oh, and Geraldine's coming into the clinic in half an hour or so," she added, wiping her hands on a towel. "Are you done with those books you borrowed?"

"Not yet," Mandy said, pausing by the kitchen door. "I hope everything's okay with her. Do you know why she made the appointment?"

Dr. Emily shook her head. "She didn't mention anything to Jean on the phone," she said, gathering her long red hair into a ponytail.

"Maybe she wants to talk about what was wrong with Martha," James suggested, following Mandy out of the room. "Sometimes it's difficult to take things in when you're upset."

"Could be," Mandy agreed. James often managed to put his finger on the way people were feeling.

"Let's try and catch her later, after we've had a look at the kittens."

"She's beautiful, isn't she?" James said, looking at the Burmese as she lay contentedly licking one of her litter. Like Mandy, he didn't risk upsetting her by picking up any of the kittens, but just watched them through the wire of the cage. Two of them were feeding, their tiny legs tangled together. The mother cat had scooped the third between her front paws and was giving him a thorough wash.

"I love Burmese cats," Simon said, glancing over. He finished topping off the food bowl of a sleepy-looking rat who was curled up in a nest of shredded paper and came over to stand beside James. "They're so elegant, but they'll play with you for hours — just like a dog."

"I'm sure this little one's going to be as gorgeous as her mother," Mandy said, softly stroking the female kitten's head as she lay in the incubator. She still looked very fragile, but at least it seemed she was feeding well now. It would only be the warmth and companionship of her family that she missed.

"How can you tell?" James asked. "I think they only begin to look sweet once their eyes have opened."

"I just know," Mandy said quietly. "There's something special about her — I can feel it." Seeing the smallest kitten all alone while her brothers were getting so much attention from the mother had really touched her heart.

The kitten had begun to meow and was trying to lift her wobbly head. It looked as though she was getting hungry, so Mandy put on her white coat and began to wash her hands in case she was needed.

"I'd better start getting ready for office hours," Simon said, looking at his watch. "Can I leave you two in charge for the moment? The rat should be fine — just coming around from his anesthetic — but Kitty's due for a meal about now."

"Sure," Mandy replied, reaching for the powdered milk. "Okay, James — let's see if we've still got that magic touch with the bottle!"

Mandy and James were on their way back from the unit, feeling very pleased with themselves for having managed to give the kitten a good meal, when they found Geraldine and Robbie sitting in the waiting room.

"Hi there, Robbie," Mandy said cheerfully, giving the beagle a pat. "Hey, what's the matter? You don't look very happy."

Instead of leaping all around her, Robbie merely raised his head and pushed it against Mandy's hand. He didn't get to his feet, even when James clicked his fingers and whistled.

"He isn't, I'm afraid," said Geraldine with a faint smile. "That's why we're here. I'm really worried about him!"

"Well, I suppose he's bound to be upset for a while," Mandy replied, settling on the chair next to them. "He'll be missing Martha, too, won't he? Just like you." Geraldine looked as though she hadn't slept well for days, and her eyes were red-rimmed.

"I know," Geraldine said anxiously, "but I've got this awful feeling it might be more than that." She put a hand under Robbie's chin and lifted his head, looking into his deep, sad eyes. "All he wants to do is lie in the basket all day, cuddled up to Mouse — exactly like Martha did when she was so ill."

"It's only been a couple of days, though, hasn't it? Since you lost her, I mean," James said, stroking Robbie's ear. "He'll probably be back to normal soon."

"No, you don't understand!" Geraldine said, her voice rising as she became more agitated. "He doesn't want to go outside and he won't eat, either. And you know how he normally loves his food. I think there's something seriously wrong with Robbie! What if he's caught what Martha had?"

Mandy looked at James, not sure how to reply. If Robbie hadn't been eating, it sounded as though he might be ill. At the very least, he must be very weak by

now, and he wasn't a young dog anymore. No wonder
Geraldine was worried. Luckily, at that moment Dr.
Emily poked her head out the door to call Geraldine
into the clinic.

"I'm sure Mom can put your mind to rest," Mandy
said, helping to coax Robbie up from the floor. He
really didn't want to go anywhere, but with Geraldine
pulling from the front and James and Mandy pushing
from behind, they eventually managed to get him into
the treatment room. Simon lifted him up onto the
table, and he stood there — his head down and tail
drooping.

"We'll wait outside for you," Mandy promised
Geraldine. The room felt crowded with so many
people in it. "Should we go and see if Jean needs a
hand in reception?" she suggested to James.

"I hope Robbie's going to be okay," he said after
he'd closed the door behind them. "He looks
miserable, doesn't he?"

Mandy just shook her head. She couldn't bear to
see the beagle so upset. "Come on, perhaps there's
some filing we can do," she sighed. "A really boring
job might take our mind off things."

A little while later, they had just pulled out
the notes for an accident-prone hamster named
Lucky, when Geraldine appeared in the reception
area again. Robbie trailed dejectedly behind her, a

look in his eyes which seemed to say, *When will this be over?*

"Well?" Mandy asked anxiously, coming out from behind the desk. "What did Mom think? Did she find anything?"

"Nothing obvious," Geraldine replied. "She's taken a blood sample to see if his kidneys and liver are working okay, but everything seems to be normal. Apart from his lack of appetite, that is, and the lethargy."

James had walked over to join them. "But surely it would be unlikely for Robbie to have caught anything from Martha, wouldn't it?" he asked, frowning behind his glasses.

"That's right," Mandy agreed. "Mom told me that viruses hardly ever pass from one species of animal to another. And FIV isn't highly contagious, anyway."

Geraldine ran one hand through her dark curly hair. "I know it sounds crazy," she said in a rush, "but I just can't get the idea out of my head that he's got that horrible disease, too. He seems to have the same symptoms as Martha. When I look at him lying there in the basket . . ." She shook her head, unable to carry on.

"Honestly, Geraldine, that's so unlikely," Mandy said positively, trying to convince her. "When Mom's tested Robbie's blood, I'm sure it'll turn out to be fine. Then you'll know for certain."

"That's true," Geraldine said. "And I suppose it won't be too long to wait. I'm bringing him back at the beginning of office hours tomorrow." She bent down to hug Robbie tightly and added, "I just couldn't bear to lose him, too — not so soon after saying good-bye to Martha. I really think it would break my heart."

"I'm sure that's not going to happen," Mandy said gently. She could see Geraldine was close to tears, and caught James's eye. Was there anything they could say that might cheer her up?

"Have you shown Geraldine your project yet, Mandy?" he asked, getting the idea right away. "I bet she'd like to see how it's turning out."

"Good idea!" Mandy replied, flashing him a grateful smile. "Why don't we go to the house? If you've got time, that is, Geraldine?"

"Of course," she said, summoning up a smile. "Let me just make this appointment and then I'm all yours. I'm sorry! I've been so wrapped up in my own problems I haven't even asked how you've been doing."

"I'm really glad I chose this subject," Mandy said when Geraldine had fixed everything up with Jean and the three of them were walking to the house with Robbie. "It was James's great idea, you know." And she patted him on the back.

James immediately started blushing, so Mandy continued quickly, "I've just started writing about all the different jobs the worker bees do. You know, looking after the queen and the grubs to begin with, and then making wax, and guarding the hive, and collecting pollen and nectar. There's so much to say!"

"This is wonderful," Geraldine said as she sat at the kitchen table and looked over Mandy's work, clipped into a loose-leaf file. Robbie had padded over to the stove and slumped against it with a sigh. "You've managed to fit in so much interesting information. Your teacher should be delighted."

"Huh!" Mandy snorted. "I'm not so sure about that. He's looking at my outline for the project at the moment, but I bet he'll find something wrong with it. Nothing I do is ever good enough for him!"

"Oh, come on," James protested, looking over Geraldine's shoulder at a page of illustrations. "He'll have to admit you've really worked hard on this. Your diagrams are amazing! They must have taken you forever."

"They did," Mandy said. "I hardly noticed the time going by, though. You don't when you're really interested in something, do you?"

"No," Geraldine agreed, gazing up from the file with a wistful expression. She sighed. "I think that's why I feel so low at the moment — not enough to think about. Bees are fascinating, but I've learned all about them now. I need to get stuck in something new to take my mind off things." She stretched her arms with a yawn and added, "I've been thinking about getting some day-old chicks to raise. There's an incubator in the outhouse, after all — might as well put it to good use."

Mandy froze. She felt like a character in a cartoon, with a flashing lightbulb over her head, and she could see that the very same thought had struck James. Of course! Why had it taken them so long to realize? Geraldine was the ideal person to raise their kitten. She'd know exactly what to do. After all, she'd taken on Robbie when he'd been abandoned by his mother, hadn't she? And if everything went well, having a new pet to love might help her get over losing Martha.

"D'you know, I've just had a great idea . . ." Mandy began cautiously, choosing her words carefully. Geraldine *had* to agree to look after the little Burmese. It would be the perfect solution!

Seven

"No, I'm sorry, Mandy," Geraldine said firmly, pushing back her chair from the table. "There's no way I could raise your kitten. I couldn't possibly take on such a big commitment just now!"

"But isn't it exactly what you were looking for?" Mandy asked desperately. "You said you needed something else to think about, didn't you? And she's such a cute little thing!"

"It would be wonderful to know you were taking care of her," James added hopefully. "I'm sure she wouldn't have a better home anywhere."

"Chicks are one thing — a newborn kitten is another," Geraldine declared, pushing her hands into the pockets of her jacket. She looked at their eager faces and her voice softened a little. "You know how much I'd love to help, but I've got Robbie to think about, too," she went on. "Even if he doesn't have FIV, what if the blood test shows he has some other disease? The kitten could easily pick up an infection."

"She wouldn't catch anything from Robbie, though," Mandy replied. She jumped up and started to fill the kettle. If they could keep Geraldine here for a cup of tea, they'd surely be able to talk her into it. "It's not as though they're the same species. If he *is* ill, you only need to worry about keeping him away from other dogs."

"Well, you know what I think about that," Geraldine replied. "I still feel as though Robbie did catch something from Martha, despite what everyone says." She closed the file and pushed it back across the table.

"Besides," she went on tiredly, "it's just too soon. I had Martha for fourteen years and it's only been a few days since she died. I need time to get over losing her. Robbie does, too. He doesn't want a little kitten rushing around and teasing him."

They all looked over to where the beagle was lying, curled in a dejected heap against the stove. "Poor boy," Mandy said, going over to stroke his smooth coat. "You need something to cheer you up, don't you?"

Robbie licked her hand a couple of times, then rested his head back on his paws. He glanced up at her, almost timidly. The furrow between his eyes seemed deeper than ever, and now he looked as though he was frowning unhappily.

"All the bounce has gone out of him, hasn't it?" Geraldine said, standing beside Mandy. "Come on, boy," she went on, encouraging Robbie to get up. "Time to go home. There's some chicken in the refrigerator, just for you."

"Won't you stay for a cup of tea?" Mandy asked, playing for time.

"Or why not come to the clinic and just take a look at the kitten?" James added. "Mandy thinks she's going to grow into the most beautiful cat."

"You two don't give up easily, do you?" Geraldine teased. She went on more seriously, "Look, I'm sure your kitten's gorgeous, and you won't have any trouble finding someone to raise her. But it won't be me, I'm afraid. You're just going to have to accept that. Okay?"

"Okay," James agreed reluctantly, and Mandy eventually nodded, too.

For now, she added privately to herself. At least she'd put the idea into Geraldine's head. Maybe if she thought it over for a few days, she'd change her mind. Mandy could just imagine the kitten in a few months' time, chasing butterflies across the lawn at Wood Vale.

She'd be so happy there, and she'd make them so happy, too! Surely Geraldine would realize that sooner or later?

The next day, Mandy and James were chatting in the hallway at the end of the school day when Mr. Marsh came hurrying toward them.

"Ah, Amanda!" he said. "Just the person! Can I have a quick word with you?"

Mandy's face must have given away her feelings, because he smiled and added, "There's nothing to worry about. I only want to talk to you about the outline you handed in yesterday, that's all."

"Oh! Fine," Mandy said, still rather suspicious. She braced herself for whatever he might say next and asked, "Do you think it's all right?"

"Better than all right," Mr. Marsh replied as he searched through his briefcase. "This outline is excellent! You've found out a lot about your subject already, and I can see how interested you are in it. If you can keep up this standard of work, your project will be very good. Here we are." He pulled the sheet of paper out of his case and gave it back to her. "I've scribbled a few comments in the margin, but they're only suggestions," he added. "Well done! I always knew you could do it."

"Thank you, sir," Mandy said as she took the sheet,

still pinching herself inside. She'd never seen Mr. Marsh look so friendly. He was positively beaming at her!

"Not at all," he replied, already starting off toward the staff room. Then he turned and called back, "I'm taking the detention class this week. We could go over your project together then, if you like. You'll be bringing it in for Friday's class, won't you?"

"Yes, Mr. Marsh," Mandy said faintly. "That would be great! Thanks."

She and James stared at each other when Mr. Marsh had gone. "I thought you said he had it in for you?" James said.

"It's like he's changed into a different person," Mandy replied slowly. "He was really nice then, wasn't he? I kept waiting for him to say something horrible and he never did."

"Just as long as he doesn't change back again by Friday," James said. "Let's go home! I've had enough of school for one day. Can I come back with you and see how the kitten's doing? I told Mom I'd probably go to your house again today."

"Perhaps you should just move in," Mandy teased, walking off with him down the corridor.

She took a deep breath as they went out into the open air, lifting her face up to the sun. A sudden rush of happiness seemed to fill her body. There had been so much to worry about recently: first Martha, then the rejected kitten, and Robbie being so depressed. Friday's detention had been lurking in the back of her mind, too, casting a shadow over everything. Now, after that quick conversation with Mr. Marsh, she felt full of hope and energy again. She was determined to do whatever she could to help Geraldine get Robbie back on his feet. And she'd find someone to look after the little Burmese, too.

"Let's get a move on," she called to James as she started sprinting toward the bike rack. "We've got places to go and people to see!"

When Mandy and James arrived back at Animal Ark, they found Dr. Emily in the residential unit. She was keeping an eye on the Burmese and her kittens while she finished writing up their notes.

"You're just in time to say good-bye to this little family," she told the two friends with a smile. "We're expecting the Brewers to come and collect them any minute."

"They look very settled now, don't they?" Mandy commented. One of the kittens was feeding steadily while the other two slept.

"Yes, I'm glad the mother's managed to bond with those three, at least," Dr. Emily said, putting down her pen.

James was peering into the incubator, where the female kitten lay snuggled under her blanket. "She's so tiny, isn't she?" he breathed.

"She's bigger than she was," Mandy said, coming to stand beside him. "I think she's growing every day." She knew how quickly things could go wrong with hand-raised puppies and kittens — they often just faded away without any warning. So far, though, this little female looked like a fighter.

Then she turned to her mother, remembering the other problem on her mind. "Have you had a look at Robbie's blood yet, Mom?" she asked. "Is everything okay?"

"Well, there's no sign of infection," her mother replied. "He's slightly anemic, but probably only because he hasn't been eating properly. There's no way he could have caught FIV from Martha, but at least now we can convince Geraldine."

"Say Geraldine was to get another cat very soon — or maybe even a kitten — could the virus be passed on somehow?" Mandy asked her mother innocently.

Dr. Emily shook her head. "No, that would be very unlikely," she said. "It might be a good idea to wash Martha's bedding and disinfect her food bowl, but only as a precaution." She shot Mandy a searching glance and added, "Why do you ask, dear? Geraldine hasn't said anything about getting another cat, has she? I'd have thought it was too soon for that."

"Oh, no reason in particular," Mandy replied vaguely. "Just thinking ahead." She shot James a warning look, in case he was about to give their plan away. She knew her mother would tell her to let Geraldine choose a new pet in her own good time. The trouble was, her own good time would be too late for their kitten.

"I know that expression on your face," Dr. Emily said, narrowing her green eyes. "You're planning something, aren't you?"

Before she could say any more, though, Simon put his head around the door and announced, "Mr. and Mrs. Brewer are in the waiting room. Are you ready for me to show them in? They've brought a big laundry hamper so we can put the kittening box right in."

"That's a good idea," Dr. Emily said approvingly. "Yes, bring them in. I know they can't wait to get Persephone home."

"Persephone?" Mandy repeated. "That's a very fancy name. I wonder what they're going to call the kittens?"

"Why don't we give this little female a name?" James asked. "If she's going to stay here for a while, we might as well."

"I'm not sure," Mandy said, gazing at the tiny, helpless creature. "Don't you think we should leave that up to whoever looks after her? I'm trying not to get any more attached to her than I am already."

"She is adorable, isn't she?" her mother said. "I must say, I don't know how the Brewers can resist her."

Just at that moment, the door opened and Simon showed the Brewers in.

"And how's my darling Persephone?" Mrs. Brewer cooed, rushing straight over to her cat without glancing at anyone else. "How's my clever girl and her dear little kitties?"

She was nicely dressed, with a swirly silk scarf knotted around her neck, and she smelled strongly of some overpowering perfume. There was something about her that Mandy didn't particularly like, and she could tell from James's expression that he felt the same.

"So these are your helpers?" Mr. Brewer said to Mandy's mom, nodding at James and Mandy. He was a short, stout man, dressed in a navy blazer with shiny gilt buttons. "Well, you've all done a fine job. Three handsome kittens for us to take home, and we've already got a line of buyers anxious to see them."

"Bring them back for the first vaccinations in about eight weeks, won't you?" Dr. Emily said. "And

I'll give you a diet sheet to help keep Persephone's strength up."

Simon carefully loaded the box carrying the Burmese and her kittens into the laundry basket, and Mrs. Brewer put a blanket over the top. "That'll help her feel more secure," she said. "We have to take care of our precious girl, don't we?"

She glanced quickly over to the incubator and added, "It's a shame about the female, but I really don't think we could manage her as well as these three. Besides, she won't be a good mother herself if she's been hand raised. We couldn't sell her for much."

"We're still looking for someone who's willing to look after her," Dr. Emily said, opening the door to the clinic. "We'll let you know what happens."

"Tell you what," Mr. Brewer said, squaring his shoulders. "If anyone manages to raise that kitten, they can keep her. We won't expect to be paid a penny, either. Someone might end up with a bargain on their hands!"

"Oh, Nigel! You're too soft for your own good," Mrs. Brewer said, sailing out and leaving Simon to carry the basket. "Now come on, let's put Persephone and her babies in the Range Rover."

Mandy followed them, fuming inwardly. She couldn't understand how the Brewers could just leave the female kitten behind without a second thought.

Didn't they feel any sense of responsibility toward her? All they seemed to think about was money!

"Oh, be careful!" Mrs. Brewer told Simon, as he took the basket through the reception area. "There's a dog! Keep Persephone away, please."

Geraldine was sitting there with Robbie at her feet, flicking through a magazine as she waited for their appointment. Mrs. Brewer shouldn't have worried, though. Robbie didn't show any interest in the cats at all — he didn't even raise his head as they were carried past.

Mandy and James said hello to Geraldine and made a big fuss over Robbie while Simon and the Brewers settled Persephone into their big, gleaming car.

"That's the Burmese I was telling you about," Mandy said to Geraldine, watching them walk to the open doorway. "Her owners are taking her home now, with the three male kittens."

She racked her brains to think of something to say that might change Geraldine's mind about raising the female kitten. This was the ideal opportunity! When the Brewers came back to settle their bill, she decided to seize her moment. Perhaps if Geraldine saw what they were like, she'd take pity on the little Burmese.

"Excuse me, Mrs. Brewer," she began, as politely as she could manage. "Are you sure you're not going to have second thoughts about leaving the female kitten

behind? My parents think she has a good chance of surviving."

"She may *survive*, dear," Mrs. Brewer replied, turning around from the desk and looking down her nose at Mandy, "but that's not really the point, is it?

We won't be able to breed her and I can't imagine anyone wanting to buy her — especially after they've heard that she was rejected. She's really not much use to anyone."

Geraldine was listening to every word of this, and a flush began to creep over her pale cheeks. Mandy could tell, from one quick glance, that she was beginning to rise to the bait.

"I bet that little one would make a lovely pet, though," she went on. "Wouldn't you like to keep her for yourselves?"

"Listen, dear," Mrs. Brewer said firmly. "We have enough to do, looking after these healthy kittens and their mother. We could spend all our time trying to raise this sickly one and there's no telling how she'd turn out in the end. If you can find someone prepared to take the risk, then fine. But frankly, it's not worth our while. She's the runt of the litter, and I'm afraid she's never going to amount to very much."

This was too much for Geraldine. She rose to her feet and said pleasantly, "Excuse me for interrupting, but don't you think you might be speaking too soon? My dog here was the runt of the litter, and look at him now!"

"Doesn't that prove my point?" Mrs. Brewer said, glancing down at Robbie. He lifted his sad eyes up to meet hers and then tried to curl himself into an even tighter ball under Geraldine's chair. "I'm sure you're very fond of him, but he is a rather miserable-looking specimen, isn't he?" she went on. "It might have been kinder to let nature take its course."

She took her husband's arm. "Now, Nigel, if we've paid our bill then we should be off. Mustn't keep Persephone waiting."

"What a terrible woman!" Geraldine exploded when the Brewers had gone. "How can she talk like that?" She crouched down and hugged Robbie tightly, muttering. "'Miserable-looking specimen,' indeed! Well, I'll show her. I've a good mind to —"

"Yes?" Mandy said eagerly as Geraldine and Robbie followed Dr. Emily into the clinic for their appointment. "A good mind to what?"

"Wait till I've had a word with your mother," Geraldine replied over her shoulder. "You'll see."

"What was that all about?" James asked Mandy curiously when they were alone. "Why did you try and make Mrs. Brewer keep the other kitten? You must have known she didn't want to."

"I wanted to show Geraldine what she was like, that's all," Mandy replied. "I thought listening to Mrs. Brewer would put Geraldine on our side and make her feel like looking after the kitten. And, James — I think I might have succeeded!"

Eight

Mandy moved around the residential unit, sweeping the floor and tidying up, with one ear open for the sound of footsteps in the corridor. James had gone home to take Blackie for a walk, but she wanted to stay around to find out whether her plan had been successful. Was Geraldine going to offer to raise the kitten herself? If so, she'd be bound to come in and have a look at her. She'd almost given up hope when Simon appeared beside her, grinning broadly.

"Problem solved!" he said, waving an arm toward Geraldine, who was following close behind. "Here's our guardian angel."

"I wouldn't go as far as that." Geraldine smiled. "But I have changed my mind about looking after your kitten, Mandy. The way that dreadful woman just left her! It made my blood boil."

"That's wonderful!" Mandy said, beaming, too.

"Oh, I knew all along you'd be the perfect person to raise her." She led Geraldine over to the incubator and told her proudly, "Look, there's Kitty. Isn't she lovely?"

"She looks so lonely, though, all on her own in there," Geraldine said quietly. "Poor little thing. I think she's going to need a lot of help."

As they watched, the kitten lifted her head and gave a weak meow. She tried to move forward across the soft blanket, but her legs weren't strong enough yet to support her and she could only wave them helplessly.

"Looks like she's hungry again," Simon said. "Would you like to feed her, Geraldine? Might as well get used to it right away."

"Where's Robbie?" Mandy asked, noticing for the first time that Geraldine was on her own. "Everything's okay, isn't it?"

"As far as we can tell," Geraldine replied. "Don't worry, he's safely in the car. You mother tells me his blood's clear, and there's no danger of him passing anything onto this little one. But if you don't mind, Simon, I'd better take him home now. Can you continue looking after the kitten till Friday? That'll give me a day to get everything ready, and I can pick her up on Friday morning."

"Sure," Simon said. "As for her next meal — I have

to go back into the clinic now, but perhaps our willing assistant can take over?" And he raised his eyebrows at Mandy.

"I'd love to," she replied. "After all, if the kitten's not going to be here for much longer, I'd better make the most of her."

"You'll come and visit, though, won't you, Mandy?" Geraldine asked, taking a last look at the kitten before she turned to leave. "I'll have my hands full with spoon-feeding Robbie and bottle-feeding this little one. Any offers of help will be gratefully received!"

"Of course," Mandy assured her. "There's nothing I'd like more, and I bet James feels the same. I'll call him in a minute. Should we come over on Saturday?"

"That would be perfect," Geraldine said, giving her a quick hug. "Well, this might turn out to be a mistake, but there's no going back now. And you know, I feel better already. This little kitten's going to be a beauty, and that snooty woman will have to eat her words."

"She will," Mandy echoed. "And we'll get Robbie back to his old self, too. Just you wait and see, Geraldine. Everything's going to be fine!"

Mandy left enough time for James to come back from his walk and then phoned to tell him the good news about Geraldine looking after the kitten. He was delighted, and Mandy felt even more sure that all their problems would soon be solved. She was almost looking forward to Friday's biology lesson!

But when Friday morning came, it was soon clear that Mr. Marsh's good mood had come and gone. He wasn't irritable, exactly, but his mind seemed to be on other things. If anyone had a question to ask him, they had to repeat it several times before getting an answer. His wavy brown hair looked more untidy than usual, and when he sat down at the desk, Mandy noticed he was wearing mismatched socks.

"I wonder what's up with him?" Vicky Simpson whispered. Mandy just shrugged her shoulders. She didn't want to risk getting into any more trouble — one detention was enough for anybody.

As soon as the bell rang at the end of their class, Mr. Marsh rushed out of the room. Mandy wouldn't have been surprised if he'd forgotten all about taking the detention class. But at the end of the afternoon, there he was, waiting for her to arrive.

"Good! I'm glad you're here, Amanda," he said. "I see from the list that it's only the two of us today. Now I just have to hurry out to my car, so start your work for the moment, please. You've brought something to do, haven't you?"

"Yes, Mr. Marsh," Mandy said, slightly surprised.

"I've brought my project. You said you'd go through it with me, remember?"

"Oh, so I did," he replied. "That's right. You're studying bats, aren't you? Very interesting."

"Well, actually I'm writing about bees," Mandy said, sitting down at one of the desks in the empty classroom and taking out her books. She couldn't believe Mr. Marsh had already forgotten what her project was about, especially after giving her such a glowing report on the outline.

"Of course, bees," Mr. Marsh said, jingling some change in his pockets as he shifted from one leg to the other. "Yes, it's all coming back to me now. Okay, well, I'll be back in a second." And with that he dashed off again, jumpy as a cat on a windy day.

Mandy began to read over what she'd written so far. She was about to begin describing how bees turned the nectar they'd collected into honey. The books Geraldine had lent her didn't explain the process very clearly, though. Mandy knew the bees stored pollen in baskets on their back legs. But where did they keep the nectar? And what did they do with it once they were back at the hive? She gazed out of the window, racking her brains to try to remember what Geraldine had said.

Then suddenly she caught sight of Mr. Marsh

outside, tinkering with something in his car. What could he be up to? He was sitting on one of the back seats, next to what looked like a large wire-mesh cage. Mandy stood up to get a better view, her curiosity aroused at once. Did he have some kind of animal in there? Just at that moment, though, Mr. Marsh glanced up toward the classroom window, so she quickly sat down again. By the time he was back in the room, five minutes later, she was reading her textbook intently.

"Fine! Working hard, I see. Well done," he said vaguely, rubbing his hands as he sat down at the desk and took a book out of his briefcase. "Let me know if you have any problems."

So much for going through my project together, Mandy
thought to herself. She looked over at Mr. Marsh,
wondering if she could interrupt him with a question.
Then she gasped out loud. A small, white, furry head
was peering inquisitively out of his jacket pocket.

"Is anything wrong?" Mr. Marsh asked, looking up.
Wordlessly, Mandy pointed toward his jacket, and his
eyes traveled downward in the direction of her finger.

"Oh," he sighed, laying down his book. "Looks like
I'll have to come clean. You've found me out,
Amanda!"

Mandy began to giggle as a second, darker head
popped out of the other pocket. "I didn't know you
kept rats, Mr. Marsh!" she exclaimed. "They're
beautiful!"

"Well, I think so," he replied, taking one of the rats
out of his pocket and stroking its head affectionately.
"But you'd be surprised how many people scream at
the sight of them. Here, do you want to take a closer
look?"

"Yes, please," Mandy said eagerly, walking up to the
teacher's desk. "I love rats — they're so intelligent
and friendly, aren't they? We often treat them at the
clinic, and one of my friends has pet rats."

"Oh, yes, I remember Ms. Temple telling me your
parents were vets," Mr. Marsh said. "Well, this is
Eenie," he went on, putting the white rat into

Mandy's hands. "And here's her friend Meenie. They're both female." He scooped the second animal out of his pocket and held her up. She was white, too, but with a dark gray head and intelligent black eyes. "Not very original names, I'm afraid."

Mandy held Eenie securely against her body and looked down into the rat's beady pink eyes. Her delicate ears were shell pink, too, but the rest of her body was pure white, from the tips of her whiskers to the end of her smooth, curving tail. Eenie stretched her twitching nose forward, sniffed Mandy delicately, and then climbed up to her shoulder. There she settled comfortably, lying around Mandy's neck like a warm furry scarf and snuffling into her ear.

"I can tell this is Eenie's favorite place," Mandy said, laughing at the tickly sensation. "She's wheezing a little, though, isn't she?" She'd noticed the rat was making a rattling sound as she breathed.

Mr. Marsh frowned, putting Meenie down on the desk and scratching her gently behind the ears. "This one's been sneezing and snuffling, too," he said. "Listen, you can hear her now. I'm worried about the pair of them — that's why I brought them to school with me today. I didn't want to leave them on their own for too long. I put their cage in the back of my car, and I've been rushing out between classes to see if they're okay."

"I'm sure you could have brought them into the lab," Mandy said. "The principal wouldn't have minded." She took Eenie down from her neck and examined her more closely, adding, "Ms. Temple used to keep a hamster as a school pet, you know."

"Well, I didn't want to ask," Mr. Marsh said. "I thought it might have distracted you from your work. I've found it pretty distracting having them around, I must admit."

"They're nice and lively, aren't they?" Mandy observed as Meenie wriggled her way up the sleeve of Mr. Marsh's jacket and popped her head out at his shoulder. "Are they eating normally?"

"From what I can tell," Mr. Marsh replied. "Apart from the wheezing and sneezing, they seem to be fine."

Mandy thought hard. "Has anything changed in their routine recently?" she asked Mr. Marsh. "You haven't started them on any new kind of food, by any chance?"

Mr. Marsh shook his head. "Not that I can think of," he said. "Why do you ask?"

"Well, they might have developed an allergy to something," Mandy replied, cradling Eenie in the crook of her arm and stroking the back of the rat's head. "Either that, or it's some sort of respiratory infection. Can you take them to a vet soon for a checkup?"

"I'm going to make an appointment as soon as I get home," Mr. Marsh said anxiously, letting Meenie run from one of his hands to the other. "It's just so difficult to fit these things in when you're at work all day."

He gazed out of the window and then suddenly jumped to his feet, tucking Meenie back into his jacket pocket. "Come on!" he said, taking Eenie from Mandy's hand. "It's a beautiful sunny afternoon, and the weekend's nearly here. Why don't I declare this detention officially over? After all, I gave it to you. Now I'm going to take it back!"

"Are you sure?" Mandy said uncertainly, unable to believe her luck. It was hard to know where she was, with Mr. Marsh changing like this all the time. And then she had a brilliant idea.

"Why don't you come home with me now?" she said to him. "Afternoon office hours will be starting any minute. I'm sure Mom or Dad could have a quick look at Eenie and Meenie for you."

"Do you think they'd mind?" Mr. Marsh asked, letting Eenie ride on his shoulder. "It would be a great relief to me, that's for sure."

"Oh, the only trouble is, I've got my bike with me," Mandy said as she began to pack away her books. Her face fell. "It won't fit in your car, will it?"

"No, but we can put it on the roof. I've got a special rack for my own bike," Mr. Marsh replied, putting Eenie safely in the other pocket and picking up his briefcase. "That's one problem with an easy solution."

Ten minutes later, Mandy's bike was safely strapped to Mr. Marsh's car, Eenie and Meenie were back in their cage, and they were all setting off for Animal Ark. Mandy fastened her seat belt, taking a look around the car. It was a real mess! Books and papers were lying everywhere, spilling out of Mr. Marsh's briefcase onto the backseat, and scattered over the floor by her feet. The air was beautifully fragrant, though. She took a deep breath, wondering if he used some kind of air freshener.

"The rats' cage smells great, doesn't it?" Mr. Marsh commented. "I've bought these wonderful cedar shavings from the pet shop for Eenie and Meenie's bedding. They must feel like they're sleeping out in a forest."

"What?" Mandy almost squeaked in her excitement. "How long ago was this?"

"Oh, a couple of days," Mr. Marsh replied. "Why do you ask?"

"Well, I bet that's it!" Mandy exclaimed. "Shavings can cause rats all sorts of problems, particularly cedar. It's the oils in the wood, you see — irritating their airways."

"You know, I think you're onto something there," Mr. Marsh said slowly. "The rats have been wheezing ever since I changed their litter. Why didn't I think of that before?"

"Well, sounds like it could be the answer," Mandy said, happy to think she might have solved the problem. "Still, it might be a good idea to get them checked over — just to make doubly sure."

"Thanks, Amanda," Mr. Marsh said, flashing her a smile. "If we can get Eenie and Meenie back to normal, it'll be a big weight off my mind."

They drove along quietly for a few minutes and then he added, rather awkwardly, "You probably feel I've been a bit hard on you lately, what with this detention and everything."

"Oh, that's all right," Mandy said, wondering what was coming next.

"The thing is, I think you could do really well in biology," he went on. "Ms. Temple told me what a good student you were, but you seemed to have switched off in my classes. I wanted to get you back on track, that's all. When you seemed to be working so hard on your project, I was delighted. Of course it was about bees — how could I have forgotten that?"

"Sometimes I find it hard to think about one thing at a time," Mandy admitted. "And there's been a lot going on at home recently."

Mr. Marsh was so much easier to talk to out of school that before Mandy knew it, she'd begun to tell him all about Geraldine and her bees, and then the whole story of Martha and Robbie came spilling out.

"My parents had a beagle when I was growing up," Mr. Marsh said. "They're wonderful dogs — really affectionate and lively. Bouncer used to wait by our gate for me to come home from school every day. I was heartbroken when he died. There probably wasn't anything we could have done, but all the same. . . ." And he shook his head sadly.

Mandy felt a pang of guilt as she remembered Robbie. She'd been so concerned about the kitten these last few days, when maybe she should have been concentrating on him. She'd last seen him a couple of days ago, and she hadn't even called Geraldine since then to find out how he was. Still, she and James were going to Wood Vale tomorrow. She'd spend lots of time with him — as long as it took to get his appetite back.

"What happened to Bouncer?" she asked Mr. Marsh, not certain whether she really wanted to hear the answer.

"He picked up some infection or other," he replied. "By the time we got him to the vet, his kidneys had been damaged and he had to be put to sleep a few days later." He gave a sad smile. "We should have realized something was seriously wrong when he stopped eating. Beagles certainly love their food!"

Mandy stared out of the car window, trying not to let herself panic. She told herself that if Robbie did have a similar problem, her mother would certainly have picked it up right away. She was too good a vet to miss any warning signs, and besides, she'd tested Robbie's blood. But Mr. Marsh's words echoed over and over in Mandy's head: "Something seriously wrong . . . stopped eating . . ."

What *was* the matter with Robbie? What if his immune system had been weakened by now, like Martha's was? There must be a strong chance that Geraldine could lose him, too. Mandy shut her eyes, trying to squeeze the thought out of her head. It was too painful to contemplate. Martha had become gravely ill so very quickly, and there had been nothing they could do to help her. Would the same thing happen to Robbie?

Nine

"Well, you were right about those rats," said Dr. Emily, smiling at Mandy after they'd said good-bye to a grateful Mr. Marsh. "I'm sure they'll be fine once their litter's been changed. Good diagnosis, dear!"

"Thanks," Mandy said, absentmindedly fiddling with a stray wood shaving that had fallen out of the cage.

"And your teacher seems very nice," her mom went on, busily spraying the tabletop with disinfectant. "Are you getting along better with him now?"

"Um, yes, I suppose so," Mandy replied, sticking the tiny shred of wood into her pocket.

"So what is it, then?" her mother asked, throwing the paper towel in the trash and washing her hands. "What's on your mind? Spit it out, dear. I can see something's bothering you."

Mandy wasn't sure what to do. She felt as though

putting her fears into words might make them come true, but she knew her mother would have something sensible to say. Besides, she wanted to hear her professional opinion. Dr. Emily leaned against the countertop, her hands in the pockets of her white coat, watching Mandy patiently.

"It's Robbie, Mom," she confided at last. "Do you think he's getting any better? Have you heard how he is from Geraldine? I know you couldn't find anything the matter with him, but surely he ought to be getting back to normal by now!"

"I agree," her mother said. "I've been worried about him, too — I spoke to Geraldine this morning when she came to collect Kitty. She says she's managed to get him to take a little of the liquid food I gave her, but he isn't very eager." She sighed. "When animals don't eat, it's a clear sign that something's wrong. I just can't figure out what it is, though!"

"Do you think he's just pining for Martha?" Mandy asked.

"Could be," her mother replied. "They did have a very strong attachment, after all. The trouble is, he's getting old, and he needs to keep his strength up. If he carries on moping around like this and not eating properly, he'll get weaker and his body won't be able to cope with infection."

Just like Martha, Mandy thought. "Perhaps I

shouldn't have suggested taking on the kitten to Geraldine," she worried out loud. "Maybe she won't be able to give Robbie all the time and attention he needs."

"So you put that idea into her head, did you?" her mother smiled. "I suspected as much. Oh, I think Geraldine can cope. And if anything does happen to Robbie, she might be glad to have another pet to help her get over it."

"I hope you're right," Mandy said, with a heavy heart. Despite her mother's reassurances, she was beginning to think that she might have done the wrong thing. If Robbie did end up suffering because of an idea she'd put in Geraldine's head, she'd never be able to forgive herself.

"Bye, Geraldine. Bye, you two," Dr. Emily called, starting the Land Rover's engine after dropping Mandy and James off at Wood Vale the next day. "Give me a call this afternoon when you're ready to be picked up."

Geraldine put an arm around their shoulders and took them inside the house. "Come and see how Kitty's doing," she said. "I've got her feeding from the bottle now, and she loves it!"

"Have you decided what to name her?" James asked, grinning. "If you're not careful, she'll stay Kitty for the rest of her life!"

"Well, that wouldn't be so bad," Geraldine replied as they went through to the kitchen. "I've been tossing a couple of names around, but nothing seems right so far. Still, there's no rush. And here she is, in her new home!"

"Oh, she does look cozy," Mandy said. The kitten was lying in a see-through plastic incubator on the countertop. She was being kept warm by a hot-water bottle wrapped up in a towel and then covered again with a soft blue blanket.

"I started off with an infrared lamp over the top of the incubator, but now she seems to prefer cuddling up to the hot-water bottle," Geraldine said. "Isn't she adorable? It looks like one of her eyes is just beginning to open, too. I could watch her for hours, even though she does seem to spend most of the time asleep."

"And where's Robbie?" Mandy asked, glancing around the room. She'd been disappointed not to see him leaping up at Geraldine's heels when she answered the door, and his basket was empty.

Geraldine sighed. "He's out in the yard," she said, pointing out of the window. "I buried Martha in her favorite spot by the pond, and Robbie seems to know she's there. He spent all day yesterday sitting under the willow tree, as though he wants to be near her."

"Poor thing," Mandy murmured, standing beside

Geraldine and watching the beagle. He lay at the foot of the tree with his head on his paws. From time to time he lifted his nose to sniff the air and gaze around, as though he was looking for someone. A light drizzle was falling, but he didn't seem to notice.

"You'd think he'd rather stay in his basket on a day like this," James said. "He must be soaked!"

"I'll go and bring him in in a minute," Geraldine said. "The trouble is, I know he'll just sit by the door and howl. I can't bear to hear him. He sounds so miserable!"

Suddenly Mandy remembered something. "I thought you said he lay in his basket all the time?" she reminded Geraldine.

Geraldine sighed. "He hasn't been near the basket for a couple of days," she replied, fiddling with the end of a scarf tied around her neck. "I'm afraid that could be my fault. I had to throw Mouse away, you see."

"Mouse?" James asked, looking puzzled.

"The funny old stuffed toy Martha used to play with," Geraldine explained, turning away from the window. "Your mother told me to clean everything Martha had been in contact with. She said there was really no danger of Kitty catching FIV, but she might pick up something else. You know how vulnerable newborns are, especially if they haven't been passed any antibodies through their mother's milk. Mouse was falling to pieces — she wouldn't have survived the washing machine. I thought it would be safer to get rid of her altogether."

"And do you really think that's made such a difference to Robbie?" Mandy asked, concerned.

"It certainly looks like it," Geraldine replied, pulling out a chair and sitting down at the kitchen table. "I suppose Mouse smelled of Martha, and that comforted him. Now that there's nothing left in the basket to remind him of her, he doesn't want anything to do with it. He sat by the door all last night. Whenever I came in to feed the kitten, there he was, in exactly the same position."

"You must be tired," James said. "Tell us what we can do to help you out."

"Should we go and bring Robbie in?" Mandy added. "Perhaps seeing some new faces might cheer him up." She didn't really believe that, but she hated to see Geraldine looking so worried. There had to be something they could do to help!

"Thanks," Geraldine said gratefully. "I really need to feed the chickens now and collect their eggs. If you two could bring Robbie in and try to feed him, that would be great. There's a special meat-and-egg dish I've cooked up in the refrigerator — he seems to have lost interest in the liquid food."

She looked at her watch and added, "Kitty will need feeding again soon, too. You'll probably have more luck with her than with Robbie!"

Mandy and James walked down the path toward the pond. On either side of them, the bushes dripped steadily. Raindrops misted Mandy's hair, and her sneakers were soon soaked. She shivered. It wasn't really cold, but the yard looked so dank and depressing. And there was Robbie, lying under the willow tree.

Mandy crouched down to pat his wet coat. "Cheer up, boy," she said encouragingly. "Why don't you come back to the house with James and me?"

The beagle looked up at her with big, mournful eyes. He pushed his nose half-heartedly into her hand and then dropped it back down to rest on his paws again.

"Here, Robbie!" James called. "I've found a stick for you. Go fetch!" He took a few steps away from the bank and hurled the stick in a graceful arc across the lawn. But Robbie just watched it land by the lavender hedge without bothering to make a move.

"Come up to the house with us, Robbie," Mandy repeated, stroking his ear. "There's something delicious for you in the refrigerator!"

Together, they eventually persuaded the beagle to

get to his feet and then they practically pushed him up the path to the back door of the house. Geraldine looked over from the chicken runs and gave them an encouraging wave.

"This must be his food," Mandy said, taking a plastic container out of the refrigerator once they were inside the kitchen. "Perhaps we should heat it up a little, in case he doesn't like it so cold."

Robbie sat by the door, watching them as they looked for a saucepan and then put his food on the stove to warm. When it was ready, James held Robbie's head steady while Mandy tried to spoon a little of the food into his mouth. It wasn't an easy job, though. If she did manage to get any morsels past Robbie's teeth, he spat them out again without swallowing.

"Oh, Robbie! Why are you being so stubborn?" Mandy said at last in exasperation, sitting back on her heels. "This is for your own good, you know. You've got to eat!"

"Let's stop for a while," James suggested. "We're not getting anywhere, and besides, I think Kitty's hungry. She's started to cry."

Mandy looked over to the incubator. The kitten was lifting up her head and meowing thinly as she struggled to move across the blanket in search of food. "You're right," Mandy said to James. "After all, we might as well feed the one who actually wants us to."

They got up from the floor. Immediately, Robbie went back over to sit by the door. He looked beseechingly up at them and whined to go out.

"You can stay here for the moment," Mandy told him, fishing a feeding bottle out of the sterilizer. "We're not giving up on you that quickly, you know."

When they'd mixed up the kitten's milk, James took a turn feeding her. He held the little kitten upright in the palm of his hand while she sucked greedily on the rubber teat of the bottle, her tiny paws wrapped around his fingers. "She's really coming along," he said, smiling at the kitten's eagerness to eat. "Her fur is so soft!"

"Dad thinks she's a lilac Burmese," Mandy said, watching him enviously. "That's a sort of pale lavender gray. She's going to be beautiful."

When James had finished feeding the kitten, Mandy took her from him and began to wipe her with some damp cotton. "You're going to have a lovely time here when you've grown up some more," she told the young animal as she massaged her tummy gently. "There's a great big yard to play in, and you've got Robbie here to keep you company."

She glanced toward the back door and caught sight of the beagle watching her intently. Hoping to keep him interested, she carried on talking quietly to the kitten in the same encouraging tone of voice.

"Yes, you and Robbie are going to be great friends," she said, nudging James's back at the same time to get his attention.

"What's up?" he asked, turning around from the sink where he'd been washing the kitten's bottle.

"Shh!" Mandy hissed. "It's Robbie. Look at him!"

The beagle had begun padding hesitantly toward her, his eyes fixed on the tiny creature she was holding. "This is Kitty," Mandy told him, crouching down on the

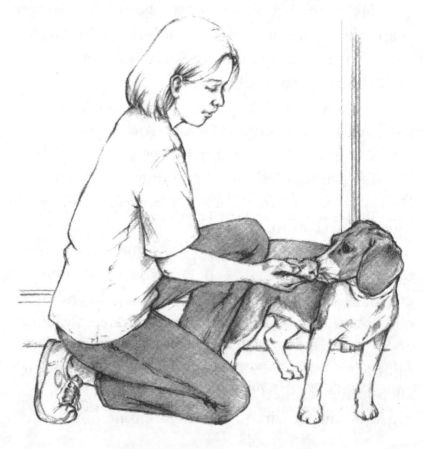

floor so she was at Robbie's level and offering him the kitten to examine. "She's come to live here with you and Geraldine. Haven't you met her before?"

Robbie sniffed Kitty all over with his damp black nose. The little creature couldn't see or hear him but managed to lift up her head toward the source of this strange new doggy smell. Robbie looked at Mandy inquiringly, as if he couldn't figure out what was going on.

"Kitty's just a baby," she said. "Are you going to help us look after her?" She patted the beagle encouragingly with her other hand, still holding the kitten close to him.

Robbie stared down at the tiny animal. Then, very gently, he licked her head a couple of times with his clean pink tongue.

James let out his breath with a whoosh. Mandy gazed up at him, her eyes shining. "I think Robbie's got the idea, don't you?" she said happily. "Hang on! Where's he going now?"

The beagle had turned away and was trotting purposefully across the room. When he'd reached his basket, he settled himself in it, looked over at Mandy, and barked. He was asking for something, and she knew exactly what that something was.

"Okay," she smiled, walking over to the basket. "Here you are."

Carefully, she laid the kitten safely between his two front paws. Robbie bent his head and began to lick her steadily all over, just as he'd done with Martha in that very same place. Then he laid his head down beside her and closed his eyes. Anyone would have thought he was asleep were it not for the steady thump, thump of his tail against the side of the basket.

"You don't think he'll squash her, do you?" James asked Mandy quietly.

She shook her head, feeling too choked up to speak, and tried to swallow the lump in her throat. "He's not going to hurt a hair on her head," she said eventually. "And neither will anyone else, if he's around. Oh, let's go and get Geraldine, James. This is something she's got to see!"

Ten

This is the life! Mandy thought contentedly, putting her arms behind her head and closing her eyes as she lay back on the grass. The sun was warm on her face, and the scent of lavender blossoms and freshly mown grass wafted over on the breeze. A blackbird was singing somewhere in the garden, and her parents were laughing as Geraldine recounted some long, complicated story about her Irish uncles.

It was the first weekend of summer vacation, and Mandy, her parents, and James had been invited over for lunch at Wood Vale. "To thank you for all the help you've given me," Geraldine had said. "I couldn't have gotten through these past few weeks without you."

"But I'm the one who should be thanking you!" Mandy had protested. "I wouldn't have done half as well in biology if you hadn't helped me, Geraldine."

Mr. Marsh had given her an A+ on her project, and he'd written her a great end-of-school report, too. It was funny how things could change, Mandy reflected, chewing on a blade of grass and remembering what she'd first thought of Mr. Marsh. In the end, the whole class had been sorry to say good-bye to him — though of course it would be great to see Ms. Temple again.

There was no need to think about school for the moment, though, Mandy decided. The long, glorious vacation lay ahead, and she was going to enjoy every second of it.

"Go fetch, Robbie!" she heard James calling, and there was the sound of something whistling through the air.

She propped herself up on her elbows to watch as the beagle raced after his ball, barking excitedly. He sniffed around the lavender bushes, ignoring a couple of bees who were busy among the flower spikes, before seizing the ball and carrying it triumphantly back to James. Wagging his tail happily, he dropped the ball at James's feet and stood with his head on one side, waiting expectantly for the next throw.

Suddenly, a small gray shape appeared from nowhere, streaking across the grass and pouncing on the ball. "Angel!" Mandy laughed, jumping to her feet. "What do you think you're doing? That's Robbie's toy — it's way too big for you!"

James rescued the ball and the kitten leaped away, skittering over the grass and shooting halfway up a tree trunk. Then she suddenly seemed to realize she'd climbed higher than she intended and looked down, meowing piteously.

Mandy hurried over and gently unhooked the kitten's claws from the rough bark, holding her slender body tight. "It's just as well you're so adorable," she told the little cat sternly, feeling the beginnings of a purr vibrate in the soft fur beneath her fingers.

"And what kind of mischief is she up to now?" Geraldine asked, walking over toward them. "I don't know whatever possessed me to call her Angel — we should have named her Trouble instead." But there was a twinkle in her blue eyes.

"Angel is the perfect name for her, and you know it!" Mandy grinned, giving the kitten one last cuddle before setting her down on the ground. At once, she began to stalk a fly, waving her tail fiercely to and fro before she jumped up in the air — and then tumbled over her paws.

"You wouldn't have said so this morning," Geraldine said, shaking her head solemnly. "She'd climbed up on one of the kitchen chairs and was trying to catch poor Robbie's tail as he waved it back and forth. Then she decided it would be more fun to jump on his back and see if he'd take her for a ride!"

"And did he?" Mandy asked, laughing at the idea. Robbie was so patient and good-tempered, she could imagine him joining in with the game.

"Oh, she lost interest and fell off a second later," Geraldine replied. She looked over to watch the beagle chasing his ball toward the orchard. "Dear old Robbie never batted an eyelid! You should see the teasing he puts up with, and there's not so much as a bark out of him."

"Angel seems to have given him a new lease on life, hasn't she?" Mandy commented.

Geraldine nodded. "From the moment he started taking notice of her, he decided life was worth living, after all." She added, half smiling at the idea, "It might sound crazy, but I sometimes think Martha's sent this kitten to look after him. That's really why I called her Angel."

"I know just what you mean," Mandy said, watching the little Burmese roll over on the grass. "I was so sure she belonged here with you two. And she *is* beautiful, isn't she?"

Angel's coat had turned the softest shade of pinkish gray, like a wisp of smoke, with darker points to her ears and nose. Her pale eyes, ringed with black, were particularly striking. It was impossible to pin down what color they were — one minute golden, and then the next as clear as a shining pool of water.

"We ought to show those horrible Brewers how lovely she is," Geraldine agreed, picking up the mischievous kitten and kissing the top of her head. "They'd probably try to take her back, though, and we couldn't have that."

James came over to join them with Robbie at his heels. "Could I have another drink, please, Geraldine?" he asked, wiping his flushed face. "This is thirsty work!"

"Of course," she replied. "There's more lemonade on the kitchen table, if you don't mind helping yourself. And if you're going that way, perhaps you could bring down some ice cream from the freezer? The bowls and spoons are out here already."

"Sure," James said, already on his way.

"I think Robbie should have a drink, too," Mandy added, noticing how heavily the beagle was panting. "Why don't we take him up with us?"

They walked back to the house. Robbie followed them, Angel zigzagging around him as she darted from one side of the path to the other. Mandy knew that she'd only just had her final vaccinations, so she wasn't used to being outside. Everything fascinated her, from a dragonfly darting across the grass to a fat worm wriggling through the soil. The yard must have seemed like one big playground.

"Come on, Angel, in you go," Mandy said, scooping the kitten up and carrying her through the back door. "I bet you'd like a drink, too."

As soon as they were inside the cool kitchen, she put Angel down by her saucer of water. Robbie went to his own bowl and began to lap noisily. When he'd had a good long drink, he padded over to his basket and settled down comfortably.

"Looks like I've managed to tire him out," James smiled, draining his glass of lemonade.

Mandy looked around from the freezer with two tubs of ice cream in her hands. "Robbie's not the only one," she said, nodding her head in Angel's direction. After a more dainty drink, the kitten was now following Robbie over to the basket. With one big leap, she jumped inside, stepped delicately over the beagle's legs, and curled herself up between his front paws and his chin. In a couple of seconds, both animals were fast asleep.

"I think Martha would approve, don't you?" James said quietly.

"Definitely!" Mandy said, smiling down at the pair of them. Then, with a happy sigh, she turned toward the door. "Let's go, James," she said. "If we stand here much longer, my hands will freeze and this ice cream will melt!"

And, together, they went happily back out into the sunshine.

Mandy Tells You All About Lucky and Other Giraffes

Did you know that . . .

- giraffes were originally thought to be a cross between camels and leopards, hence their scientific name *giraffa* (one who walks swiftly) *camelopardalis* (camel marked like a leopard).

- giraffes are very fast and can gallop at speeds of up to 35 miles per hour.

- giraffes are the tallest mammals in the world, growing up to 18 feet in height.

- a giraffe's tongue is very flexible, and around 17 inches in length!

- giraffes are herbivores and mainly eat leaves, particularly from the acacia tree.

- giraffes have excellent eyesight and can see farther than any other land-based creature.

- giraffes were first brought to Rome in 46 BC, though they didn't appear in France until 1826, when a female giraffe called Zarafa was given to the king of France as a present.

- giraffes are most vulnerable to attack when they're lying down or bending over to drink, as they have to splay their legs and find it very hard to get up quickly. As a result, they tend to sleep and give birth standing up! If they ever do lie down to sleep, it's usually only for about 20 minutes, and another giraffe is normally standing guard.

- each giraffe has an individual pattern to its coat, which is unique to itself.

🐾 FUNNY FOX BUSINESS 🐾

"Race you to Grandma's!" Mandy shouted as she bent forward over the handlebars of her bike and sped down the road.

"You're on!" James called back. He took up the challenge and began pedaling hard.

Mandy laughed as the wind tugged at her blond hair. But as Lilac Cottage came into view, she frowned and slowed down. "Oh! Look at that!"

Pieces of wet cardboard littered the road outside her grandparents' cottage. Plastic bags and other bits of rubbish were being whipped into the air.

"What's happened?" asked James.

Mandy shook her head. "I have no idea," she replied.

As they drew closer, Mandy saw that her grandpa was sweeping broken glass into a pile with a stiff yard-brush. Just then, her grandma came out of Lilac Cottage. She was wearing yellow rubber gloves and carrying a plastic garbage bag.

Mandy and James dismounted beside the front gate. "Hi, Grandpa. What's going on?" Mandy asked.

"That's what we'd like to know!" Tom Hope replied, straightening up and putting his hands on his hips.

Dorothy Hope came over. "Hello, dear. Hello, James. Don't mind your grandpa, he's feeling a bit grumpy. To tell you the truth, we're both a bit fed up. This is the second time in a week that someone's tipped over our garbage can and left the gate open so that trash has blown everywhere."

Mandy blinked. The usually neat front yard, Grandpa's pride and joy, looked awful. She spotted an empty food can that had rolled under a bush and stooped to pick it up. "What a mess. And this trash could be a real danger to wildlife!"

"And to me, with my blood pressure to consider!" Grandpa muttered crossly.

"Blood pressure, indeed! You're as fit as a fiddle, Tom," Grandma said.

Mandy grinned and gave her grandpa a hug. Mr. Hope was tall and straight, always on the go. "Never mind, Grandpa. We'll help you clean up the mess."

"Trash-picker-uppers at your service, Mr. Hope!"

James said cheerfully, and shot into action. He grabbed a handful of wet paper that had wrapped itself around a pine tree and thrust it into the garbage bag.

"What would we do without our favorite granddaughter and her best friend?" Mrs. Hope said.

"Have a quiet life?" Mandy suggested innocently.

"No more animal emergencies? No more unwanted pets to rescue? That sounds very boring!" Grandpa had brightened up already.

Mandy smiled at him. He could never stay in a bad mood for long.

Ten minutes later, the trash had all been picked up and Lilac Cottage's front yard was restored to its usual neat appearance.

"I'm going to lock the garbage can in the garage. I'd like to see anyone get at it there!" Grandma said, a stern glint in her eye.

Mr. Hope winked at Mandy and James. "I wouldn't like to be in the phantom can-tipper's shoes once your grandma finds out who it is! Let's go inside, okay? I think you've earned your lunch."

After a lunch of crusty bread and homemade mushroom soup, Mandy and James offered to do the dishes.

When it was time to leave, Grandma and Grandpa came out to the front gate to see them off. "Say hello to your mom and dad, Mandy. Thanks for your help, James."

"That's okay," James said. "And thanks for lunch."

Mandy thought that James seemed thoughtful as they got on their bikes and cycled back up the road. "I don't get it. Why would anyone overturn your grandma's garbage can? Unless . . ."

"What is it, James?" Mandy asked curiously.

"Unless it's an animal looking for food," he said.

"That's it! James, you're brilliant!" Mandy gasped.

"Hmm. It would have to be something very strong to knock over a garbage can," James observed.

"Not necessarily. If a stray cat or dog jumped up it could easily knock over a can," replied Mandy.

"That's true," James agreed. "We could ask around. Find out if anyone has lost a dog or cat. How about checking the post office first?"

Mandy smiled at her friend. He was thinking logically as usual.

A few minutes later they were peering at the cards in the post office window. "No luck," Mandy said. "These cards are all advertising things for sale." She felt disappointed. James's idea that an animal was raiding the can had made perfect sense.

Two women were coming across the town square toward them. One was Mrs. Ponsonby, resplendent in a lilac coat and matching hat. Pandora, her

Pekingese, was tucked under her arm, and Toby, her sweet-natured mongrel, trotted by her side. Her friend Mrs. Platt was with her.

"Sam Western was outside the Fox and Goose. He was trying to convince anyone who'd listen that foxes are causing trouble around here again." Mrs. Platt looked disapproving. Her poodle, Antonia, was yapping excitedly as she tried to get at Pandora.

"I know it's annoying to have trash strewn every-where," Mrs. Ponsonby replied. "But you can't just go blaming any animal you please . . ." She stopped as she drew level with Mandy and James. "Oh, hello, Amanda dear. Hello, James."

"Hello, you two." Mrs. Platt smiled at the two friends.

"Hi," they replied, exchanging looks. It seemed as if other people were having the same problem as Mandy's grandma and grandpa.

"Trust Sam Western to stick his nose in!" James whispered to Mandy. Mr. Western was a local farmer and landowner who had upset many people in the past with his overbearing manner.

"I know," Mandy answered. "I think he regrets his decision not to hunt foxes." She looked at Mrs. Ponsonby. "Have you heard about any stray dogs or cats?" she asked politely, explaining the problem.

Mrs. Ponsonby shook her head. "The only dogs

I've seen around lately belong to Jude Somers," Mrs. Platt said. "It wouldn't be them."

"No," Mandy agreed readily. "Jude doesn't let Joey and Spider run loose. Dad says the dogs are in good condition. They wouldn't go looking for food."

Jude Somers and his family lived in an old red trailer in the park. Mandy and James were friends with them. And her grandma was more than happy to let them fetch fresh water from Lilac Cottage's outside tap.

Mrs. Platt raised her eyebrows. "It's certainly a mystery. I hope someone solves it before Western suggests we bring back foxhunting."

"Oh, dear. I couldn't go along with that." Mrs. Ponsonby shook her head so that the lilac feathers on her hat trembled. "But if it *is* foxes then we'll have to do something."

James looked horrified. "Bring back foxhunting?" he hissed.

"No way!" Mandy felt her blood run cold at the very thought. She knew from experience that Sam Western could be very determined.

"Well — we must be off, dear," Mrs. Ponsonby was saying. "I have an article to write for the church magazine. Good-bye, Amanda, James."

"We've got to do *something*," James said as the two women and their dogs moved away.

Mandy nodded. "Come on!"

"Where are we going?" James asked.

"To the park!" Mandy wanted to hear what Jude Somers had to say. He did odd jobs around the town. Nothing much escaped his notice.

As they biked along the lane, Mandy and James spotted a colorful group in the distance.

"It's Jude and the kids!" James said as they drew closer.

Skinny, long-limbed Jude had a water jug in one hand. His two small children were running and skipping along beside him. Two lean dogs were sniffing out rabbits along the hedges.

Jude turned around as Mandy and James dismounted. He grinned, his teeth white in his sunburned face. "Hey, look who it is, kids!"

Five-year-old Skye and her three-year-old brother, Jason, scampered up. Their wind-reddened faces beamed and their mousy hair hung in their eyes. Mandy smiled at them and reached down to pet the dogs. Jason tugged at Mandy's hand, demanding to be lifted up onto her bike.

"Pipe down, Jason," Jude said, trying to look stern. But Jason took no notice.

"I want a ride!" he demanded.

"Okay," Mandy said, grinning as she lifted him up. She pushed the bike along, steadying the little boy on the seat. Jason leaned forward, clinging to the handlebars. Skye skipped along behind the dogs, slashing at the hedges with a stick.

"Come on over and say hello to Rowan," Jude said when they reached the park.

Soon they were all sitting outside the red trailer, enjoying cups of tea and Rowan's homemade pancakes. Skye and Jason were sprawled on a knitted patchwork blanket, sharing their pancake with the dogs.

"Ah, this is the life," Jude said happily, sipping his tea.

Rowan's silver earrings glinted as she nodded in agreement. Jude's wife was small and slight and her short hair was dyed bright orange. "Everything's going right for us at the moment," she told Mandy and James. "We've got a few weeks' work up at The Riddings, so Jude and I spend the mornings there. And the Spry sisters don't mind if we bring Skye and Jason. Although not everyone is as easygoing as they." The twin Spry sisters were eccentric ladies who lived in The Riddings, a rambling old house on Walton Road.

"No," Mandy agreed, thinking of Sam Western.

Jude gave one of his narrow grins. "The Sprys are as crazy as they come, that's why we get along! Joan was a little upset just before we left today, though."

"Why?" Mandy asked.

Rowan answered her. "Oh, she was complaining

about their garbage can having been tipped over. She insisted that it was all right when she came outside first thing in the morning. Marjorie eventually managed to calm her down."

Mandy and James exchanged a knowing look. Marjorie was usually the one in charge!

"Something's been tipping over garbage cans in town," Mandy said. "We wondered if you'd heard or seen anything unusual." She told them their idea about missing pets and the conversation with Mrs. Ponsonby and Mrs. Platt. "At least we were all sure it wasn't Joey and Spider."

"No! Not Joey and Spider . . ." Jason echoed decisively. The little boy petted the dogs' long, pointed noses. Mandy noticed Skye glance sharply at her brother and poked him in the ribs. "Ow!" he complained. "Mom, tell her — !"

"Stop bickering," Rowan said mildly.

"It's good to know that people are sticking up for us," Jude said to Mandy and James. "Some people are too quick to condemn."

Rowan touched her husband's arm. "Not everyone. There are some friendly people in Welford!"

"The worst thing is that Sam Western's getting involved," James said.

"He's got it in his head that foxes are to blame," Mandy added. "Have you seen any around?"

Jude rubbed his chin. "One or two. I caught sight of a vixen a week or so ago. But I've not seen her lately."

Mandy noticed Jason glance sideways at his sister. Skye jumped to her feet and grabbed her brother's hand. Together they took off across the park, the dogs loping along behind them.

"Don't go out of sight," Jude called after them tolerantly. He turned back to Mandy and James. "I know Western. He's the type to steam in and take over."

Mandy nodded worriedly. "He'd just love to have foxhunting in the area again."

Jude tossed back his dark hair and frowned. "I'm definitely against killing animals for sport. Rowan and I will keep our eyes and ears open, won't we?"

Rowan nodded. "We'll let you know if we see anything."

"Thanks," Mandy and James said in unison. Getting up to head for home, they waved to Skye and Jason, who were still racing around with the dogs.

Mandy felt an idea taking shape in her mind as they parted at the top of the lane.

"What is it?" James said, looking closely at her.

She tapped the side of her nose. "I've got a hunch. Meet me at the crossroads tomorrow morning."

James blinked at her, obviously dying to hear more. But Mandy only grinned mysteriously as she got on her bike and zoomed off.

The following morning, Mandy was up early, eager to find out if her hunch was right. After helping clean out the cages in the residential unit, she set off to meet James. He was waiting outside the Fox and Goose when she arrived.

"Where are we going?" By now James was almost bursting with curiosity.

"To The Riddings," Mandy said. "I think Skye and Jason know more about all of this than they're letting on."

"What makes you say that?" James asked as they headed toward the hilly road on the outskirts of Welford. He eased down into low gear to tackle the steep incline.

"Well, remember how Rowan told us that Joan was all in a fluster about finding their garbage can tipped over?" Mandy recapped their conversation with the Somerses. "That was just before the Somerses left yesterday morning, right? So the bins must have been disturbed while they were actually there working."

"Er . . . right," James agreed, looking a little confused.

"And did you notice that little Jason seemed very sure that his dogs weren't responsible? 'Not Joey and Spider,' he said, remember?" Mandy said.

"Because — he knew who it actually was!" James said, catching on.

"Exactly!" Mandy grinned at her friend. "I rest my case!"

James chuckled. "You'd make a great lawyer!"

A few minutes later, they had reached Walton Road and The Riddings came into view. Jude's red van was parked on the driveway of the big old house. Long leashes secured the dogs to a nearby tree and there was a bowl of water within easy reach.

Mandy and James waved at Jude, who was cutting the lawn. Voices came from the direction of the conservatory and the Spry sisters came into view.

Joan came right over, her sharp face jutting forward on her thin neck. "Visitors! We're not expecting anyone!"

Marjorie smiled. "Mandy and James are friends, Joan. They're welcome anytime."

"Thanks," Mandy said. "We came to see Skye and Jason, if that's okay."

"Who?" said Joan, waving a skinny arm. "No one around here named that."

"She means the Somers children," Marjorie

explained. "You go ahead and find them, dear. And come and visit us soon."

"We will, thanks," Mandy and James promised.

Skye and Jason were nowhere in sight. Mandy noticed an old barn set inside a walled yard, in the field beyond. "Let's go and look over there," she suggested.

As they drew nearer, they heard the faint sound of voices. Mandy peered around the wall and saw the kids in the yard. They were filling a dish with scraps of food. A battered bucket filled with water was nearby.

As Mandy and James stepped into view, Skye and Jason froze.

"Hi," Mandy said brightly. "You two look busy."

"We're feeding our pets," Jason said, grinning up at them through his tousled bangs. Then he put his fists to his mouth as Skye scowled at him.

"Can we help?" James said in a friendly fashion.

"No!" Skye's eyes snapped defiance. "They're our pets. We found them."

"Of course they are," James said, careful not to upset her. "We just want to see them."

Jason hesitated, then he ran up and tugged at Mandy's hand. "I'll show you."

"Well, don't let them out!" his sister warned. Skye opened the barn door just wide enough to slip inside.

Jason put one finger to his lips. "Shhh!" He led them over to a pile of straw.

"Oh . . ." Mandy opened her eyes wide in amazement as a fox lifted her head and gazed at her with amber eyes. Nestling close to their mother's fur were two fluffy apricot-colored cubs. They yawned, showing needle-sharp teeth and small pink tongues. "They're adorable!" she breathed.

Skye beamed proudly. "We're looking after them. We keep them in here so they'll be safe."

Everything fell into place. "And you've been raiding people's garbage cans to get food for them, haven't you?" Mandy guessed.

Skye blinked up at her. "It was just stuff people threw away. They didn't want it anymore."

"She's got a point," James said.

Mandy bent down, so that she was level with Skye. "It's dangerous to keep a mother fox and her cubs closed up in a barn," she said gently. "And it's very, very bad for the foxes, too."

"Why?" Skye asked, scowling. Jason's bottom lip trembled. Skye slipped her arm protectively around his shoulder.

"Foxes are wild animals," Mandy explained. "They need sun and fresh air. The mother needs to teach her cubs to hunt or they won't be able to adapt to the wild."

Jason's face crumpled. "Will they die?"

Mandy shook her head. "Not if you let them go right away. The mother will take very good care of her cubs."

Skye frowned mutinously. "*We* can take care of them," she said.

"Not like their mother," Mandy said firmly. "The cubs won't grow strong if they're fed on scraps. They could get sick."

Skye's face was set and unmoving. Mandy's spirits sank. She didn't want to force the kids to release the foxes.

Just then Jason gulped and a tear ran down his cheek. "I don't want the cubs to get sick!" he wailed.

Skye took a tissue from her shorts pocket and wiped her brother's face. "It's all right, Jason," she said gently. She turned to Mandy. "Okay. The foxes can go," she said in a matter-of-fact voice.

James helped to open the barn doors wide and Mandy explained that the foxes would slip away when everything was quiet.

"Bye-bye, foxes," Jason said over his shoulder as they all trooped back toward the Spry sisters' garden.

"Wait until your grandma hears about this!" James said with a grin.

Mandy chuckled. "And Sam Western!"

A couple of evenings later, Mandy and James were back at The Riddings, taking up the Spry sisters' offer of a visit. The Somerses had been invited, too. Spread out on a table on the lawn were sandwiches, cookies, and fancy cakes.

"Have a blueberry muffin, Mandy," Marjorie said. "They're delicious."

"The lemon cake is better." Joan's sharp nose jutted forward.

"No, it's not!"

"Yes, it is!"

Jude winked at Mandy and James. "I'll have one of each!"

"Look!" Skye and Jason pointed toward some bushes.

Mandy saw a pointed red nose poke out. A dainty, long-legged body followed. The mother fox! And, snapping playfully at her heels, the two cubs.

They came right onto the lawn and began rolling over and over, kicking and biting at each other. Two healthy, fluffy balls of trouble!

Everyone laughed at the cubs' antics.

Mandy winked at Skye and Jason. The little boy came over and sat down next to her. "I'm glad we let them go," he said softly.

"Isn't it strange, Joan, that the garbage cans aren't being knocked over anymore?" Marjorie said, nibbling delicately on cake.

James looked at Mandy. "I expect your grandma and grandpa are relieved about that, too!" he said with a wide grin.

Rajiv Tells You All About Chhota and Other Tigers

Did you know that . . .

- tigers are the largest living cats.

- a tiger's stripes are like a human's fingerprints.

- not all tigers are yellow with dark stripes: there are white tigers with dark stripes,

black tigers with light-colored stripes, and
even white tigers with no stripes at all.

- the heaviest tiger recorded was a 1,028-
pound male Siberian.

- tigers are good swimmers and, unlike most
cats, actually like water.

- tigers can eat as much as 40 pounds of
meat at a time. After such a big meal, days
may pass before they are hungry again.

- in the dark, a tiger's vision is six times
better than a human's.

- tigers do not purr like domestic cats. They
make a noise referred to as a "chuff."

- a group of tigers is called a "streak." Tigers
are mostly loners, though, and rarely join
groups.

- a tiger's canine teeth are at least 10 times
longer than a human's.

- tigers have white spots on the backs of their
ears which help to protect them from
predators. They look like eyes and deter

other animals from attacking from behind — because they don't know whether the tiger is coming or going.

- the same method can be used against tigers, because they don't normally attack from the front, either. Placing a mask on the back of the head can deter man-eating tigers — though man-eating tigers are very rare!

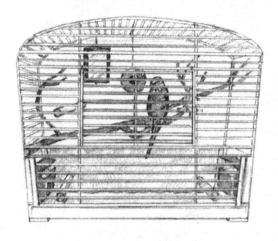

 BUDGIE BABIES

"Hello, Mandy," Mrs. McFarlane said, appearing from the back room of the general store.

"Hi, Mrs. McFarlane," Mandy said as the door tinkled shut behind her. "How are you?"

"Fine, thank you." The shopkeeper dusted her hands on her blue overalls. "What can I get you?"

"Just some lemon candy, please," Mandy said.

Mrs. McFarlane began to unscrew the old-fashioned container of hard candy. Mandy often thought that the general store was like an Aladdin's cave. The shelves overflowed with interesting things — candy, comics, cans of food, pet chews, and toys.

"So where's James today?" Mrs. McFarlane asked. James Hunter was Mandy's best friend.

"He's gone to visit his aunt for the weekend,"

Mandy explained. She looked at the shelf of pet things and saw a tray of bells and mirrors for budgerigars. It made her think of Mrs. McFarlane's green budgie. "How's Billy?" she asked.

"Not too good actually," Mrs. McFarlane sighed. "He's been plucking out some of his chest feathers with his beak. It's a sign of boredom. I've tried moving his cage so he can see some different things and giving him some new toys but it hasn't stopped him."

"Poor Billy," Mandy said. "What are you going to do?"

"I don't know, dear," Mrs. McFarlane replied.

Suddenly Mandy had an idea. "You should get another budgie to keep him company. Then he wouldn't be bored."

The shopkeeper considered Mandy's idea. "That's a good idea. It *would* stop Billy from being bored and it would be nice to have two budgies. I've always fancied owning a blue budgie as well as a green one." She nodded. "Yes, maybe I'll go to Walton next week and see if I can get one there."

That evening, over supper at Animal Ark, Mandy told her mom and dad about poor Billy. "I hope Mrs. McFarlane gets another budgie," she said. "I'm sure Billy would like to have a friend."

Dr. Adam, Mandy's father, nodded. "Budgies normally accept other budgies very easily."

"In fact, they seem to thrive on the company," Dr. Emily said as she began to dish out a delicious-looking vegetable lasagna. "Speaking of budgies, I've got an appointment to visit a budgie breeder tomorrow morning. Her name is Kathleen Tibbit. One of her birds has an eye infection."

"Where does she live?" Mandy asked.

"Just outside Walton," Dr. Emily replied. "Would you like to come there with me?"

"Yes, please!" Mandy said, taking the plate her mother handed her. "How many budgies does she have?"

"Oh, over sixty," Dr. Emily said.

"Wow!" Mandy said, impressed. "Maybe we could find one for Mrs. McFarlane." She picked up her fork and began to eat her lasagna. Sixty budgies — she couldn't wait!

The next morning, Mandy and her mom set off for Mrs. Tibbit's house. Just before Walton, Mrs. Hope turned off the main road onto a bumpy path. "Mrs. Tibbit lives down here," she said. "I've visited a couple of times now. She's won a lot of prizes with the birds she's bred. She's very highly respected in the budgerigar world."

They bumped around a corner and a large, old house came into view. It was built of gray stone and had diamond-shaped panes of glass in the windows. Dr. Emily stopped the four-wheel drive and Mandy jumped out. "Should I ring the bell?" she asked, seeing a doorbell by the front door.

Dr. Emily nodded.

Mandy tugged the rope. She heard the bell echoing inside the house, but no one came to answer it.

"Maybe Mrs. Tibbit is in the yard," Dr. Emily said. "The aviaries are around the back."

Mandy followed her mom around the house.

"Gosh!" she gasped as they walked into the back yard. To one side of the house were two huge aviaries like outdoor rooms. Their wooden frames were covered with wire mesh and they had been built around two old trees. Inside each were lots of budgies — green ones, blue ones, white speckled ones. They flew through the leaves, clung onto the mesh, and perched on the branches, twittering and chattering.

"They're amazing, Mom!" Mandy exclaimed.

Each aviary had an open-air section and then a shed with a rectangular hole for the birds to fly in through. Just then, one of the shed doors opened and a woman came out. She had gray hair clasped in an untidy bun at the base of her neck and a yellow silk scarf with pictures of parrots on it wound around her neck. Her face looked worried.

"Dr. Emily!" she exclaimed in surprise.

"There was no reply at the front door, so we decided to come and find you," Dr. Emily explained. "This is my daughter, Mandy. I hope you don't mind her coming, too."

Mrs. Tibbit hardly even glanced at Mandy. "Oh, dear, oh, dear."

Dr. Emily frowned at the older woman. "Are you all right, Mrs. Tibbit?"

"Yes . . . no," Mrs. Tibbit stammered. "Oh, Dr. Emily, a terrible thing's happened. I think two of my birds have been stolen!"

Stolen! Mandy stared at the gray-haired lady.

Mrs. Tibbit quickly let herself out of the aviary. "I've been looking everywhere," she said, rubbing her forehead in distress. "It's Salt and Pepper — my most valuable breeding pair. They were here yesterday but today they've just vanished."

"Out of the aviary?" Dr. Emily said.

Mrs. Tibbit nodded. "Someone must have gotten in and taken them."

Mandy looked at the crowd of budgies flying around the two aviaries. "What do they look like?" she asked.

"They're pied violet budgerigars," Mrs. Tibbit replied. "They have white backs and heads, gray and blue speckles on the wings, yellow bills, and violet-blue plumage under their wings down to the base of their tails."

"Like that one," Mandy said, seeing a bird that just about matched Mrs. Tibbit's description landing on the mesh of one of the aviaries. It clung to the wire, chirruping at her.

Mrs. Tibbit nodded. "I have eight pied violet pairs all together, but Salt and Pepper are my most valuable. They've both won Best in Show awards."

Mandy spotted two more of the violet pied budgies. "How can you tell which ones are Salt and Pepper, Mrs. Tibbit?"

"Salt, the cock bird — the male — has a pure white back with no speckles and Pepper, the hen, has lots of light gray speckles on her back and wings. They're very easy to spot," Mrs. Tibbit said. "And they're definitely not here."

"So you think someone's stolen them?" Dr. Emily asked in concern.

"They must have," Mrs. Tibbit said, agitated. "I saw both Salt and Pepper when I was removing the nesting boxes from the shelter yesterday." She must have seen Mandy's puzzled look because she explained: "They're wooden boxes that go in the shelter — the enclosed section of the aviary — for the birds to nest in. I didn't want the exhibition birds to mate in the aviary because it makes it difficult to be sure of the chicks' parentage, so I took the nesting boxes out. Today I was going to move Salt and Pepper and one of my other exhibition pairs to the breeding cages." She shook her head. "I should have put a lock on the door. But I've never had any trouble before and I'm a light sleeper." She put her hand on the wooden frame. "I feel sick at the thought of someone taking them."

Dr. Emily looked at her sympathetically. "Maybe you should sit down, Mrs. Tibbit. Would you like me to make you a cup of tea?"

"That's very kind of you, but I don't want to hold you up," Mrs. Tibbit said.

"It's no problem. We're not in a rush," Dr. Emily said. "Let's go inside."

"Can I stay and look at the birds, Mom?" Mandy asked, looking longingly at the cages full of their colorful inhabitants.

Dr. Emily looked at Mrs. Tibbit. "Would that be okay?"

"Of course," Mrs. Tibbit said. "But if you go inside the aviaries, please make sure you shut the doors, dear. I couldn't bear it if any more budgies disappeared."

"I'll be very careful," Mandy promised.

As her mom and Mrs. Tibbit disappeared up the path, Mandy let herself into the aviary that contained the pied budgies. She unbolted the door leading into the safety porch and then went through a wooden door into the shelter. The air in the wooden room smelled strongly of birds. Food containers hung from the wall and there were roosting bars for the birds to perch on. Another door led to the outside area.

Mandy gasped as she stepped out. The air was alive with budgies! They flew and swooped and perched on the branches of the old hollow tree. Some sang and some twittered. Mandy ducked as one just missed her head. It was like being in a different world!

Mandy looked at one bird and then another. Although at first they looked the same, gradually she began to see differences — some birds had more white, some had larger patches of blue, some had lots of speckles, some just a few.

She thought about Salt and Pepper. There were so many similar birds, it would have taken a thief ages to find the right ones, particularly in the dark. It was very odd that Mrs. Tibbit hadn't heard anything.

She counted the pied violet birds. It was hard because they kept flying around, but after the third count she was sure that there were fourteen. Two were definitely missing.

She looked around the aviary. There was no way the birds could have gotten out unless they'd been stolen, but then she was back to the question — how had the thief done it without Mrs. Tibbit hearing anything?

Just then a budgie flew past Mandy's nose and landed a few feet away from her on the branches of the tree and chirped loudly. Mandy smiled at the handsome little bird. His chest was puffed out and he looked full of confidence and pride. He hopped along the branch, bobbing his head. The feathers on his back were a beautiful glossy white.

White! Mandy stared. There wasn't a single speckle all the way from his neck down to his tail. She was sure she hadn't seen him before when she was counting birds. *Could it be . . . ?*

With a loud twitter the little bird flew off the branch and swooped down almost to the bottom of the tree where there was a split in the gnarled trunk. To Mandy's astonishment, he fluttered his wings and disappeared inside.

She ran to the foot of the tree and crouched down. Inside the tree trunk there was a dark hollow. She gasped. In the hollow was a nest. The budgie with the white back was perched on one side and sitting on the nest was a pretty hen budgie with lots of small gray speckles all over her wings and back.

"Salt and Pepper!" Mandy breathed in delight.

Hearing her, Pepper looked up and ruffled her feathers protectively — giving Mandy a glimpse of two perfect little eggs.

Not wanting to disturb the two birds, Mandy withdrew as quietly as she could but inside her heart was leaping. Salt and Pepper hadn't been stolen, after all. They'd just been nesting in the only place they could find!

*   *   *

Mrs. Tibbit was astonished when Mandy told her the news and wouldn't believe it until she had seen the little family for herself. "Well!" she exclaimed as she straightened up after looking into the little hollow. "So that's where they've been. I *thought* they were getting ready to nest. I just wasn't expecting it to be this soon."

"What will you do?" Mandy asked her.

"I'll leave them there," Mrs. Tibbit replied. "I'm sure it's just as good a place as any for them to bring up a family. If I tried to move them they would abandon the eggs. But at least now I know where they are, I can make sure they get all the nutrition and care they need." She smiled gratefully at Mandy. "Thank you so much for finding them."

"That's okay," Mandy said. "I'm just glad they're safe."

Dr. Emily smiled at her. "Maybe Mrs. Tibbit will let you come and see the chicks when they've hatched."

"Oh, yes, please!" Mandy said, turning to Mrs. Tibbit. "I'd love to! And so would my friend, James."

"Then you're both very welcome to come." Mrs. Tibbit smiled. "And as a present today, just to say thank you for helping me find Salt and Pepper, you can choose a budgie to take home with you, if you like."

Mandy looked hopefully at her mom, but Dr. Emily shook her head. "You know the rules, Mandy."

Mandy sighed. She did. Her mom was very strict about not letting her have any pets at Animal Ark apart from her three rabbits, Flopsy, Mopsy, and Cottontail.

"I can't," she said to Mrs. Tibbit. "I'm not allowed to have any more pets. But I do know someone who *would* like a budgie!" she said. "It's Mrs. McFarlane, who runs the general store in our town. She has one budgie, but he's lonely. She'd love another! Can I choose one for her instead?"

"Of course," Mrs. Tibbit said. "What sort would she like?"

"A blue one," Mandy said, remembering what Mrs. McFarlane had said.

"Well, look in the other aviary then," Mrs. Tibbit said. "There are quite a few in there. You can choose whichever one you like."

Mandy went and stood outside the other aviary. In the highest branches of the tree a bright blue budgie was singing. "Can I have that one, please?" she said, pointing.

Mrs. Tibbit looked. "Of course," she said. "He's named James."

"James!" Mandy exclaimed.

"I wonder what human James will think of that!" Dr. Emily said, raising her eyebrows.

"I'll go and fetch a box for you," Mrs. Tibbit said. "And we'll get him down."

Mandy looked at the budgie singing in the tree and grinned happily. Now all she had to do was to give him to Mrs. McFarlane — and tell James the news, of course!

James Tells You All About Peanut and Other Chinchillas

Did you know that . . .

- the chinchilla originally comes from high up in the Andes mountains in South America, where it lives in rock crevices.

- chinchillas are excellent jumpers and have been reported to clear six feet in a single bound.

- chinchilla fur is very dense. They have about 80 hairs per hair follicle, whereas humans have only one! Because their fur is so dense, chinchillas can't get fleas.

- about 150 chinchillas have to die to make one fur coat. The wild chinchilla was almost made extinct by fur trappers, before protective laws were passed.

- chinchillas' tails are one third of the length of their entire body and help provide balance for high-speed escapes.

- chinchillas keep clean by taking dust baths. In the wild they bathe in volcanic ash. As pets, they need special chinchilla dust from pet shops so that their coats don't get matted.

- chinchillas can live for up to 15 years when kept as pets.

- chinchillas have no odor at all, as long as they are kept clean.

🐈 THE CONTENTED CAT 🐈

"Gangway! Watch out . . ." Jean Knox, Animal Ark's receptionist, backed slowly into the consulting room.

Mandy's eyes widened. *What was going on?* She was helping out her dad with morning office hours, because school was closed for a teacher training day. It had been a busy session and Dr. Adam had just called in the next patient.

"Almost there . . ." Jean did a sideways shuffle, easing one end of a large pet carrier around the open door. A tiny, nervous-looking woman, whom Mandy didn't recognize, had hold of the other end.

"Here. Let me." Dr. Adam hurried forward to help.

"Oh, thank you!" the tiny woman gasped as Dr. Adam took over. "Pumpkin's so heavy!"

"One. Two. Three!" Dr. Adam and Jean swung the carrier onto the examination table.

Mandy had her first clear view of the patient. Staring out of the front grille were two bright amber eyes set in a face as round as a full moon. The entire carrier seemed to be stuffed with ginger fur.

"Oh, wow!" Mandy suddenly realized that she was looking at the fattest ginger cat she had ever seen.

"Thanks, Jean. Mandy and I can manage now," Dr. Adam said with a smile.

"Okay then." Jean dusted off her hands, her glasses bobbing on their chain against her sweater. She glanced toward the owner as she went out. "Call me if you need a hand out to the car, Mrs. Walker."

"I will. Thank you so much." Mrs. Walker's fragile white hands fluttered up to her throat. Her neatly permed hair was barely level with Dr. Adam's shoulder.

Mandy stood beside her dad as he smiled down at the owner. "Now, what's the problem with Pumpkin?" he asked kindly.

"It's his weight. He keeps getting fatter and fatter. I just can't understand it. I'm so careful with his food." Mrs. Walker's whole body seemed to droop. "I'm so worried. I'm sure there must be something seriously wrong with him."

"I find it's best not to jump to any conclusions," Dr. Adam said in his calm, level way. He snapped open the pet carrier's fastenings. "Let me take a look at him. Out you come, Pumpkin."

Pumpkin didn't need much encouragement. Blinking placidly, he squeezed himself out of the carrier. After a couple of steps forward he yawned, then flopped onto his side on the table.

"Gosh! You really are enormous," Mandy said, petting Pumpkin's head.

The ginger cat's legs looked small and stubby in comparison to his huge, round body. Closing his eyes to slits, Pumpkin began purring loudly.

Mandy turned to Mrs. Walker. "He's very friendly, isn't he?"

"Oh, he is," Pumpkin's owner said fondly. She seemed pleased to talk about her pet. "He's as soft as butter. I live alone and he keeps me company in the evenings. He has his very own armchair."

Mandy wasn't surprised. There was no way Pumpkin would fit on his owner's lap!

"Our records show that you live in Walton, Mrs. Walker." Dr. Adam was checking the records on his computer. "Has Pumpkin been seeing the vet there?"

"Yes — for his routine vaccinations and things. I would have taken him there this time, but the clinic is closed for building work."

"No problem," Dr. Adam reassured her. "I can certainly take Pumpkin on as a temporary patient, but you'll have to inform Dr. Hughes that I'm treating him. All right?"

"I'll do that. Thank you." Mrs. Walker plucked at the belt of her flowered dress with a birdlike hand. "What do you think could be causing his weight gain?"

"It could be a number of things," Dr. Adam replied. "Let's start with a process of elimination. What do you feed him?"

"Well, he has two meals a day. A dish of chicken or fish in the morning, and some canned food at night." Mrs. Walker ticked off items on her fingers. "Oh, and sometimes I put a sprinkle of those crunchy cat treats on top. He likes those."

"That sounds fine. And what else do you give him?" Dr. Adam waited for Mrs. Walker to go on.

By now, Pumpkin had heaved himself into a sitting position. He sat there, a big, furry orange mound, licking his paws and washing behind his ears.

"That's all he has," Mrs. Walker said.

"It's important that I know exactly what you give Pumpkin to eat, including treats. Small amounts of rich food like pieces of cheese or cookies can easily add up," Dr. Adam explained tactfully. "Do you give him milk to drink?"

Mandy knew that some owners gave their pets unsuitable treats. Sometimes they were embarrassed to admit that they fed them chips and table leftovers.

Mrs. Walker looked put out. She shook her head, so that her permed hair trembled. "Good gracious me, no! Milk's bad for cats, isn't it? And sweets would rot his teeth. He only drinks water and I never give him tidbits between meals."

Mandy was impressed. Mrs. Walker certainly seemed to know what was healthy for cats to eat. But now she felt worried, too.

"Pumpkin shouldn't have grown to this size on that diet, should he?" she asked her dad.

"No," Dr. Adam agreed, looking baffled. "Would you give me a hand, Mandy? I'm going to do a routine examination."

Mandy petted Pumpkin and spoke to him gently while her dad took his temperature and listened to his chest. He shone a light in his eyes, then looked in his ears and down his throat.

"Everything looks normal," Dr. Adam said as he finished his examination. "His coat's good and there's no sign of fleas or other parasites. I think we need to rule out certain medical conditions, so I'm going to do some tests. Would you steady him while I take some blood, please, Mandy?"

"What conditions are you going to test for?" Mandy wanted to know.

"Diabetes and kidney problems among others," her dad replied. "Some of this weight could be fluid retention." He took some blood, then patted

Pumpkin. "That wasn't too bad, was it? Okay. Let's put him on the scale."

Mandy helped her dad lift Pumpkin onto the floor and Mrs. Walker coaxed him onto the scale. "Come on, Pumpkin," she encouraged. "That's a good boy."

Mandy stood and watched as Pumpkin strolled sedately over to the weighing machine. Then he plonked himself down onto the metal plate and curled into a ball, as good as gold.

"Wow! Almost twenty-nine pounds!" Mandy exclaimed, reading the digital display. She thought Pumpkin must be the fattest cat in Walton and Welford combined.

Dr. Adam seemed surprised by Pumpkin's weight, too. "He needs to lose at least half of that weight," he told Mrs. Walker. "Otherwise he's heading for heart trouble, among other things."

"Oh, dear." Mrs. Walker's delicate pointed features twitched nervously.

"I don't think you should worry too much, though," Dr. Adam said. "Pumpkin seems pretty healthy despite his size, but we'll know more once we get the test results. I'll be in touch with you in a few days."

Mandy scratched Pumpkin under the chin. He had uncurled himself now and was all stretched out. He purred loudly as Mandy fussed over him, not at all put out by being poked and prodded. "He's so laid back, isn't he?" she said, smiling.

Mrs. Walker nodded. "Nothing worries him. But he isn't really a lazy cat. Most of the day he's outside in the yard or roaming around. He generally only comes in for his meals and then settles down for the evening."

"That makes his weight gain even more of a mystery," Dr. Adam said, shaking his head. "From what you've told me, Pumpkin should be a regular slim Jim."

Mandy helped put Pumpkin back into his carrier.

"Well, thank you for seeing us. I'll wait to hear from you," said Mrs. Walker, giving Dr. Adam a grateful smile.

Half an hour later, when the last patient had been seen, Mandy went into reception. She found Jean working at her computer.

"Let me give you a hand," Mandy said, tidying up the leaflets and booklets on animal care.

"Oh, thank you, Mandy. Wasn't that Pumpkin a whopper!" Jean said suddenly. "A regular fat cat! There's something about him, though — that cat has charm."

Mandy smiled. She couldn't agree more. "He's certainly got a purr to match his size!" She thought

Pumpkin had to be one of the friendliest cats she'd ever met.

"Mandy Hope, are you planning on camping out in the lab all weekend?" Ms. Temple, the biology teacher, asked, a twinkle in her eye. It was Friday afternoon at Walton Moor School and classes were finished for another week.

Mandy had been thinking about Pumpkin and hadn't heard the bell ring. "No way!" She grinned and jumped up. "Sorry, Ms. Temple!" She stuffed her books into her schoolbag and joined the end of the scramble for the door.

Her friend, James Hunter, was waiting for her by his locker outside the coatroom. "Hi! I'm starving," he said, the moment he saw her. "Can we go to the store and buy some chips before we catch the bus?"

"Okay." Mandy grinned. James was always hungry. Her grandmother said he had what she called "a very healthy appetite."

They went to the store and Mandy bought her favorite treat — lemon candy. James began munching his chips as they retraced their steps to the bus stop.

Suddenly, Mandy spotted a huge ginger cat waddling down the street. His big, furry tummy swayed back and forth, almost touching the ground. "Look! That has got to be Pumpkin!" she burst out.

She had told James every detail of the portly pet's visit to the clinic on the way to school that morning.

"Wow!" James almost choked on his chips. "That is one megacat!"

Mandy went over to Pumpkin. "Hello again, boy! Want some attention?"

Pumpkin meowed a welcome. He rolled onto his back and presented his pale underside for tickling.

James closed his chip bag and put it in his pocket. "You weren't kidding about his size, were you?"

"Me?" Mandy grinned. She knew that she had a tendency to exaggerate sometimes. She ruffled Pumpkin's belly fur. "Are you heading home for your dinner?" she asked him.

Pumpkin put his head on one side. A purr rumbled in his chest and he got heavily to his feet. As he continued his stately walk down the street, Mandy and James walked along behind him.

"We're going the same way," Mandy said. "Should we go and say hello to Mrs. Walker?"

"If you like," James said good-naturedly.

They had only gone a few yards when Pumpkin stopped outside a bungalow with cheerful window boxes. He ambled slowly up the yard path and began scratching on the front door.

"That must be Mrs. Walker's house," Mandy said to

James. But then the door swung open and a man appeared. Mandy's eyes widened in surprise.

"Come to see Fred for your usual, have you?" the man said fondly to Pumpkin.

Pumpkin purred and rubbed himself against the man's legs. He looked up at him and meowed loudly, as if to say, *Yes, please. I'm starving.*

"Wait there, then," Fred said, going back into the house.

Mandy frowned at James. "That's funny. I'm sure Mrs. Walker said she lived alone."

"Maybe Fred's looking after him for her," James suggested.

"He might be," Mandy reasoned. "But Mrs. Walker didn't say she was going away." Somehow she couldn't imagine Pumpkin's meticulous owner going anywhere without him. Besides, there were the tests. She was sure that Mrs. Walker wouldn't go away without knowing the results.

"Well, whoever Fred is," James said, "he seems to know Pumpkin very well."

The man reappeared with a dish of food. He put it down on the ground and Pumpkin began eating. Mandy and James could hear the cat smacking his lips.

"You're enjoying that, aren't you?" the old man said with a broad smile on his wrinkled face as he watched Pumpkin gobbling down the food.

"Come on," Mandy said, digging James in the ribs.

"Where to?" James asked.

"I'm going to have a word with Fred." Mandy walked boldly up the path.

James reddened, shy as usual, but he followed her at a slight distance.

The man looked up and smiled in a friendly fashion. "Hello there, little girl. What can I do for you and your friend?"

Mandy smiled back. "Excuse me," she began politely. "But we were wondering about your cat . . ."

Fred gave a rusty laugh. "Oh, he isn't my cat. He just visits me. We're good friends, aren't we, Rascal?"

Mandy looked at James. *Rascal?*

Fred grinned at her expression. "That's my name for him anyway. I don't know where he lives. But we're good pals, him and me. I always have his food ready when he turns up. Regular as clockwork, aren't you, Rascal?"

"Oh!" An idea sparked in Mandy's head.

"What?" James whispered.

"I'll tell you later," Mandy hissed back.

They said good-bye to Fred and left Pumpkin to finish his food.

"So what was all that about?" James looked curiously at Mandy as they went to catch the bus back to Welford.

"I think I might have cracked the case!" Mandy was full of excitement.

"Don't worry. Superglue's supposed to fix anything!" James grinned. "Sorry. Couldn't resist that."

"Ha ha! No, listen." Mandy eyes narrowed in concentration as she relayed her suspicions to James. "You remember I told you that Pumpkin's really friendly? Well Jean was impressed by how good-natured he was, too. And Mrs. Walker said that Pumpkin stays out most of the day and only comes in at night to eat."

"Okay. So, he must be going somewhere . . ." James was concentrating now, reasoning things out in his logical way. "He'd have plenty of time to amble around and visit anyone he likes. I get it! Maybe other people are feeding him, too, just like Fred?"

"Exactly!" Mandy said. "That would explain why he's so enormous."

"It does make sense," James agreed. "But how are we going to find out if we're right?" Suddenly he grinned at her through his glasses. "I know! We could put a tail on him. Get it? It means to follow him . . ."

Mandy groaned. "I know. That's what they say in old gangster films. Your jokes are as bad as my dad's!"

"Oh, thanks!" James replied, pretending to be offended.

"But I think you're right about following Pumpkin," Mandy added. "That way we can find out exactly where he goes."

James pushed his bangs back from his forehead thoughtfully. "I read somewhere that cats can roam over a large territory. We wouldn't be able to follow him very far after school each day."

"No, but it's Saturday tomorrow," Mandy reminded him. "How about if we bike over here first thing in the morning?"

"Okay. That'll give us lots of time."

Mandy grinned. "I'll meet you at your house as soon as I've done my chores."

Mandy had finished sweeping the floors. Now she squirted disinfectant on all the surfaces and wiped them clean. "All done!"

She went to say good-bye to her dad before leaving to meet James.

Dr. Adam was in the kitchen, ironing his white lab coat. "Where are you off to in such a big hurry?" he asked, ruffling her blond hair.

"I'm meeting James, then we're biking to Walton," she told him. "We've got a theory about Pumpkin."

"Sounds interesting. I don't suppose you're going to tell me what it is?" Dr. Adam coaxed.

"Nope! Not until we're sure!" Mandy rushed out the door. "See you later, Dad," she called over her shoulder.

James was outside in his yard, brushing Blackie, his pet Labrador, when Mandy arrived. "Mom's complaining about having pet hair all over the furniture," he said, making a face. James also had a pet kitten named Eric.

"Hello, boy." Mandy patted Blackie's head and petted his velvety ears. The Labrador looked up at her, with soft brown eyes. He gave her a big doggy grin.

"Should I bring him with us?" James asked.

Mandy put her head on one side. Blackie got along well with cats, especially Eric, but she didn't know how Pumpkin would react. "Better not this time," she replied. "If Pumpkin gets spooked and runs off, we'll be wasting our time."

"Somehow I can't see Pumpkin running anywhere!" James commented, but he agreed that Blackie should stay behind. "He won't mind. Mom will take him with her to the pet shop. She needs to stock up on his favorite food."

Mandy chuckled. "He'll love that. And I expect she'll get him a doggy treat."

Blackie's ears pricked up. He gave a short bark.

James finished brushing his dog, then wheeled his bike around to the front gate. He was already wearing his bike helmet. Mandy buckled on her helmet and they set off.

"Where to first?" James asked as they pedaled toward the outskirts of Welford.

"I don't know," Mandy replied. "Maybe we should go back to where we saw Pumpkin yesterday. He must live somewhere nearby." She wished she had thought to ask Jean for Mrs. Walker's address.

But she shouldn't have worried. As soon as they reached Walton they spotted a familiar figure padding slowly along the pavement outside Walton Parish Church.

"Pumpkin!" she exclaimed.

"Looks like he's already out on his rounds," James said.

Mandy watched Pumpkin turn down a side street. She and James dismounted and wheeled their bikes after him.

After turning into a cul-de-sac, Pumpkin ambled up the drive of a red-brick house.

"Let's sit on our bikes and watch from across the street," Mandy said to James.

"Tom!" two children called, rushing out to meet

Pumpkin. They were both boys. One looked about seven, the other about five. They had fair hair and were dressed in T-shirts and jeans. "Come on, Tom. Come and have your breakfast!"

Mandy glanced at James. How many names did Pumpkin have?

A woman came out of the house. She smiled at her kids. "Have you two been waiting for Tom?" She put a dish of food on the floor. "There you are, boy. Tuna fish, your favorite."

Pumpkin plodded over to the dish. He took a sniff and began eating.

"Look at him chomping away," James said. "You wouldn't think he'd already had one breakfast at his real home."

Pumpkin polished off the tuna and stood, licking his lips, beside the empty dish. The two little boys darted about, trying to get him to chase a toy mouse. Pumpkin gave them a look that seemed to say, *No chance.*

The boys' mom took the empty dish into the house, then reappeared in the drive. "Daniel, Oliver," she called, waving a set of car keys. "We have to go shopping now."

"Aw! We want to play with Tom," the elder of the two complained.

"He'll be back the same time tomorrow. Just like always. Get into the car, please."

Daniel and Oliver each gave Pumpkin a final cuddle. "Bye, Tom. See you tomorrow," the small boy called as he got into the car.

As the vehicle pulled out of the driveway and sped away, Daniel and Oliver waved frantically from the back window.

Pumpkin washed himself in a leisurely fashion, then rose to his feet. He yawned. He stretched. And then he set off again, plodding cumbersomely down the road.

"Here we go again!" James said.

They followed at a distance. This time Pumpkin went to the back door of a house. A woman with flowing silk clothes and dark red hair held up with fancy combs came out to feed him.

"She looks like she might be a painter or something. I wonder what *she* calls him?" James said.

Once again, Mandy and James watched as Pumpkin was petted, pampered, and fed.

Then the artsy lady waved good-bye to him. "See you tomorrow, Rossetti."

"It's a good thing we didn't have a bet on *that* name!" James said, laughing.

Pumpkin was off again. He made his way, plodding slowly and heavily down the street.

"Phew! I'm surprised he can even walk after that feast!" James commented in amazement.

"He's on his way to Fred's bungalow, now." Mandy recognized the route the cat was taking. "If he carries on eating three extra meals a day he could get dangerously ill," she said worriedly.

James made a face. "Never mind getting ill. *I'm* afraid he's going to burst!"

"We have to do something," Mandy said, ignoring James's joke.

"Yes. But what?" her friend asked.

Mandy had an idea. "Why don't we go and talk to all the people who are feeding Pumpkin," she suggested. "I'm sure they don't realize what harm they're doing to him."

"It's worth a try," James agreed. "We could start now, by having a word with Fred. He seemed friendly the other day."

Fred saw them from his living room window and came out to meet them in the driveway. "Hello again, you two. Oh, you've arrived with Rascal. Ready for your food, are you, boy?"

"Rascal's real name is Pumpkin," Mandy began. "His owner brought him to Animal Ark — my parents' veterinary clinic in Welford."

"Pumpkin, you say? And he was at the vet's?" Fred looked concerned. "Is he sick?"

"Dad doesn't think so. But he's very overweight and that could be dangerous." Mandy explained about Pumpkin going to all the different homes and being fed at each one. "So, you see, it really would be best for him if you all stopped giving him food."

Fred had been listening closely. He rubbed his chin. "Oh, dear," he said sadly. "I'm afraid that he'd stop coming to see me if I didn't feed him. And I'm really fond of him."

Mandy's spirits fell. She could see what Fred meant. Maybe if Pumpkin was having just *one* extra meal a day he'd still lose most of his weight. Perhaps she and James would have better luck persuading the two boys' mom. They thanked Fred politely and left.

In the cul-de-sac, Mandy saw that the car was back in the driveway. Daniel and Oliver were helping their mom unload bags and boxes of groceries. They saw Mandy and James pull up on their bikes and came over curiously.

"Hi!" they chorused.

"Hi," Mandy and James replied.

"Oh, hello." Their mom came to speak to Mandy and James. "Didn't I see you two around here earlier?"

"Yes," Mandy said. "We've been following Pumpkin to see where he goes. We wondered if we could have a word with you about him."

"Pumpkin?" The woman looked puzzled.

"He's the enormous ginger cat who comes to visit you."

"Is that his name?" The woman laughed. "I like Tom better. The boys gave him that name. But Pumpkin certainly suits him. Why don't you come in? We can talk while I make the boys their lunch. I'm Jennifer Kemp, by the way."

Mandy and James followed her into the kitchen.

Mrs. Kemp unwrapped a pizza and put it into the oven. She gave each of the kids an apple to tide them over, then turned to Mandy and James. "Okay," she said. "Fire away. What's all this about?"

Mandy went through the whole saga again. She explained about Pumpkin's visits to different homes and how his health was at risk because of all the extra meals.

"I can see what you're getting at," Mrs. Kemp said when Mandy had finished. She looked sympathetic. "It's a bit tricky, though. The kids just spent their pocket money on meals for Tom — I mean Pumpkin. And they would be really upset if he stopped coming to see them."

Mandy and James exchanged glances. It was just the same as Fred. They thanked Mrs. Kemp before they left, and Daniel and Oliver came outside to wave them off.

"Two down, one to go," James said as he climbed on his bike.

But the artsy lady had a similar attitude. She told

them her name was Celia Pollard. She listened, she understood, and then she apologized. Just like the others. "You see, I wouldn't want Rossetti to stop visiting."

By now Mandy was feeling angry and frustrated. No one seemed to want to endanger Pumpkin's health, but no one wanted to miss out on the friendly cat's visits.

"There has to be some way to keep all Pumpkin's friends happy and for him to have a healthier lifestyle." Mandy sighed dejectedly. "Come on, let's go back to Animal Ark. Dad might be able to think of something."

"Hello, you two," Jean Knox said, when Mandy and James came into the waiting room. Office hours didn't start for another half an hour and she was pinning up a poster reminding pet owners about the importance of booster shots.

"Hi, Jean," Mandy replied. "Is Dad in the kitchen?"

"No. He's in one of the consulting rooms with a sales rep. It's that nice Mr. Butler again from Healthi-Pet suppliers. Why don't you wait? I don't think they'll be long."

Mandy was just about to sink onto a seat when suddenly an idea shot into her head. She leaped up and grabbed James's arm. "Come with me!"

"Where are we going?" he asked, looking confused.

But, without stopping to explain, Mandy rushed ahead into the consulting room. Dr. Adam and the sales rep looked around in surprise. There were samples of Healthi-Pet products all over the table.

"Hi, Mr. Butler! Do you want any help promoting diet food for cats?" Mandy got straight to the point.

Mr. Butler blinked at her in surprise. "Er . . . hello, Mandy. Have you got something in mind?"

"She usually has," Dr. Adam said wryly.

Mandy rushed on. "I've thought of a great way for you to get publicity around here. It's Pumpkin — "

"Pumpkin?" Mr. Butler looked blank.

"An overweight cat," James said, coming through the open door.

"Ah, I see," the sales rep replied.

"He has about five different homes and he gets fed at each one of them." Mandy was in full swing now. "James and I have asked everyone, apart from his owner, not to feed him, but none of them really wants to stop — because then Pumpkin won't visit them anymore . . ." She paused for breath. "So I thought, if we could persuade everyone to feed him diet food . . ."

Mr. Butler caught on fast. "Then the cat will lose weight so he's healthy, and yet he'll still keep making his regular visits to his surrogate owners. Bingo, everyone's happy! It's brilliant. What a story! The marketing people at Healthi-Pet are going to love this."

Dr. Adam looked bemused. "Did you know about this, James?"

"I do now!" James said, grinning. "I agree with Mr. Butler. It's a brilliant idea, Mandy."

A slow smile spread across Dr. Adam's face.

"What's so funny?" Mandy asked him.

"I was just wondering how Mrs. Walker is going to react to the news that her beloved pet has been sharing his affections with half of Walton! Some owners can be very possessive."

"Oh." For the first time, Mandy experienced a moment of doubt. "We'll go and have another word with Pumpkin's surrogate owners first, before we tell Mrs. Walker," she suggested.

"Good idea," Dr. Adam said. "If they agree, then half of the battle is won."

Dr. Adam decided to visit Mrs. Walker in person when the test results arrived. Mandy and James went with him.

"Come in. How nice of you all to visit us," Mrs. Walker said, showing them into her living room. The small room was neat and tidy. Flowered curtains hung at the windows.

Mandy spotted Pumpkin at once. He was sprawled

in an armchair, his huge ginger body nestling against a soft cushion. As soon as he saw Mandy and James, he began purring loudly.

"Look who's come to see us, Pumpkin," Mrs. Walker cooed, beaming around at them all. Then a shadow passed over her face. "Oh, I hope it isn't bad news."

"Quite the opposite," Dr. Adam reassured her. "All Pumpkin's test results were normal."

"Oh, that's wonderful!"

"Yes, it is," Mandy said fervently. "And we've

discovered the reason why Pumpkin has put on so much weight, haven't we, James?"

James nodded. "And Mandy's had a great idea about how he can lose weight, too."

"Really? You seem to have been very busy!" Mrs. Walker said, with a smile.

Dr. Adam chuckled. "They always are when there's an animal involved! I think you two had better explain."

So Mandy told Mrs. Walker how she and James had followed Pumpkin and discovered that he had a number of homes. "He's so fat because everyone he visits feeds him. No one wanted to miss out on his visits, so I thought we might be able to persuade everyone to give him diet cat food instead." She paused. Pumpkin's owner was looking a bit stunned.

James took over. "Mandy has arranged with Mr. Butler, a sales rep from Healthi-Pet, for you to get a free supply. He says it will be good publicity for his products."

"Enterprising, aren't they?" Dr. Adam said. "It seems like a good solution to me, but of course, as Pumpkin's real owner, you'd have to agree."

Mandy was hoping for Mrs. Walker to see the merit of their idea. "We've had another word with Pumpkin's part-time owners. They said they'd be happy to feed him just a small portion of diet cat food. That way, Pumpkin will still visit them."

"Ah, the part-time owners." Mrs. Walker's hands began fluttering toward her sweater buttons.

"You could call them admirers," James said helpfully.

"Oh, yes. They all love Pumpkin," Mandy rushed on. "They even have different names for him. Rascal, Tom, and Rossetti . . ." She bit her lip as Mrs. Walker crossed to the armchair and looked down at Pumpkin, a frown knitting her brows together. She could see that her narrow shoulders were trembling.

James threw Mandy a worried look. Was Mrs. Walker upset? Mandy held her breath. Suddenly a soft, trilling noise rose into the room.

"It's Mrs. Walker. I think she's laughing," James whispered.

"Well, Pumpkin! Or should I say Rascal? Tom? Or . . . Rossetti? I had no idea you were so popular. Why — you're almost famous!" Mrs. Walker wiped her eyes. She stretched her thin arms around the enormous cat and gave him a hug. "You always were too friendly for your own good. I don't mind sharing you, you old rogue. But from now on, there's going to be a lot less of you to go around!"

As Pumpkin purred with contentment and began to wash himself in a leisurely fashion, Mandy gave a soft chuckle. And she could have sworn that Pumpkin closed one eye in a mischievous wink.

Brandon Gill Tells You All About Ruby and Other Pigs

Did you know that . . .

- pigs have existed for at least 45 million years!

- pigs live on every continent on Earth except Antarctica.

- pigs were probably domesticated in China in 4900 BC, but maybe even as early as 10,000 BC in Thailand.

- the smallest wild pig is the pygmy hog, which is 12 inches tall and weighs around 13 pounds, while the largest is the giant forest hog — 43 inches tall and weighing 300 pounds.

- the heaviest domestic pig on record weighed over 2500 pounds!

- pigs are surprisingly fast runners.

- the average pig litter contains between seven and 12 piglets — but the largest on record contained 37 — of which 33 piglets survived.

- pigs are not only used for meat but also for medical purposes: pig insulin is used for treating diabetics and pig hearts have been used in experimental transplants.

- pigs have a very good sense of smell and are actually smarter than dogs!

🐈 FOLLOWED BY A FOAL 🐈

Dr. Adam stood by the tail of the dapple-gray mare, his chest heaving for breath. "How's she doing, Nick?"

Mandy glanced at the tall young man who was holding the mare's head. "Okay," Nick Summers muttered anxiously. "But she's not going to be standing for much longer." As he spoke, the mare's legs trembled, and for a moment Mandy thought she was about to collapse in the straw. "She's exhausted."

"I almost got it that time," her dad gasped. "One more try and we might be there. Good girl, Rosie." Turning back to his work, he began again. Mandy knew that he needed to ease the unborn foal's head around inside the mare. At the moment its neck was bent backward and Rosie couldn't push it out.

Oh, please, please come around, Mandy pleaded

silently. She looked at Rosie's hot, damp neck, and at
the sweat running down her dad's face as he grappled
with the foal. She pulled her heavy winter coat tighter
around her. It was early in the morning and still dark
outside, and a thick night frost had coated every
blade of grass and every bare branch. She and her
dad had been in the stable at Drysdale Farm for over
an hour now. She wondered how long the mare could
go on.

Fiona, Nick's young wife, came into the stable with
four mugs of tea on a tray. "Any luck?" she asked,
worried.

Nick shook his head.

"Almost there, almost there," Dr. Adam panted.

Go on, Dad, Mandy thought fervently. She felt so
helpless just standing there watching. She dug her
hands in her pockets, wishing there was something
she could do.

Suddenly her dad staggered backward. "Got it!" he
exclaimed.

Hope sprang into Nick's eyes. "It's turned?"

Leaning his hands on his knees and taking in deep
lungfuls of air, Dr. Adam nodded. "Come on, Rosie,
girl," he gasped. "It's up to you now."

Mandy watched as Nick let the mare sink down on
her knees. She collapsed on her side, her breathing

heavy, her coat matted with sweat as the birth contractions swept through her. Mandy looked at her dad anxiously as he came to stand beside her. "Will she be okay?"

"I hope so," he said, peeling off his rubber gloves and wiping his forehead with his arm.

Little by little, the foal began to emerge in its white transparent amniotic sac. Through the white membrane, Mandy saw the hooves and could make out a dark head and muzzle.

Her dad stepped forward. Breaking the sac, he took hold of the foal's legs and each time the mare pushed he gave a tug.

With one last push from the mare, the foal slid out onto the straw. Mandy saw its tiny bay ears flicker. "It's out!" she gasped.

Leaving Fiona by Rosie's head, Nick came around to help Dr. Adam. The two men gently cleared away the amniotic sac and wiped away the mucus from the foal's nostrils, so that it could breathe.

"Oh, isn't he beautiful?" Mandy breathed as the foal struggled onto his chest. His damp coat was dark bay, and in the middle of his forehead was a snowy-white star. Mandy swallowed the tears that sprang to her eyes as she watched the foal blink and look around for the first time. Nick and her dad clapped each other on the shoulders, relief on their faces.

"Adam!" Fiona said urgently. "I think there's something wrong with Rosie!"

Mandy saw the delight fade abruptly from her dad's face. He moved swiftly to the mare's head. She was still, her flanks heaving with exhaustion and pain. "She feels cold," Fiona said to him anxiously, her hands massaging the mare's ears. "All wet and clammy."

Dr. Adam ran a hand over Rosie's neck, then checked her gums. Grabbing his stethoscope from his black bag, he kneeled in the straw and began listening to her heart.

"She's going into shock," he said, getting quickly to his feet. "I think she's hemorrhaging. The birth must have been too much for her."

"Oh, Dad!" Mandy whispered. Icy fingers clutched at her heart. She knew that a hemorrhage was heavy bleeding and that in this case, Rosie must be bleeding internally. She also knew that it could be fatal.

"Can you do anything?" Nick asked quickly.

"Depends on the hemorrhage," Dr. Adam said grimly, pulling on some fresh gloves. "If it's burst into the peritoneal cavity, then we'd have to operate." He crouched down on the straw behind Rosie and began to do an internal examination.

Mandy's stomach churned as she looked at the mare's dark eyes, which were wide with pain. She couldn't bear it if anything happened to Rosie. There was a tense silence in the stall while her dad worked.

"It's okay," he said at last, his voice relieved. "There's a swelling that suggests that the hemorrhage is being contained. Providing it doesn't burst then she should be okay." He rummaged in his bag. "I'll give her a cortisone injection to combat the effects of the shock. It will also reduce the pain and swelling. It will take a few weeks for her to recover properly, but she should be fine in the end. Now the most important thing is to get her dry and keep her warm."

"I'll fetch some blankets," Fiona said, getting up and hurrying out of the stable.

Nick picked up a handful of straw and began to rub the mare's sides.

A movement in the straw behind her made Mandy look around. "What about the foal, Dad?"

"He needs drying off, too," Dr. Adam said. "Rosie's going to be out of action for some time yet."

"I'll help!" Mandy said eagerly. She crouched down by the foal and, picking up some straw, began to rub his sides like Nick was doing with Rosie.

"Thanks, dear," her dad said. "If you keep going with him, I'll fetch some colostrum from the car. He's going to need to have his first meal by hand."

Mandy rubbed the foal's damp coat in firm circles. The foal looked up at her with big, dark eyes. "Good boy," she murmured. The foal poked his muzzle forward and pushed his nose under her coat, seeking the warm darkness. Mandy let him snuggle in under the flap against her chest. "You're going to be okay," she whispered to him. "You really are."

Fiona came back. She had brought some towels as well as a blanket for Rosie. "How's he doing, Mandy?" she asked, handing her a towel.

"Okay," Mandy replied. Dropping the straw, she began to rub at the foal's neck with the towel. "What are you going to name him?"

"I don't know," Fiona said, crouching down to help Nick with Rosie. "Got any ideas?"

Mandy looked down at the little foal. "Well, he's very friendly."

"How about Amigo?" Nick suggested, looking up. "It means 'friend' in Spanish."

"I like it!" Fiona said.

"Well, that's settled then," Nick said. "Amigo it is."

Mandy kissed the little foal's forehead. "Hello, Amigo," she whispered into his tiny ear. She liked the name. It seemed to suit him. As she worked, she gradually felt him drying off and warming up.

When her dad came back, he had a bottle in his hand. "He needs feeding," he said. Mandy nodded. She knew how important it was for foals to eat within a few hours of being born. All the antibodies a foal needed were in the first milk, called colostrum. It helped protect them against disease. Dr. Adam held up the bottle. "This contains colostrum collected from another mare. It'll give him all the protection he needs."

Mandy looked longingly at the bottle. "Can I feed him, Dad?"

Dr. Adam looked inquiringly at Nick.

"Of course," Nick said, still busy with Rosie. "Thanks, Mandy."

Feeling delighted, Mandy took the bottle and gently brought Amigo's head out from under her coat. As soon as the little foal felt the soft nipple against his lips he began to suck clumsily. Milk spurted down his face as he lost the nipple. Mandy steadied his head and tilted the bottle slightly. Amigo grasped the nipple more firmly and quickly began to take long sucks. His lips were strong and Mandy had to hang on tightly to the bottle so that he didn't manage to pull it out of her hands. "Good boy," she murmured as the milk went down.

Dr. Adam went over to Rosie to examine her. "She's looking a bit better," he said. He slipped his hand under the blanket that Fiona had laid over Rosie's prone body. "And she's warming up a bit."

Just then, his cell phone rang. Whisking it out of

his pocket, Mandy's dad walked to the door. "Adam Hope speaking," he said briefly.

Mandy watched him listening and nodding. "Okay, I'm on my way," he said at last. Turning the phone off, he swung around. "There's a sheep having trouble lambing at Fordbeck Farm. I've got to go over there. I'll come back here when I'm done."

Nick nodded. "We should be okay now."

Dr. Adam fixed up his bag. "If Rosie shows signs of being interested in her surroundings and sitting up, bring the foal around to her head so that she can bond with it. And if she wants to get up and nurse, let her — but she'll probably be down for a bit longer. Any trouble, just call me on my cell phone." He looked at Mandy. "Are you going to come with me or do you want to stay on here until I get back?"

"Stay here," Mandy said quickly, stroking the foal, who had almost finished his bottle. "Is that okay, Nick?"

"Fine," Nick replied. "We could use the help." He looked at Fiona. "You're going to have to leave for your dentist's appointment soon, aren't you?" His wife nodded. "And I need to feed the other horses."

"Well, Mandy can stay and keep an eye on these two for you then," Adam said. "Okay, dear?" he asked Mandy.

"Of course!" she replied. She couldn't think of anything she'd rather do!

Her dad kissed the top of her head. "See you later then." And with that he strode out of the stable.

"Would you mind sticking some more dry straw down in here, Mandy?" Nick said, following him. "There's some in the next-door stable."

"Sure," Mandy said.

It was quiet when they had all gone. Having finished the bottle, Amigo rested his head against Mandy's lap, his eyes half closed. Mandy stroked his ears.

After a while, she eased his head onto the straw and stood up, stretching her cramped legs. For a moment, Amigo opened his eyes and looked at her, but then he relaxed again, his eyelashes fluttering.

Mandy checked Rosie. The mare was still lying on her side, but her breathing was more regular and the pain in her eyes had eased.

Fetching clean straw, a pitchfork, and a mucking-out box from the stable next door, Mandy began to work around the horses, replacing the dirty bedding with fresh straw.

As she shook out the last wedge of straw, she heard a rustling behind her. Amigo had woken up. She turned and saw that his front legs were stretched out and he was trying to stand.

Mandy went over. "Come on, then," she encouraged him.

Amigo heaved with his back legs. On the third attempt he managed to stand up. He swayed from side to side, looking almost comical, his long, slender legs stretched out, his eyes wide.

Suddenly his knees trembled and with a soft thud he collapsed back onto the thick straw. But it didn't scare him. Shaking his head, he put out his front hooves again. Fixing his eyes on Mandy, he levered his body up. He staggered. He swayed. But this time he managed to stay upright.

"Good boy!" Mandy praised.

Amigo lifted one hoof and then the other and then started walking toward her.

"Hello," Mandy said in delight. With a tiny snort, he buried his head in her coat. Mandy stroked his fluffy forelock and stepped back. Amigo followed her. She giggled and stepped back another three steps until her back met the stable wall. Amigo nuzzled her coat. "You *are* friendly!" Mandy said.

Catching sight of the last wedge of straw that she had been ready to shake up when Amigo had distracted her, she began to spread it around the bed. Wherever she went, Amigo followed, his steps still slightly unsteady, his tiny ears pricked.

"You silly foal," Mandy said, rubbing his forehead. "What are you doing?"

Just then there was a rustle in the straw behind her. She looked around. Rosie had lifted her head and neck. "Oh, good girl!" Mandy breathed.

With a heave of her legs, Rosie rolled onto her chest and sat up and looked at the foal.

Mandy moved quickly to the side of the stable. She didn't want to interfere with Rosie and Amigo's first meeting.

Rosie stretched out her muzzle. Her nostrils quivered and she whickered softly.

Mandy held her breath, but to her surprise, Amigo ignored Rosie and came over to her instead. "What are you doing?" Mandy asked. "Go and see your mom."

Amigo nuzzled her coat.

Mandy frowned. This was strange. Why wasn't he going to Rosie? She turned the foal's head so that he looked at the mare. Rosie whickered again. Amigo turned away from her and butted Mandy in the stomach.

Mandy tried to push Amigo toward Rosie. "Go on!" she urged, but Amigo didn't move. Mandy began to feel worried. This was really odd.

Just then, Nick looked over the stable door. "How are they?" His blue eyes lit up. "Hey, look at Rosie!"

Mandy was very relieved to see him. "She just sat

up a few minutes ago," she said, going to the door. "But Amigo won't go to her."

As she spoke, the foal hurried after her.

"What do you mean?" Nick asked.

"He just keeps following me!" Mandy said as Amigo began nuzzling and pushing at her again.

Nick came into the stable. "Come on, Amigo," he said, crouching by Rosie and holding out his hand. But Amigo ignored him, his head still burrowed inside Mandy's coat.

"He's been doing this constantly," Mandy said to Nick. "Ever since I dried and fed him."

Nick stared at her. "Of course!" he exclaimed. "That's it. He's imprinted on you!"

"Imprinted?" Mandy echoed, not quite sure what he meant.

"He thinks that you're his mother!" Nick said. He quickly explained. "Newborn foals aren't born with an automatic bond to their mother. It's only when they suckle that they start to recognize their mother's shape and movement. You fed Amigo, and now he's convinced that you're his mom."

Mandy stared. So that's why Amigo wasn't going to Rosie! She glanced at the mare. *Poor Rosie!* She was whickering again to her little foal, her dark eyes confused and distressed.

"What can we do?" Mandy asked.

"If we can get him to suckle then they should begin to bond," Nick said. "But first we need to get Rosie up on her feet." He pulled off the blanket and took hold of the mare's headcollar. "Come on, girl," he said. "Let's see if you can do it. Up you get."

At first, Mandy thought that Rosie wasn't going to be able to manage the effort. But the trusting mare seemed to know that her master was trying to help her. She slowly thrust out her front legs and then with a tired groan heaved her hindquarters up. "Try and bring Amigo over," Nick told Mandy.

Mandy tried to lead Amigo toward the mare's belly. "Come on, Amigo, there's milk here for you to drink." But Amigo refused to move.

"Try putting your arms around his hindquarters and shoulders and moving him closer," Nick said, after a few minutes.

Mandy did as she was told. Feeling the pressure on his hindquarters Amigo scrabbled backward, almost sitting down in her arms. "Steady, steady," Mandy gasped, letting go.

"Here, you hold Rosie," Nick said, looking worried. "I'll try to guide him around."

"What's going on?" a voice said.

Mandy swung around. "Dad!" she exclaimed. "You're back!"

"The sheep had lambed by the time I got there." Dr. Adam looked over the stable door, his eyes concerned. "But what's happening here?"

"The foal's imprinted on Mandy and won't bond with Rosie," Nick explained.

"He just keeps following me," Mandy said, feeling increasingly guilty and upset.

Dr. Adam came into the stable. "I should have thought about that," he said, putting his bag down and looking worried. "It does happen occasionally and you *were* with him for a long time while Rosie was down." He looked at Mandy's face. "Don't blame yourself, dear. It's not your fault. It's just one of those things. Now we have to figure out what to do about it." He turned to Nick. "You've been trying to get him to drink?"

Nick nodded. "But he won't."

"He doesn't seem to want to go anywhere near Rosie," Mandy said. Warm from her efforts with the foal, she pulled her coat off and threw it over the stable door. "What can we do, Dad?" she asked anxiously.

Rosie stamped her foot and shook her head up and down. She was beginning to get agitated.

"Come over here, Mandy," her dad said quickly. "If you stand near Rosie then Amigo may follow."

Mandy did as she was told. "Come on, Amigo!" she called, expecting the foal to follow. To her surprise, he didn't. He just stood where he was, looking uncertain. He looked at Mandy and then he looked at her coat on the door. Taking a step forward, he nudged the coat with his muzzle. It slipped from the door and fell in a heap on the floor. Amigo began to nose it hopefully.

Mandy looked at her dad in astonishment. "What's he doing?"

"It's the coat!" Nick said suddenly. "He's imprinted on your coat, Mandy, not on you! When you dried him he put his head in the dark underneath it and then you fed him. He must associate it with being fed."

"I think you're right," Dr. Adam said, looking at the little foal nuzzling the coat. "The question is — what do we do now?"

Mandy suddenly had an idea. She picked up the coat. "Will Rosie mind if I put it over her?" she asked Nick.

Nick shook his head, his forehead creasing. "But why — ?" he began.

Mandy didn't answer. She wasn't sure if her idea was going to work but it was worth a try. She approached Rosie carefully and, after patting the mare to reassure her, she placed her coat gently over the mare's loins so that the flaps hung down behind her belly.

"Amigo!" she called softly.

The little foal pricked his ears and stepped forward. Mandy held the flap of the coat out. Amigo stopped and looked at it. She held her breath. Would her idea work?

Suddenly Amigo buried his head underneath the flap and straight underneath his mother's tummy. There was a pause and then his fluffy tail swished. Just like Mandy had hoped, he had smelled Rosie's milk!

His legs suddenly stiffened, and with quick, jerky movements of his head and neck, he began to nurse greedily.

At last! Mandy's legs felt shaky with relief. Moving as quietly as she could, she crept to the side of the stall.

"Good idea," her father said softly. "Now that he's drinking, they should bond just fine."

Nick nodded. "Brilliant!" He edged forward and carefully slipped Mandy's coat off Rosie's dapple-gray back.

Amigo was drinking so fast that he didn't even notice. Now that he had found his mother's milk, it looked as if he wasn't ever going to leave her side.

Mandy sighed with relief and looked at her dad.

"Well done," he said, his eyes shining proudly.

Mandy stood beside him and Nick, watching Amigo nurse. Seeing the mare's dark eyes brimming with love and delight as she gently nuzzled her foal was all the thanks she needed.

🐈 TARANTULA TROUBLE 🐈

"How much longer do we have to wait?" Imogen Parker-Smythe's voice rang out in the waiting room of the Animal Ark Veterinary Clinic. "We've been here for ages."

Mandy was helping Jean Knox in reception. It was Saturday morning and there was a long line of patients waiting to see her mom and dad.

"I thought Imogen and her mom only came in about five minutes ago," Mandy said to Jean as she reached for a bottle of medicated shampoo. One of the patients was a guinea pig with a skin condition.

Jean nodded. "You're right. Imogen's very assertive for a seven-year-old, isn't she?"

"That's one word for it," Mandy replied, glancing at the little girl. *For your information, Imogen used to be* really *spoiled. She's a lot nicer nowadays,* Mandy thought. She wondered why she seemed so impatient today.

Imogen was balancing a pet carrier on her knee. Peering out of the front was a bad-tempered-looking Persian cat.

"So you'd better make an appointment for a week from today for a checkup. But that paw's doing fine." Dr. Emily appeared at the door of the treatment room followed by Ken Hudson and Tess, his sheepdog.

"Now, Mrs. Platt, if you'd like to bring Antonia in," Mandy's mom called to the next patient. She glanced around the packed waiting room and gave her daughter a grateful smile. "Good thing you're here to lend a hand, dear!"

Mandy grinned. "One down, fifty to go!" she joked as Mrs. Platt led her poodle away.

"Mom-my, my arms are aching!" Imogen whined. Her face started to crumple as she tugged at her mother's coat with chubby fingers. "And we're going to be late for the horse show."

"Give the carrier to me then, Immi darling," Mrs. Parker-Smythe soothed. "I'll hold Bella until it's our turn. WHICH WON'T BE LONG NOW." She raised her voice so that there was no mistaking her meaning.

Mandy tried to ignore the pointed remark. There were at least six people to be seen before the Parker-Smythes.

Just then, Dr. Adam stuck his head out of the consulting room. "Mandy, I need an extra pair of hands in here. I don't suppose you're free?"

Mandy leaped into action. A large rabbit was fussing about having her temperature taken. Mandy held her gently on the table and calmed her down while her dad continued the examination.

Five minutes later she was back in reception, dealing with owners waiting patiently with their pets. Most of them were Animal Ark regulars, but there was one man whom Mandy didn't recognize sitting quietly in a corner. He had a small cardboard box on his lap.

Suddenly a high-pitched noise rang out. Mandy jumped before she realized it was a cell phone.

"Hello?" The man with the cardboard box fumbled in his coat pocket and spoke into his cell phone. "Can't hear you! Must be a bad reception in here . . ." He cut off the call. A moment later the phone rang again.

A puppy whined nervously and there was a loud hiss from the pet carrier on Mrs. Parker-Smythe's lap. The man jabbed his phone impatiently and it gave another high-pitched warble.

"Settle down, Bobby," the puppy's owner said as she tried to calm the frightened dog.

But it struggled free and sprang to the floor. Quick as a flash, Mandy stooped to catch the puppy as it bolted toward her. Its claws slid and scratched on the smooth floor as it fought for a foothold. Suddenly it skidded sideways and shot beneath Mrs. Parker-Smythe's chair.

"Uh-oh!" Mandy murmured.

There was a rumbling growl from the pet carrier, followed by a loud hiss. "Bella doesn't like this noise," Imogen said worriedly.

"Would you *please* hurry up and catch that dog?" Mrs. Parker-Smythe said. "All this commotion is unsettling poor Bella. She's a very sensitive cat."

What about poor Bobby? He must be terrified, Mandy thought. She was on her knees, peering under the chairs. The whimpering puppy was crouching in the darkest corner, trying to make himself as small as possible.

"Come here, Bobby. Don't be frightened," Mandy encouraged. At last she felt her hand close around the puppy's fat tummy. She drew him out gently from his hiding place.

Bobby's owner gave Mandy a relieved smile as she handed him back. "Thanks. That cell phone going off really frightened him."

As Mandy went over to the reception desk, she noticed the man in the corner talking urgently into his cell phone. By now Dr. Emily had come out to call her next patient into the treatment room.

"When's it going to be our turn?" Imogen seemed to be having difficulty controlling her impatience. Mandy felt sorry for her. She was obviously very excited about going to the horse show.

"Now don't worry, Immikins," Mrs. Parker-Smythe said reassuringly. "I'll make sure we get there in time."

She strode toward the desk, a determined look on her face. Ignoring the line of people waiting to be served, she spoke directly to Jean. "I'm sure no one would mind if Imogen and I went in to see the vet next. It is an emergency." She patted her blond hair with a manicured hand.

"An emergency? Okay. I didn't realize." Jean seemed flustered. She reached for the chain that held her glasses and began checking the appointments.

Just then, the man with the cell phone came over to ask where the bathroom was. Mandy pointed it out to him and he disappeared, taking the small cardboard box with him.

"Ah, here's the entry," Jean was saying to Mrs. Parker-Smythe. "Apparently you've only brought Bella in for a routine examination."

"That's right. She seemed a bit out of sorts. We're minding her for a friend, you see, and I'd hate for her to get sick. Bella's a pedigree. I don't expect anything's wrong. But one has to be certain."

"Then — there isn't really an emergency, is there?" said Jean, looking puzzled.

"Yes," Mrs. Parker-Smythe insisted. "Yes, there is. The horse trial will be starting in an hour or so. We really need to see a vet right away."

Mandy saw Jean blink with surprise.

"I'm sorry, but in that case you'll have to wait your turn," the receptionist said politely. "Dr. Adam and Dr. Emily have their hands full. Of course, you could always come back another day."

Good for you, Jean, Mandy thought silently. *Don't let Mrs. stuck-up Parker-Smythe bully you!*

Mrs. Parker-Smythe drew herself up and Mandy held her breath, waiting for the cutting reply.

Suddenly the bathroom door flew open and an agitated figure emerged, a cell phone held to his ear. "I'LL BE THERE IN A MINUTE!" the man shouted, his face red and angry-looking. "All right. You win! I'll leave now . . ." He rushed past Mandy, calling over his shoulder that he'd be back shortly.

"I'm going to speak to the vet about your attitude," Mrs. Parker-Smythe said curtly to Jean. She swept toward the bathroom, her smart shoes clacking on the floor.

"Phew!" Mandy whispered to Jean. "How are the appointments going?"

"We're getting through them now," Jean said. "Mrs.

Parker-Smythe probably won't have long to wait now, but I didn't feel like telling her that!"

Mandy chuckled. "I don't blame you! Look out, she's coming back over here!"

Mrs. Parker-Smythe had emerged from the bathroom and dumped a small cardboard box in front of Jean.

"I found this by the sink. That man who rushed out must have left it behind."

"Thank you," Jean said. "I expect he'll come back for it."

Mandy frowned in puzzlement, wondering what had been in the empty box. "Who was that man, Jean? And what did he bring in?"

Jean smiled secretively and answered in a low voice. "His name's Slater. And he brought in his pet tarantula, but I wouldn't advertise the fact, if I were you."

"Oh, right!" Mandy opened her eyes in astonishment. *A tarantula — how fascinating!* Then she bit her lip. *But if the box is empty — where is it?*

Just then, Dr. Adam came out of the consulting room. He looked up and smiled. "Mrs. Parker-Smythe? Would you come in?"

"About time, too! Come along, darling." Mrs. Parker-Smythe lifted the pet carrier and stalked toward the consulting room, her daughter in tow.

Mandy caught her breath. "Excuse me," she began, trying to catch the snobbish woman's attention. "You've got —"

"I'm sorry, Mandy, dear. But I don't have time to stand around talking now." Mrs. Parker-Smythe followed Dr. Adam into the room and closed the door in Mandy's face.

"Oh, my goodness! Did you see — ?" Jean began, pointing at the closed door.

"Yes!" Mandy replied. "I did!"

This is no time to be polite, she thought, rushing forward. She pulled open the door and went straight into the room, just in time to hear her dad announce that Bella had fleas.

Mandy's eyes locked onto the dark hairy shape that was crawling upward from Mrs. Parker-Smythe's shoulder. She took a gentle hold and pulled the tarantula carefully away from her neat blond hair.

"And I'm afraid *you* have spiders, Mrs. Parker-Smythe!" she said, her eyes sparkling. She just had time to step out of the way as Imogen screamed and her mother crumpled in a faint on the floor.

Mandy Tells You All About Wolves

Did you know that . . .

- all domestic breeds of dog are directly descended from wolves.

- wolves are an endangered species in the wild.

- wolves are very sociable and loyal to one another. They live in packs of between seven and 10 animals, though packs of 20 are not unknown.

- wolves are primarily carnivores and mainly eat hoofed animals, such as deer or bison. Because they hunt animals larger than themselves, they generally hunt in packs.

- wolves have very strong jaws, with a crushing pressure twice as strong as that of a German shepherd dog.

- wolves have a very developed sense of smell and can detect prey from almost two miles away!

- a wolf's howl carries several miles. Wolves howl to locate their packs when separated and to excite and bond the pack before hunting.

- a wolf's hearing is very powerful. Out in the open, they can hear sounds up to 10 miles away.

- wolves have a double layer of fur to keep them warm in the snow. The underfur grows thicker in the autumn and insulates them, while the outer fur prevents snow and water from getting through, keeping them dry.

- most wolves live to be around eight years old, though they can live up to 13 years in the wild and 16 in captivity. The record lifespan for a wolf is 20 years.

 OTTER ANTICS

"Are you awake, Mandy?" Claire Esson was already up and dressed when she peered around the bedroom door.

For a moment, Mandy didn't know where she was. It had been late when the Hopes arrived at Claire's family's farm the previous night, and they had gone straight to bed. Now she was eager to get up and explore.

She threw back the covers. "What time is it?"

"Nearly time for breakfast," Claire replied with a grin, coming into the bedroom. "Dad's been up for a while tending to the animals."

Mandy smiled. "Vets and their helpers *usually* get up as early as farmers! Except when they're on vacation!"

Claire's dad, Greg Esson, was Emily Hope's cousin.

His sheep farm was near Campbeltown, not too far
from Oban on the west coast of Scotland.

"I'm so glad that you and your parents are
spending Christmas with us." Claire grinned. "We're
going to have a great time." She was a year younger
than Mandy and great at Highland dancing. Mandy
had seen her take part in the Highland games one
summer vacation.

Claire went across to open the curtains, her long
fair braid swinging back and forth. Cold winter light
poured into the room. "Look, it's just started to snow
again."

Mandy padded across to stand beside Claire. An
untouched blanket of snow covered the farm buildings
below them. Beyond the farm, the mountains and the
flat gray sea seemed to blend into the sky. "Oh." Mandy
caught her breath. "It's beautiful."

"Sometimes you can see deer on the hillsides from
here," said Claire. "And I think there's a colony of
otters nearby."

"Really? Do you think we could go and watch
them?"

Claire nodded. "I'll ask Dad where to look. He was
the one who told me about them."

"Great." The snow was falling thick and fast now.
Mandy had a sudden thought. "Won't the sheep need
to be brought in?"

Claire shook her head. "It has to be a lot worse than this before we bring them into the barn," she said. "They have stone-built huts up on the hills for shelter — and Dad will be checking on them later. We can go with him if you like."

"I'd love to," Mandy answered at once. "I like sheep. I've helped Dad out with lambing a few times."

Claire grinned, her blue eyes dancing. "Of course you have! I can see that your dad's right about you!"

Mandy frowned. "What do you mean?"

"He says you're more fond of animals than people!"

"That's true with certain people." Mandy flashed Claire a grin. "But there *are* some exceptions!"

Claire moved away from the window. "I said I'd help Mom with breakfast. See you downstairs in a minute."

"Okay." As soon as Claire had left, Mandy used the sink in the corner of the room. She pulled on jeans and a T-shirt, with a thick sweater on top, then stuffed her feet into stout boots.

It was warm and cozy in the big farm kitchen. There was a Christmas wreath on the door, and swathes of ivy leaves and shiny red ribbons festooned the walls.

Claire was making toast while her mom, Ella Esson, stirred a steaming pan of porridge. "Did you sleep well, Mandy?"

"Yes, thanks," Mandy replied.

"Morning, dear." Dr. Emily and Dr. Adam were sitting at the wooden table. Dr. Adam looked up from reading his newspaper and gave Mandy a lopsided smile. "Sleep? I would have thought you'd have been counting sheep!"

"Ha-ha." Mandy was used to her dad's terrible jokes. "I'm surprised you didn't say counting woolly jumpers!"

Everyone laughed. Just then the back door opened. Mr. Esson paused in the doorway to take off his boots and outdoor coat.

"Food's ready, Greg. Sit yourself down." Ella Esson smiled a greeting. She ladled creamy porridge into bowls and passed them around. There was toast, too, and rich yellow butter and honey to spread on it.

Greg sprinkled salt on his porridge and began eating. "Have you two made any plans for this morning?" he asked Mandy and Claire.

Dr. Emily looked up at her cousin. "I'll give you one guess."

"A tour of the farm to get to know all the animals?" Greg's blue eyes crinkled as he smiled.

Mandy and Claire exchanged glances. "What else?"

As soon as breakfast was finished and cleared away, Mandy and Claire put on warm coats and hats. "Does anyone want to come with us?" Claire asked.

Dr Emily shook her head. "No, thanks. I'm looking forward to chatting with your mom and dad. We've got some catching up to do."

"What about you, Dad?" Mandy asked.

Dr. Adam stroked his dark beard. "I think I can manage to resist meeting any animals for a few hours! I *am* on vacation from being a vet!"

"Okay." Mandy grinned at him. "But you don't know what you're missing!"

It had stopped snowing. The air felt clean and still. Mandy was following Claire. They trudged toward the barns through snow that was several inches high. Claire showed her everything — the chickens, the farm cats, two sheep who were being kept in the barn because they had foot trouble, and Greg's sheepdogs, Jake and McCloud.

"Hello, you two." Mandy bent down to pat the dogs, who were curled up in snug hay nests. They crawled out, tails wagging, for some attention. She stroked their black-and-white heads and laughed when they licked her face with their warm tongues.

"What do you want to do now?" Claire asked when they had finished exploring the farm buildings.

Mandy was warm, bundled inside her coat and hat. And the snow on the hills looked so inviting. "Let's go for a walk!"

When they reached the top of a steep slope, Mandy paused to look around. She could see the curve of the river and the road that led to Campbeltown.

"Who lives there?" Mandy pointed to a small stone house nestling in the fold of two hills.

"That place has been empty for ages. Dad says some people find it too isolated around here."

"Oh, look!" Mandy suddenly noticed a woman and a dog come out of the house.

"Looks like we've got a new neighbor," Claire said delightedly. "She must have just moved in. Let's go over and say hello."

"Okay," Mandy agreed.

As the woman came toward them, Mandy frowned, puzzled. She couldn't decide what breed the dog was. It was a long, low shape against the snow. *Maybe it's a dachshund,* she reasoned. But long sausage-shaped dogs didn't move in that graceful, fluid way.

Suddenly, her eyes opened wide. *Surely not. It couldn't be . . .*

"I think she's got an otter on that leash!" she gasped.

Claire's jaw dropped in disbelief. "Are you sure?"

But Mandy was already hurrying forward, the snow dragging at her boots. As the woman drew near, Mandy saw that her guess was right. The otter wore a leather harness that fitted snugly around its middle and over its front legs. Its thick brown pelt was fluffed up against the cold.

"Hi!" Claire's new neighbor had a bright, friendly smile. Her wispy brown hair was escaping from a fake fur hat. She wore a long red velvet coat and black boots. "Have you come from the farm?"

"Yes. My mom and dad own it. I'm Claire Esson," Claire introduced herself.

"And I'm Mandy Hope. I'm here with my parents. We're staying with Claire's family for Christmas."

"Pleased to meet you both. I'm Charlotte Figg. And this is Oswald. He comes everywhere with me."

Oswald gave a snuffle and reared up. He held his body very straight and rested on his hindquarters as he looked curiously at Mandy and Claire.

"I bet no one ever ignores *him!*" Mandy said, admiring the way Oswald used his muscular tail for balance.

"You're right! He's a real show-off," Charlotte replied. She gave a chuckle. "See what I mean?"

By now, Oswald had dropped onto all fours. He scrabbled a pile of snow into a ball with his webbed front paws. Dipping his nose, he pushed the snowball around, dribbling it like an expert soccer player.

"Wow!" Claire said delightedly. "Isn't he great, Mandy?"

"He's fantastic," Mandy answered, but she couldn't help thinking that Oswald would probably prefer to be swimming in a fast-flowing river, chasing slippery fish instead of snowballs.

Oswald gave the snowball another shove. It rolled toward Charlotte's feet. She tried to move out of the way, but Oswald had other ideas. Mandy could have sworn he gave a whiskery grin as he dashed in circles around his owner's legs.

"Oh, dear! Now neither of us can move!" Charlotte looked down as the leash tightened around her boots. Oswald squeaked in complaint.

"I'll untangle it." Mandy bent down to help.

Her nimble fingers soon finished the job. Oswald studied her with round black eyes. He twitched his small, wide-set ears and made a soft whistling sound.

"He's saying, 'Thanks, Mandy,'" Claire said.

"You could be right." Charlotte patted Oswald's head. She was obviously proud of her unusual pet. "He's very intelligent and always into everything. One of his favorite things is going for car rides."

Mandy felt a stab of concern. "But does he have access to fresh water?" She hoped she didn't sound rude, but she just had to speak up.

"Mandy's mom and dad are vets," Claire explained.

"Ah." Charlotte Figg's face sparked with interest. "So you're a bit of an animal expert? Why don't the two of you come back to my house for a cup of tea? Maybe you'd like to see where Oswald lives."

"Thanks, we'd love to," Claire answered at once.

"Yes, thanks." Mandy jumped at the chance to check out Oswald's living arrangements.

As they walked along the crest of the hill, Oswald kept pace, his peculiar loping run making long tracks in the snow.

Charlotte chatted as they walked. "I'm a writer," she told them. "I need peace and quiet for my work. A house out here is just perfect for Oswald and me."

A few minutes later they reached the valley bottom. Charlotte unfastened the front gate. "Here we are."

Mandy saw that the stone house was surrounded by a large yard. The shapes of bushes, trees, and flower beds were visible beneath the snow.

"What's that?" Claire pointed to a multilevel arrangement of logs, planks, and sections of concrete pipe.

"Oswald's activity center?" Mandy guessed. She was impressed. There was also a sloping lawn that led down to a frozen stream.

Oswald strained against his harness, making excited little chirrups.

Charlotte unclipped his harness. "Off you go then, you rascal!"

Oswald didn't need telling twice. He bounded across the lawn and headed straight for the stream.

"Won't he hurt himself on the ice if he dives in?" Claire whispered to Mandy as Oswald paused on the frozen bank.

The otter's whiskers twitched. He stretched out his front paws. Balancing his weight perfectly, he thumped up and down on the ice. Suddenly the ice broke with a cracking sound. Oswald scooped up chunks of ice and crunched them up in his strong jaws.

Mandy chuckled in amazement. This otter was a real character!

"Let's go inside and get warm." Charlotte unlocked the front door and led the way into the kitchen.

"What about Oswald?" Mandy asked.

"Oh, he'll come inside when he wants to. He has his own way into the house." She showed them the flap in the bottom of the door.

"Doesn't he ever try and get out of the yard?" Mandy asked.

Charlotte shook her head. "He has no reason to," she said firmly. "I can give him everything he needs."

Mandy thought it best to say nothing. Charlotte was obviously devoted to Oswald. But, in the back of her mind, she still felt uneasy. It just didn't feel right to keep a wild animal as a pet.

Charlotte brought them tea and lemon cake in her

tiny living room. Framed book covers were displayed on the walls and there was a large bookcase crammed full of books of different sizes.

Mandy was just finishing her cup of tea when she heard the door flap bang. A few seconds later, Oswald poked a whiskery snout around the door. He bounded into the living room and leaped onto the sofa. Mandy just managed to put down her cup of tea before it went flying. Oswald dug his nose under the cushions and tipped them all onto the floor.

"No, Oswald," Charlotte said firmly. Oswald grinned, showing powerful teeth. Then he jumped onto the floor and began to chew the corner of a rug.

Charlotte distracted him by giving him a piece of dried fish. As soon as the otter had gobbled it up, he made a dash for the stairs. They could hear him thumping around in the bedrooms.

Charlotte rolled her eyes. "Excuse me. I'd better go and check on him. He's got a thing about climbing onto my dressing table, then jumping onto the dresser."

Mandy and Claire laughed. It looked as if it was a full-time job keeping a mischievous otter amused!

Mandy could have stayed all day, just watching Oswald play. But Claire reminded her that her mom would be getting lunch ready at the farm. Charlotte came out to wave good-bye to them at the gate. She had Oswald in tow, winding around her legs like a playful kitten.

"Oh!" Charlotte narrowly avoided being tripped up. "Bye, you two. It was lovely to meet you. You must come and see us again."

"We will!" Mandy and Claire promised.

"Charlotte's nice, isn't she?" Claire said as they walked along.

Mandy nodded. "And Oswald's really great. I just think he'd be better off living in the wild."

Back at the farm, she found that her parents had just returned from a shopping trip in Campbeltown. The Hopes were in their bedroom, wrapping Christmas presents for the Essons. There was an antique gelatin mold for Ella and a new jacket for Claire.

"What do you think of this?" Dr. Emily held up a fluffy terrycloth bathrobe. "It's for Greg."

"He'll love it," Mandy said distractedly. She sat on the bed and began telling them about meeting Charlotte Figg and Oswald. ". . . Charlotte has the perfect yard for an otter to live in. It has a stream and everything . . ." she finished.

"Why do I have the feeling there's a but?" her mom asked.

Mandy sighed. "I know Oswald seems happy living with Charlotte. But I still think it's cruel to keep him as a pet when there's all this countryside for him to live in."

Dr. Adam nodded. "I must say, I agree with you, dear. And you say he was chewing carpet and tipping over cushions? Sounds to me like he could be getting a bit bored. Otters are very social animals in the wild. Ideally they'd spend most of their time fishing or interacting with other otters."

"Oh." Mandy felt worried for Oswald and Charlotte. "Animals can get destructive when they're bored, can't they?"

"Yes, but it sounds as if Charlotte is trying to give him all the stimulation he needs. Of course, if Oswald's high spirits became a real problem, she'd have to do something about it."

"Yes." Mandy hated to think of the special bond between Oswald and his owner becoming strained.

"But there's no law against Charlotte keeping Oswald as a pet, dear," Dr. Emily said, practical and levelheaded as usual.

Mandy chewed at her lip. *Maybe not, but that doesn't mean it's right.*

"I know that look, Mandy Hope," her mom said. "What are you thinking?"

Mandy jumped up from the bed. She had made up her mind. "I'm going to try and persuade Charlotte that it's kinder to let Oswald go."

"Uh-oh. Mandy has spoken!" Dr. Adam gave a pretend wince. "That could be very tricky."

"I know." Mandy gave her dad a determined grin. "But I'll think of something."

By now it was lunchtime. Ella served up a chunky farmhouse stew and homemade bread. Everyone ate heartily. After lunch was cleared away, Mandy and Claire decided to go with Greg to check on the sheep.

They helped load bales of hay into the back of the Land Rover, then set out along a narrow, snow-carpeted path. Greg stopped the Land Rover in the top field, and Mandy and Claire piled out.

"Oh, look." Mandy saw that the sheep had pawed at the shallow snow to uncover the tough mountain grass. "Aren't they clever?"

Greg smiled agreement. "Sheep are underrated, if you ask me."

Mandy helped Greg break the ice in the water troughs. Then she and Claire piled the hay in the shelters.

"Just in case the weather gets worse," Greg explained. "This will keep them warm and provide food if the ground gets too frozen for grazing."

As the Land Rover bumped its way back toward the farmhouse, Mandy began thinking about Charlotte and Oswald again. There had to be a way to get

Charlotte to see that the otter would be happier living in the wild.

Suddenly, she sat bolt upright. "The colony of wild otters!" The words burst out before she could stop them.

"Come again?" Greg threw Mandy a puzzled glance.

Claire shrugged. "Don't ask me, Dad!"

Mandy gave them an embarrassed grin. "Sorry! I got carried away. But I think I know what to do about Oswald. Remember this morning, Claire, when you said there was a colony of wild otters around here?"

Claire nodded. "Yes, but I'm not sure where they are. We'd have to try and find them."

"Oh, that's okay." Mandy rushed on. Finding the otter colony seemed like a minor problem. "My dad was saying earlier that bored pets need companions. I think Oswald needs some friends. Otter friends."

"Oh, I get it!" Claire opened her blue eyes wide. "We can introduce Oswald to the wild otters."

"Right!" Mandy rushed on, eager to finish explaining her idea. "And when Charlotte sees how happy Oswald is, she'll want to let him go and live with them."

Claire looked doubtful. "Do you think so? She's very fond of him."

Greg glanced across at Mandy. "Claire's got a point. It's a good plan, but it sounds a bit unlikely to me. I wouldn't get your hopes up about her letting her pet go."

"I won't." Mandy knew that Greg was right, but this was the best idea she could come up with. "When can we go and look for the otters?"

"How about now?" Claire looked at her dad.

Greg rubbed his chin. "Not a good idea. It'll be dark in a couple of hours. Why not go tomorrow morning? When I saw them, they were downriver from the rapids. There's a deep pool there with plenty of fish in it."

"And where there are fish, there might be otters!" Mandy was bursting to put her plan into action.

Right after breakfast the following day, Mandy and Claire set out for the river. It was crisp and frosty. A weak sun glinted on the patches of heather showing through the snow. Mandy heard the rushing water before she saw it. Then she and Claire crested the brow of a hill — and there were the rapids.

"Wow." Mandy looked in awe at the torrents of foaming water, pouring down a series of natural rocky steps.

"Come on. It's this way." Claire strode along the wide bank.

As they followed the course of the river, the water

became less turbulent. Soon it widened into a quiet, dark pool.

"Look!" Mandy spotted a movement in the water. "Strings of bubbles. I think otters are fishing over there!" She ducked down and kept very still.

"Oh, yes. I see them!" Claire crouched down beside Mandy.

Ripples snaked across the water. A distinctive blunt head broke the surface a couple of yards away and another head appeared. And then a little farther on there was another one.

Mandy could hardly believe her eyes. This was incredibly good luck.

"How many can you see?" Claire whispered.

"Three. No — four. Look, there's one on the bank."

One of the otters had climbed out of the river. It was crunching up a fish that it held in its front paws. The otter on the bank dived into the water. Mandy followed its bubble trail.

"I think it's chasing the others."

Sure enough, the three otters were playing a game. They rolled over and over — one minute surfacing, the next diving. Mandy wished that Oswald could be here. She was sure he would love to join in. "We must get Charlotte to come here with Oswald."

"But she might not want to come," Claire said.

Mandy brushed aside such details. "We'll worry about that when we get there. Come on."

"Okay." Claire gave in. "The river curves back on itself here. I'll show you a shortcut across the fields. It's not far."

Charlotte answered their knock almost at once. She had a towel in her hand. "Hello again. Come on in. I was just upstairs in the bathroom."

As they stepped into the hall, Oswald came running down the stairs. His pelt was plastered to his body and drops of water speckled his whiskers. Wet paw prints splotched the stair carpet. Charlotte bent down and began rubbing Oswald dry with the towel.

Mandy chuckled. "I thought you meant it was you who'd been having a bath!"

"It was meant to be me. But Oswald had other ideas!"

They all laughed.

Mandy saw an opportunity. "Oswald seems to be in a swimming mood. We could take him down to the river."

Oswald pricked up his ears at the sound of his name. He gave a low fluting whistle. "He's saying, 'What a good idea!'" said Charlotte, smiling at Mandy and Claire. "Just a minute. I'll get my coat."

Claire looked at Mandy, openmouthed. "That was sneaky!"

Mandy gave her a sheepish grin. "I know."

As Claire led the way across the fields, Mandy wished that the wild otters would still be there. Charlotte let Oswald out of his harness. He bounded along, inquisitive as usual, snuffling at heaps of snow and poking about beneath fallen logs.

As soon as they rounded the bend in the river, Mandy saw the otters. All four of them were gamboling about on the far bank. Oswald stopped in his tracks. He lifted his nose and his whiskers twitched.

"Oh, dear!" Charlotte said, sounding worried. "Wild otters."

"Aren't they wonderful? We thought they might be here," Mandy said.

Charlotte took the harness out of her pocket and moved toward him. "I better put him on his leash . . ." she began.

Mandy held her breath. It was up to Oswald now.

Oswald looked at Charlotte. He looked at the leash. Then he gave a joyful whistle, flicked up his tail, and bounded toward the river. Charlotte watched in concern as her pet dove in and swam powerfully across to the other side.

Charlotte put her hands up to her cheeks. "Oh, my gosh, what if the wild otters attack him?"

Mandy's heart skipped a beat. She hadn't thought of that.

By now, Oswald was shaking himself dry on the opposite bank. He gave a warbling cry and scampered toward the other otters. For a couple of seconds the wild otters just stared at him. Then one of them ran over to meet him. It had a distinctive dark patch near its tail.

"I think that's a female," Mandy said.

"How do you know?" Charlotte and Claire asked.

"Females are usually smaller," she replied. "It looks like she's friendly. Let's call her Patch."

"Patch. It suits her," Claire said.

Patch sniffed Oswald and gave little grunts of curiosity. Then she suddenly darted away toward the river. Oswald gave chase and the rest of the wild otters trooped after him. With hardly a splash, they all slid into the water.

Mandy let out a long sigh of relief. She could see him leaping and darting in a froth of bubbles, playing boisterously with others of his kind. "Looks like Patch has persuaded the others to accept Oswald."

A few moments later, Oswald surfaced, clambered onto the bank, and began to eat a fish. Patch climbed out after him. She approached Oswald, her head weaving from side to side. Oswald snickered and nudged the fish with his nose. Patch came forward boldly and took a bite.

"He's sharing the fish with her!" Claire said in amazement.

"Yes. And he's having the time of his life," Charlotte said in a small voice. "I thought he had everything he wanted. But I could never give him this."

"You've done your best," Mandy said generously.

Charlotte gave her a level look. "Yes, I know. But this is what he needs, isn't it?"

Mandy nodded. "It's a good place for an otter to live. There's lots of food and shelter. And he wouldn't be far away from you."

"You're right." Charlotte looked sad, but determined. "You've helped me make a decision I've been putting off for some time. I think I know what I have to do — and pretty soon, by the looks of it."

She whistled to Oswald to call him to her. He raised his head and hesitated before answering her call. Behind him, Patch looked up and chittered, then went on eating the fish.

A few days later, Mandy, Claire, Charlotte, and Oswald were once again standing by the riverbank. Over the previous few days, they had been accompanying Charlotte when she brought Oswald to play with the wild otters. Now it was Christmas Eve, and they had all come back one final time.

"Thanks to Patch, the colony has completely accepted Oswald now," Charlotte said. "I think it's time to let him make a choice."

Oswald was rolling in the snow at Charlotte's feet. Suddenly he reared up. Balancing himself on his back legs, he peered around.

"Look!" Claire whispered, pointing toward a clump of reeds.

Mandy saw that a single wild otter was waiting there. "It's Patch!"

A fluting whistle rang out on the still air. Oswald's ears twitched. He looked up at Charlotte with round black eyes.

"She's calling you," Charlotte said softly. "Off you go."

Oswald gave a chirrup and bounded toward the reeds. Halfway there, he paused and looked over his shoulder. Mandy thought he seemed to be saying, "Are you sure this is okay?"

"Go on," Charlotte encouraged him gently. Oswald blinked, then ran toward Patch.

Charlotte managed a brave smile, but Mandy saw the tears in her eyes. "If you don't mind I'll be getting back now. I'd like to be by myself for a while."

"Okay," Mandy said. She had a lump in her throat.

"The poor thing," Claire said, when Charlotte had gone. "She's really going to miss Oswald."

"I know," Mandy said. "It's awful, isn't it?" She had felt so sure that they had done the right thing for Oswald. So why did she feel so miserable?

Christmas morning dawned bright and clear. The Hopes and the Essons exchanged presents in the farmhouse kitchen. The room smelled of mince pies, oranges, and spices.

"Wow! A new bike helmet and a book about endangered animals!"

"Oh, great! In-line skates!"

Mandy and Claire thanked everyone for their presents.

Greg was delighted with his robe and Ella loved the gelatin mold. "It'll look wonderful on the kitchen counter," she said.

Breakfast was even more scrumptious than usual. Mandy did justice to cheesy scrambled eggs and mushrooms, followed by bread, butter, and Ella's homemade marmalade. At last, she pushed back her chair. "I'll never be able to eat anything again!"

"I hope you will," Claire's mom said, laughingly. "I'm making a huge Christmas dinner with all the trimmings!"

Everyone helped clear up, then Dr. Adam suggested that they all go for a walk.

"Why don't we stop to visit Charlotte Figg?" Dr. Emily suggested. "She must be feeling a bit low. Oswald was a big part of her life."

"That's a good idea." Mandy smiled. She had been worrying about Charlotte, who was bound to be missing Oswald.

"I'll just put a few things in a basket." Mrs. Esson began packing mince pies, pots of jam, and a tub of butter.

Greg winked at Mandy. "Just in case siege conditions are announced and we can't get home."

"I heard that!" his wife said.

Everyone laughed. They all set out toward the slope behind the farm buildings.

"Good King Wenceslas looked out . . ." Mandy's dad's rich baritone voice echoed around the snowy hillside. "On the Feast of Stephen . . ."

"Oh, Dad!" Mandy winced. He could be so embarrassing at times.

They reached Charlotte's house and all trooped in through the front gate. As she opened the door to them, they called out, "Merry Christmas!"

"Oh." A rather shaky smile spread across Charlotte's face. "I wasn't expecting visitors. To be honest, I'm feeling rather low and really missing Oswald."

"Of course you are, dear," Claire's mom said kindly. "We won't stay if you'd rather be by yourself. But I always find it cheers me up to chat."

"I'm sure you're right." Charlotte seemed to gather herself together. "And it's so kind of you all to visit. Come in and get warm. I'll make some tea."

Everyone piled into the tiny house. "Mom thought you might enjoy these," Claire said, handing over the basket of Christmas treats.

"Thanks very much. You shouldn't have . . ." Charlotte looked as if she might burst into tears. Suddenly she turned and dashed into the kitchen.

"Come on, Mandy. We'll give Charlotte a hand." Dr. Emily steered her daughter into the tiny, spotless kitchen.

Charlotte was filling the kettle at the sink that overlooked the garden. Mandy saw her glance wistfully over at the stream. Then suddenly Charlotte froze and gave a cry. "I don't believe it. Look!"

Mandy went to stand next to her. She thought she could see movement at the bottom of the yard. There was something near the stream. A long dark body appeared from behind a bush and a blunt whiskery snout began nosing around in the snow.

"Oswald!" Mandy breathed, as a smaller otter ran up to him and bit him playfully on the neck. The two otters rolled about, muscular tails thrashing. "He's brought Patch along with him!"

"There are three more behind that tree," Dr. Emily observed. "It looks like he's brought the whole colony to visit you, Charlotte."

"I thought you weren't expecting visitors!" Mandy joked.

"I wasn't!" Charlotte beamed at her. "But these are a welcome surprise. Thanks, Mandy. I might have lost a friend — but I appear to have gained an entire family!"